BEGUILED, BEWITCHED, & BROKEN

THE SISTER WITCHES URBAN FANTASY SERIES
BOOK 4

CORALIE MOSS

PINK MOON BOOKS

Published internationally by Pink Moon Books, British Columbia, Canada.

ISBN: 9781393317357

Cover Design: Elizabeth Mackey

 Formatted with Vellum

To Mr. Moss
and all the car rides that have brought us story ideas, book titles, boxes
of berries, and dips in the sea.

ACKNOWLEDGMENTS

Every book is group effort, and this one was no exception.

I'm forever grateful to my editor, **Michelle Meade**. She's guided me through all four books of the Sister Witches series and it has been a pleasure to work with her.

Laurel Buchanan, Debra Byrd, Kim Kennard, and Leslie Mart, THANK YOU. The Beta Belles get a standing ovation. I needed their eyes and their feedback earlier than usual in the editing and polishing process, and they came through.

Thank you to my friend, **Meka James,** for being a daily source of inspiration and support.

Many thanks to copy editor, **Warren Layberry,** for his ability to organize a manuscript, and to proofreader, **Lillie's Literary Services.**

CONTENTS

GLOSSARY

Cast, in order of appearance (more or less):
Beryl Brodeur: Witch. Spellcaster. Wields a wand. 32 years old. Middle sister. Nickname: B
    Kostya Arkadi: Fire Demon. 34 years old. Middle of the Arkadi brothers. Nickname: Koz
    Clementine Brodeur: Witch. Binder. Thread Seer. 28 years old. Youngest sister. Nicknames: Clemmie, Sissy
    Alderose Brodeur: Metal Witch. Prefers knives and daggers. Unbinder. 34 years old. Oldest sister. Nicknames: Rosey, Rós
    The Reformed Realm: An ancient demon realm attempting to catch up to modern times in terms of governing.
    Sidan: Fae. Girlfriend to Alderose. Nickname: Sid.
    Laszlo Arkadi: Ice Demon. Mate to Clementine. Oldest of the Arkadi brothers. 38 years old. Nickname: Laz
    Iván Arkadi: Ice Demon (with other elements). Husband to Dagur Birgitsson. 32 years old.
    Tanner Marechal: Druid. Connected to the Goddess Idunn.
    Magicals: General term for those with magic in their veins.
    Chamonix, France: Site of both Château du Blanc, home of the Du Blanc Order of Druids; and Lionel Vigne's fortress.

Jake Winslow: Dragon Shifter. 28 years old. Has a thing for Alderose.

Lionel Vigne: Fae. AKA The Collector, The Imperator. Resides in Chamonix, France. Would never allow anyone to call him by a nickname.

The Facility: A state-of-the-art laboratory. Also provides housing for Magicals in Lionel's breeding program.

The Demesne: Family curse for the Brodeur family that causes one to fall to their knees at first sight of the fated mate. Has variations. Has been known to be wrong.

Moira Brodeur (deceased): Witch. Binder. Mother of Alderose, Beryl, and Clementine.

Maritza Brodeur: Witch. Binder. Beloved of Alabastair Nekrosine. Professor of Necromantic Studies. Nicknames: Mari, Tía Mari.

Malvyn Brodeur: Sorcerer. Master Jeweller. Specialty is collars that restrain wearer's magic. Enforcer for the Board of Magical Governance. Nickname: Mal.

Alabastair Nekrosine: Necromancer. Portal Keeper. Beloved of Maritza Brodeur. Wears capes all the time. Nickname: Bas.

Jadzia/One-Becomes-Three/Laurentine: Fae who murdered the Brodeur sister's father.

BEGUILED, BEWITCHED, & BROKEN

1

"Did I die?"

Worried faces studied me from behind clear face shields. I wrinkled my nose at the overwhelming smell of pungent antiseptics and medical supplies and tried to breathe away the banging inside my head. Worry flickered to annoyance before one of the hovering faces turned away.

"Please let the prince in before he bashes through the window," they said.

A door clanged against something metal. Kostya materialized at my side. My gorgeous demon stopped just shy of grabbing me, pillows and IV lines and all, and pulling me off the bed.

"Beryl."

"Hey," I said, working to unstick my tongue from the inside of my mouth. "What happened? Where's Clementine?"

I didn't know why I was flat on my back, but I knew with certainty that something had happened to my younger sister. The last memory I had was seeing her talking to a mystery man while a string quartet played in the background.

"She's okay. She's okay, and so is the kid. But you..." Kostya's face crumpled behind his surgical mask.

"But me *what*?" Relieved as I was that Clementine was okay, I had no memory of a kid.

"You don't remember?"

I went to shake my head, but it wasn't going anywhere. My skull was wedged firmly in place and Kostya's gaze was darting back and forth and up and down like he was cataloguing a sequence of facial fault lines.

"Is there a mirror in here?"

"Why do you want a mirror, Beryl? You just—"

"I want to see what's going on, Kostya. Please." Nothing in his gaze or his tone was instilling confidence in my appearance and my arms weren't cooperating with my attempts to examine the condition of my chin and cheeks. "Because the look on *your* face is telling me something's wrong with *my* face."

Another memory slid in. I had been invited to a royal ball. That explained why Clementine was wearing yards of silvery white brocade. Two demons had done my hair and makeup. I'd been given a gown and shoes and sparkly accessories, including a satin clutch.

"Can you bring me that little purse I was carrying?"

He shook his head. Messy hanks of auburn hair fell forward from where he'd pushed them behind his horns.

"There's nothing wrong with your face, Beryl. It's your neck they're worried about, and I'm not leaving your side for a bloody mirror. Not today. Not tomorrow. Not ever."

Joy blossomed across my chest. Whatever had happened to me hadn't damaged my hearing, and it sounded a lot like my favorite demon in all the realms was proposing. My shoulders sank back into the pillows, and I attempted a grin. Okay, maybe it wasn't a proposal exactly—but it was more of a commitment to the concept of an 'us' than anything he'd said in the past.

. . .

Once I was awake and moderately alert, every moment was taken up by an exam or a consult or another bag of blood. When the healers were getting ready to go, they left the night shift with firm instructions that, if Kostya stayed, he had to let me sleep. I thanked them for taking good care of me and begged Kostya to tell me what happened that landed me here in the first place.

He had a reclining chair delivered to the room. Pushing it right up against my bed, he wrapped himself in a blanket and shared the unadorned details: I had been bitten and almost drained of blood by a male vampire. A different kind of Magical —a jaguar shifter who was taken from the palace the same time as me—had likely swiped her claws across my belly, leaving a trio of cuts.

Nothing about the details startled me, which meant the healers had me on painkillers. Not only was I not reacting to Kostya's story, no part of my body hurt. Though the gentle loopiness buoying me almost—*almost*—masked the faint sensation that something vital was flowing out of a spot to the left of my bellybutton.

Under the cover of my blanket and still holding Kostya's concerned gaze, I made a second attempt to move my arm. It took a few tries to get my hand onto my belly, where my fingertips searched for a way to connect with bare skin. Whatever material the demons used for wound care was thin enough I couldn't feel the edge of a bandage. By following the sensation of leaking magic, I was able to trace three raised ridges I was sure hadn't been there before.

"Did you see the claw marks?" Giddy with success, I slid my arm out from underneath the covers and reached for Kostya. He took my floppy hand in both of his and slowly kissed my knuckles. His eyes were watery when he looked up.

"I did," he said. "I saw the claw marks on your belly and the puncture wounds on your neck, and I vow to never again let anything like that happen to you."

As much as I wanted to ask him more questions about what else he'd seen and what he meant about never leaving my side, the drugs took over and ushered me to sleep.

BY THE NEXT morning it was apparent to my treatment team that the blood donated by my family, plus the blood products developed by demon researchers, had done an excellent job of accelerating my healing. Once I was fitted with a modest neck brace and given a salve to help with the bruising, I got the green light to leave. I was cautioned by a kind-eyed demon to not overdo physical activity for at least a week.

Which was laughable, considering the next bit of news. My older sister had decided to pursue the Magicals whose actions landed me in the medical center in the first place—by herself. The departure timeline from the Reformed Realm to France was moved from *in a few days* to *as soon as possible*. My hope that Kostya and I could have a deeper conversation about the course of our relationship was shoved to the back burner in favor of following Alderose.

ONCE EVERYONE'S bags were packed, our group, which consisted of me, Clementine, Kostya, and his brothers, Laszlo and Iván, were summoned to my uncle's estate near Vancouver for a family meeting. I secretly dubbed the gathering, *What To Do About Alderose*. From Canada, an expanded version of our group was sent *back* to Massachusetts, to the building my sisters and I now owned and the site where so much of the current drama started.

Most helpful to our urgent need to locate Alderose was the

discovery my mother had practiced geomagick in her third-floor workroom. Five deliberately placed mannequins marked the five points of a pentagram and once we figured out the proper dot-connecting sequence, the pentagram became a portal.

Clementine, the three Arkadi brothers, a druid named Tanner, and I activated the pentagram. We arrived in Chamonix, France at the region's primary portal tree, where the reason behind my uncle's insistence that the druid join our group became crystal clear.

Tanner knew the area intimately—he'd studied Druidry there for decades, maybe longer—and he was able to guide us through a series of little-used tunnels that originated underneath his teacher's château and wended their way out. Some led upward, deeper into the Alps. Others sloped down into the valley. The tunnel route we took led to a newly-built tower known as the Facility.

Tanner's first gift to our rescue mission helped us locate Alderose within the Facility, where she was being held prisoner. His second gift helped us free her. The druid's lanky, barefooted appearance belied his prowess with earth magic and blade work. He wielded a set of short swords that could cut through fae constructs, whether they were invisible wards or imbued objects.

Guarded by Iván, the fastest and fiercest of the demon brothers, Tanner used the wavy-edged blades to carve doorways into invisible walls. He sliced through the locking systems on the glass walls separating patients in a sterile medical ward. And he made single, clean cuts in the arm, chest, and leg restraints holding Alderose to an examination table.

The entire rescue mission was fast and at moments, frantic. Clementine and I were completely absorbed with getting to our sister and getting her out. Along the way, Kostya and Laszlo freed a woman I recognized from the Reformed Realm, the mother of the little shifter kid who had the meltdown at the end of the parade. We also freed a mud-coated man named Jake, who elected to stay within his below-ground cell and act as an inside contact for us and the bigger mission—which was to take down Lionel Vigne, the fae who built the Facility and populated it with captured Magicals, and put an end to his twisted project.

Jake made an impression on the Arkadi brothers with his bravado and with his admission that his other form was a three-headed dragon. He swore he could, and would, eat his captors for lunch.

We made it out of the Facility and followed Tanner back through the tunnels to the druids' modest château. He assured us the healers were equipped to run tests on Alderose and would tend to the obvious wounds, as well as any we couldn't see.

I didn't say out loud that I wished them good luck with that last piece. My heart was in my throat as Tanner and a white-robed woman whisked Laszlo and his armful of unconscious witch into a treatment room within the main building and shut the door.

I stared at the rustic infirmary's heavy wooden door and wished my sister speedy healing. No sounds penetrated from the other side. I was shaking from the late hour and the sustained energy our hastily put-together rescue mission had required so soon after I was discharged.

Loosening the neck brace, I gently palpated the area where the vampire's teeth had entered. My skin and fingers were numb from the cold, and I was beyond ready to become as one with a horizontal surface. All Kostya, Clementine, and I needed was to be shown to our guestrooms.

Beds, and privacy, were moments away.

A man about my age approached us. I couldn't tell if he was a druid-in-training or a staff person. Like everyone we'd seen so far, he was attired in a generic uniform of canvas drawstring pants, a sweater knit from natural wool, and felted slippers. His dark blond hair was long and held away from his face with a leather cord.

"I am the night host." He gestured for us to follow him into a round tower. "Please come with me."

We trudged single-file up narrow, twisting steps that brought us to a dimly lit hall. I was sure I wasn't the only one looking forward to the end of the druid's *Welcome to Chamonix* spiel so I could indulge in a hot shower before collapsing into bed.

"All bathing in the main areas of the castle is cold water only," our guide said, before I could voice my desire to bathe. "Should you prefer hot water, there is a communal bathhouse fed by natural hot springs in one of the outbuildings. Because this is a place of study and worship, we ask that you confine yourselves to our guest wing and the dining hall. Unless you are accompanied by one of our senior staff."

Kostya stopped him from leaving. "Could you give us directions to the bathhouse, please? This is our first time here."

The night host directed our attention to the hand drawn map on the back of our room's roughhewn wooden door. "Food and drink await you in the sitting room at the end of the hall," he added. "There is always fruit, bread, butter, and cheese available should you become hungry between meals."

I dreaded the answer to my next question. "Is there wine?"

"This is France. There is always wine."

I hugged Clementine once the druid left and waited for my sister to close and latch her door. I took two steps into the room Kostya and I had been assigned and paused. Any other time, spending the night an in ancient castle in the French Alps might have felt quaint. Romantic even. Especially if our hosts had thought to drop a stem of wildflowers into the empty vase on the room's lone table or leave a lit candle in the window.

But right now, with the adrenaline of Alderose's rescue mission retreating, spoiled me was having a hard time accepting the lack of hot water. And the fact that an essential component of my magic-management system might need an emergency repair. I unzipped the leather pants I'd pilfered from Alderose's duffel bag—and worn on the mission for good luck—and lifted the hem of my turtleneck sweater.

The seamless material of my corset hugged my torso as always. Even though I could no longer see two of the claw marks, the center cut hadn't mended completely. Magic continued to leak out. I didn't know if the faintly pink mist signaled a dire situation, nor did I know how to return the garment to its pristine state.

The sea witch who made the corsets lived near the Caspian Sea. When we were done here in France, I could ask Kostya to head west rather than east and visit the witch with me. First, I would have to explain to him why I was wearing the invisible garment to begin with.

"Beryl? Come here. I think I can rig up a tub and hot water for you."

I zipped the pants and patted my belly. The situation with my magic hadn't reached code red…and this I had to see. Tucked into a corner of the bathroom and given a bit of privacy by a half-wall was a white porcelain toilet with an overhead tank. In the opposite corner was an old oak dressing table topped with a matching ceramic bowl and pitcher. Between the toilet and makeshift sink was a beaming, handsome demon pointing to a large copper contraption.

"What's *that* supposed to be?" I asked.

Kostya waved me closer and pointed out the obvious. "It's a *tub.* You sit on the wood slats and a parade of ladies-in-waiting bring buckets filled with water that's been heated over an open fire in the castle's kitchen. Look, there's even a bar of soap. It was probably made by barn wenches from goat's milk and fresh herbs procured by hand on the new moon."

"Are you finished?" I was giggling. It was that, or cry. We'd traversed Chamonix's network of underground tunnels in order to get to Alderose, then again to bring her out. The damp cold had made itself at home in my muscles and joints.

"I'm just getting started. Here," he said, "aim the showerhead toward the tub. As soon as there's a couple inches of water in there, I'll heat it for you."

I could believe in miracles. I hopped to it and let Kostya know the castle had surprisingly decent water pressure. He ducked out of the bathroom, leaving the door wide open. I watched him strip down to his boxer briefs and managed to get water all over the floor gawking at his thick thighs, tapered waist, and lascivious smile.

"How can you *do* that to me?" I asked. "We're in this...this situation and you're practically naked and all I can think about is—"

"Sex?" He placed a folded towel on the floor, sat, and embraced the tub with his legs, chest, and arms. A chant in Demonish fired up the flame-shaped tattoos running along his forearms. Designs I'd never seen in our ten years of knowing each other lit up his inner thighs and the front of his chest.

"Your demon lines come in *so* handy," I said. "Why did I not know about this feature of dating a fire demon before?"

"You've never struck me as the kind of witch who dreams of roughing it." Kostya glanced up at me and chuckled. "In France or in the woods or anywhere else. You focus on filling the tub. I'll focus on heating the water. While you soak, I'll check on Clementine, and if Laszlo's with her, I'll see if he has an update on Alderose."

"Insolent beast." I sprayed him. Steam rose from his chest as Kostya poured more magic into his fiery lines. Keeping an eye on the rising water, my thoughts lingered on my younger sister and her beau.

The Demesne—our family curse, if you could call it a curse at all—had recently paired her with Kostya's older brother. The fact the demon prince had responded to the curse by growing an enviable set of wings was a clear sign their magics were compatible. I hoped their bond would encompass their bodies, hearts, and souls and last their entire lives. I also wished the Demesne had provided *me* with that kind of happiness.

Instead, the Demesne had brought me nothing but trouble, causing me to make a terrible wrong I had yet to fully right, and it had completely ignored my relationship with Kostya.

I turned off the shower, folded my clothes as I undressed, and stepped into the knee-high water. Groaning, I slowly lowered myself onto the slotted seat and leaned back. Kostya removed the neck brace and draped a towel over the tub's rounded back support, providing my pounding head with a deliciously soft cushion.

"Your neck's healing nicely. Remind me to apply the salve when we go to bed," he said, placing the bar of soap in my hands. "Be right back."

Before the door fully closed, I caught a glimpse of the matching set of raised ridges on either side of Kostya's spine. Those bumps were the primary reason we weren't having sex. When the true mating response arose for demons, a pair of nascent wings appeared. And according to secrets shared when demons got drunk, there was nothing tender about the way the wings ripped through the skin of their upper backs.

Kostya's had begun to appear during our recent whirlwind trip to the Reformed Realm. We'd arrived at the palace and gone straight to his walk-in closet for some wickedly quick sex before making our command appearances at the ball. We stopped midway through our stand-up act when I noticed what was happening on his back reflected in the mirrors.

My big, beautiful demon had withdrawn, thinking abstaining would delay the inevitable and, at the same time, protect me. He never finished explaining what it was he wanted to protect me *from*. With my added uncertainty over how the rip in my corset might affect *my* magic, I swore to whatever goddess watched over me I would lay out all my secrets for Kostya tonight.

Because I knew in my heart it was *he* who needed protection from *me*.

2

_____

I LEFT THE WATER IN THE TUB WHEN I FINISHED BATHING—THERE was no drain that I could see—wrapped one linen towel around my torso and draped the other over my shoulders. Kostya hadn't returned from checking on Clementine and getting us a pitcher of drinking water.

Anxiety roiled in my empty belly. I stepped to one of the room's small, square windows. The late-night sky beyond the bubbled glass was pitch black and starless. I wasn't going to turn off the single lamp or get into bed until Kostya returned. I dried off, got into my nightshirt, and slipped my feet into one of the smaller pair of slippers provided for guests.

Perched on the edge of a single bed, I touched the polished tip of my elk antler wand to the center of my forehead, thinking a few minutes of meditation and breathwork would help. The little bed jiggled and rocked. Magic rippled through the room, like someone or something big had slammed against a far-off door in a subterranean cellar. I quickly jerked my feet off the floor and tucked them under me.

Kostya burst through the door and paused, half in, half out. "Did you feel that?"

"I did. Any idea what it was?"

"No. Laszlo said he heard things while he was in the infirmary with Alderose. We're both wondering if the repercussions of our rescue mission have begun."

"Do you think we're in danger?" I tucked my wand under my pillow and drew the bed's thin coverlet tighter around my shoulders.

"Yes," he said, setting a dented metal pitcher on the table. "And no. Tanner's promised we'll have a detailed meeting once the sun's up and we've eaten. Oh, and he sent a message along with Laszlo. Someone he referred to as the Crone wants to meet with you and Clementine in the morning, which is only a few hours away."

"Did he say who this Crone is, and do you really think any of us are going to *sleep*?"

"Yes, he did. And yes, we have to sleep, darling." Kostya pressed his shoulder to the door to get the latch to snug tight. "The Crone was the head of the order a long, *long* time ago, before Tanner joined. When she retired, leadership went to her daughter. Tanner said we'll meet Ni'eve tomorrow. Today, I mean."

I nabbed the glass with two guest toothbrushes encased in cellophane and the jar labeled *Poudre dentrifice-menthe* off the bedside table and followed Kostya. I wasn't excited about being left alone in the bedroom after that big *boom*.

"Do you think we could push the two beds together?" I asked. Cuddling up against a big, warm demon would help me sleep better.

"Your wish is my command," Kostya said, grinning at our fractured reflections in the mercury glass mirror. "Stay awake until I've had my shower?"

"Yes. And there's something I want to talk to you about." I ran my hand across the small of his back and stood on tiptoes to kiss his jaw. In the middle of forcing myself to tear my gaze off his incredibly fine chest, I managed to spill half the pot of tooth powder in the rinsing bowl.

Maybe it was the view. Maybe it was my nerves.

True to Kostya's usual style, he was finished with his shower in minutes. A few droplets of water clung to his chest, and the room's low light made the rose gold bars in his nipples and the rings in his ears and horns glow. I had to force myself to pat the nearest bed and stick to my plan.

"Come on, the sooner we get these pushed together, the sooner we can talk."

Kostya moved the table out of the way, carefully lifted one of the beds and snugged it against the other and swept his arm in an arc.

"After you."

I chose the side closest to the exterior wall. He set the jar of salve near my pillow, shifted onto his hands and knees, and crawled over to me. My nipples pebbled in anticipation of what was coming next. My demon had a ritual he followed most every time we slept together. If he stuck to it now, I'd lose my momentum.

I pressed my hand to his chest. "Can you save that for later?" I asked. "Otherwise you're going to distract me."

"Would that be such a bad thing?" He nuzzled the unbitten side of my neck and took my earlobe between his teeth while his hand explored the fullness of one breast, then the other. I had to scratch my nails up his sides and push him away to get him to take my request seriously. He gave me a playful stink-eye before uncapping the salve and rubbing a small amount over the tender skin.

If I were a cat, I would have purred. Kostya knew my body well, and he knew just how to shift his touch from the erotic to the healing. He wiped his hands on a towel when he finished and slid under the covers beside me.

"Now, you have my complete, undivided, not-at-all-sexual attention," he said.

My palms went sweaty. Kostya had a high opinion of me, one I wanted to maintain. I took a deep breath and tucked the covers around my hips.

"I have something I've been wanting to share with you, and ever since you said that thing back at the palace—"

"What thing, babe?" he asked, kicking at the far corner of the mattress to liberate the tightly tucked sheets. Distracted, I lifted the hemmed edge to my nose. Our bedding had been line-dried and ironed.

Stop it, Beryl. Seize the moment.

I swallowed hard. "That thing about never leaving my side? You know, when we were in the medical center and I asked you to get my purse?"

Kostya went still. The weight of his hand landing on my leg settled my flighty heart. "I meant that, Beryl. And when the time is right, when this situation with Lionel and the Magicals he's captured is resolved and sorted, I'll show you just how serious I am."

I melted. He wrapped his arm around my waist and pulled me onto his chest. I took a deep breath and began.

"Once upon a time, there was a little girl named Beryl. She was a middle child, she was a witch, and she could be very bossy." Narrating in third person put necessary distance between me and, well, me.

"Beryl lived with her mother and father and her two sisters in an old Victorian house on the outskirts of Northampton, Massachusetts. There were other old houses lining their street, with lots of maple trees between them and lilac bushes that made perfect hiding spots. Beryl's house had a backyard with a sandbox and a swing set, a toolshed and a chicken coop, and a thicket of overgrown raspberries.

"Beyond the berries was a forest. Beryl thought the forest went on forever, and she was very intimidated by its size. To calm her fears, she would make up stories about the creatures that lived among the tall pine trees and the clumps of wild blueberries, and the patches of swamp grasses and skunk cabbage.

"One day, when Beryl was seven, she was playing in her sandbox. It was a very sunny afternoon, and her mother was with her in the backyard, hanging laundry to dry on the clothes lines."

I darted a glance at Kostya. He was wide awake and staring at me.

"Little Beryl heard a sound in the woods. She was feeling brave that day. Adventurous. So she brushed sand off her hands and walked to where the grass met the beginning of the woods. She didn't say anything to her mother, she just...got up and walked. And before she stepped over the property line and into the woods, she held out her arms and opened her heart. Whatever creature was making those sounds seemed very, very sad, and she wanted them to know she was coming to help."

Memories of that moment fluttered up the front of my chest, of seeing my mother's elongated silhouette behind the big sheets she was trying to wrangle. I dropped the pretext of telling my story as though it had happened to someone else.

"My parents set perimeter wards to keep us safe and contained when we were kids, kind of an expandable outdoor safety gate. I remember feeling a gentle zap any time I got too close. That day, right on the other side of the wards, four or five of the most adorable fox kits were rolling all over each other. They couldn't come onto the lawn, so I went to them.

"Though I barely felt the wards as I passed through, I did feel another layer of magic working to warn me away. I had second thoughts and turned to go back, but I was quickly overwhelmed by the kits. I was small for my age, and they were very, *very* bouncy. I stumbled. And then I started to cry because the foxes wouldn't leave me alone. They kept licking me and nipping at my legs and my elbows like I was one of them. They were so cute, but they scared me and made me cry.

"I managed to crawl away but because of the protective wards, I couldn't get back to my yard. I ended up running the other way, deeper into the woods. The foxes thought I was playing a game and they chased me, and the more they chased me, the more lost I got.

"I finally stopped running and curled into a ball. The kits snuggled around me and shared their warmth. And then both our mamas found us at the same time."

Kostya stroked my back. "Is that the whole story?"

"No," I whispered. "After my mom brought me inside the house, she made me tell her what I'd done to make the kits want to follow me. I told her they were crying and seemed so sad and lonely. I admitted I'd ignored her previous verbal warnings and the wards. She didn't have much to say other than to remind me never to go into the forest without her or my dad. But the foxes kept returning, every single day. And every single day, I kept wanting to disobey my mom, whether I was in my bedroom or in the sandbox or standing as close to the invisible line as I could get without getting zapped.

"Until one day the foxes didn't show up. And it was my turn to be sad. I asked my mom why they had disappeared. She didn't give me a satisfactory answer. A couple days after that, my dad put up an actual fence and completely enclosed the back yard."

Kostya traced my kneecap under the blanket. "So that's your big secret? The woman I love had a thing for foxes long before she met me?"

"I wish," I said, watching him explore the contours of my

leg. "Fast forward seven years. I was fourteen. My mom always made me go with her when she ventured onto the college campus near our house. The school had one of those beautiful, old glass and iron greenhouses, and there were a lot of tropical plants and trees growing inside. A few of those provided ingredients required for certain potions. My mom needed the components to be fresh, and she didn't have the proper growing environment at our house, so she'd go on these foraging missions.

"I'd act as a distraction, which allowed her to harvest or dig for what she needed, and then we would go."

Realizing I was getting wound up and long-winded, I stopped and took another deep breath. Kostya had closed his eyes. I stroked his wavy hair and traced the arc of his horn.

"I'm listening," he assured me. "I'm still enjoying the image of you playing with a bunch of cute little foxes."

"That day in the greenhouse, my mom made me stand guard at the interior door to the room with the big banana tree. She was taking a long time, and I got bored, so I made up a game. I timed how long it took me to walk the path inside the adjoining room, and I kept doing it over and over, faster and faster, trying to beat my best times.

"I was pretty far from the door I was supposed to be watching when I heard metal hinges squeak, and then I heard this boy's voice calling. I couldn't stop myself from careening around the corner and whipping out my wand to scare him away.

"I fell and hit the gravel walkway the moment I saw him. I skinned my knees and shredded my tights, and because I had no idea what was happening, why I had this overwhelming urge to...to *absorb* him, I tossed out a defensive spell, one I'd been practicing on the mice in the toolshed.

"The spell was meant to stop him, not—"

I clenched the bedsheet and stuffed it into my mouth. Kostya sat up and slowly pried my fingers apart.

"Not *what*, Beryl?" he asked, rubbing my icy hands.

"Not turn him to stone," I said.

Once I got going, I couldn't stop. "He turned to stone, Kostya, right there on his knees in the middle of the doorway to the tropical greenhouse. I remember seeing cacao pods hanging from the trunk of the tree behind him and some other monster purple flowers. I think I screamed, because next thing I knew my mom was trying to pick *me* up, and I couldn't unbend my arms or my legs. I felt so...so *heavy*."

"Did your mom fix it, fix you?"

"No." I was having a hard time looking at Kostya. I sat up and hugged my knees to my chest. "She couldn't fix it. Him. Not right then. Not...there. The first thing she did was hide me under one of the potting tables in the room where I'd been racing. She found the boy's mom—whom it turned out she knew and who was also a Magical—and together they were able to pick him up and hide him under the table next to mine until they could figure out what to do.

"His mom said his name was Micah."

I had frozen in place, my knees and elbows locked in reaction to what I had done, and I was the lucky one. I could still feel how my heart had beat so hard against chest and recall how I convinced myself the poor boy next to me couldn't feel his. How could he? He was stone. He looked like he'd toppled into the greenhouse from a pedestal in the nearby bank of flowering shrubs. The only thing missing were patches of lichen on his shoulders and knees.

"So then what did your mom do? Was she able to reverse the spell?"

I snugged my fingers into Kostya's armpit and squeezed my eyes shut. "First, my mom sealed the two doors to the room.

There was so much glass in the doors and the upper half of the cinderblock walls and also overhead that she had to do a cloaking spell. While she was doing that, Micah's mom turned him so he was seated and facing me, not lying on his side."

I stopped my storytelling for a moment. More details than I usually remembered were coming back.

"My mom confiscated my wand and asked me to explain every spell I had cast over the past few days. There weren't many and after I described them she made me squat in front of Micah. I had to hold my arms out straight and grip my wand tight in both hands. She sat behind me, and she had Micah's mother sit behind him. I remember feeling very squished.

"She put her hands over mine and whispered a spell, over and over. I could feel the power building and building until she snapped my wand in half. Micah broke apart at the same time."

I had to stop and focus on my breathing. My racing heart was trying to fly out of my chest and find refuge in Kostya's.

"Did the boy survive?"

"Thank goddess, he did. The stone broke. Just...crumbled into chunks and Micah the boy became Micah the naked gargoyle, with tiny horns and these sticky wet wings. He looked so surprised. I think I fainted. Because the next thing I remember was being in my bedroom. My mom grounded me for a month and forbade me from practicing any spells until she had time to supervise.

"It was the Demesne that triggered the whole thing, Kostya. Both times. First with the foxes, and then with the boy. I never saw him again. Though my mom did say he was okay."

"Demesne, like what happened with Clementine and Laszlo?" he asked.

"Yes, like that only different. I have Binder magic like Clementine and my mom and Maritza. The way my mom explained it to me, my Binder magic morphed into this...

anomaly which meant that *any* living being I felt attracted to could bring me to my knees.

"And which meant the *opposite* was also true, that any living being attracted to me could end up on their knees, wanting nothing more than to bind with me forever. I know it would have made more sense if she'd also explained about the Demesne. Because now that I know about the family curse, I'm convinced it was the influence of the Demesne that altered my Binder magic."

I relaxed my legs, let go of the covers, and made my way off the mattress. I had to reveal my ever-present corset to Kostya.

"My mother eventually found a solution to my problem. It was to wear this," I said, pulling off the nightshirt I'd worn to bed and pointing to my midsection, "or never let me out of the house."

"What's *this*?" Kostya asked, throwing off the sheet and blanket. He moved to the end of the bed, pulled me over, and positioned me between his knees.

I ran my fingertip under the bottom edge of the invisible garment and pulled the material slightly away from my skin. The moment I let go, the material sighed and reclaimed its hold on my ribs, waist, and hips. I took Kostya's hand, brought it to my belly, and showed him how to locate it.

"It's a corset. My mom and a friend of hers, a sea witch, created it to keep my magic contained. My mom said—" I shook my head and rested my hands on the rounded part of my belly. "She said we couldn't take the chance my magic would turn another boy to stone. Or worse. This protects everyone out there from me and me from myself."

Kostya smoothed the curve of my hips and pulled me close enough he could kiss my chest. I sank into him, rested my elbows on his shoulders, my forehead on the top of his head.

Though I wasn't ready to share my secret with the world, sharing it with Kostya was a relief.

"How does this affect your spellwork, babe?" he asked. "I've seen you use your wand for making light, like back in Northampton and again in the tunnels. But when I think about it...that's it. I can't recall the last time I witnessed you doing something big."

"I perform spellwork at about ten percent of what I'm capable of. Ten percent and below feels safe. When I attempt anything that requires more wattage, I can feel my insides warring against my mother's incessant warnings to never remove the corset."

Kostya cupped the sides of my waist with his hands, one of my favorite ways of being held, and made space between our bodies. He traced the barely visible cut, the one that was taking the longest to heal, with his thumb. I went still as he spread his fingers and hovered his palm over the same spot.

"Any chance you're losing some of that power?"

"Yes," I whispered. "Right there, right underneath your hand. The other cuts sealed up after the healers sutured my wounds, but this one won't fully close and I can feel magic leaking out. I've got to get this closed back up before you and I have sex again. If we can even have sex again."

"What do you mean, 'if we have sex again'?"

I cupped his sculpted jaw in my hands and stared into his trusting brown eyes. "I would never forgive myself if the reason your wings were trying to explode out of your back was because my magic is forcing them, not because your demon nature and my Demesne have declared that we're fated to be together."

Kostya circled his arms around my lower back. "Beryl, how long have we known each other?"

"Ten years?"

"Have you had other relationships in those ten years?"

"Kind of? I mean I've gone on dates. Lots of dates." I stroked his horns to their tips and delighted in the way my demon melted into my touch.

"I've gone on lots of dates too. And every time you and I have gotten together, even if it was only our annual weekend in July, I've felt like I was home."

Kostya released me enough that he could again trace the barely visible flaw in the corset. His voice went softer, deeper as he spoke.

"When your uncle offered me the promotion that would give me more authority *and* keep me based on the east coast, I didn't think twice about accepting. Being closer to you carried far more weight in my decision-making than a bigger paycheck and greater responsibility within the Board of Magical Governance."

"I still think we should wait on the sex thing," I said, gasping as the demon lines on his arms lit up. The coppery fire reflected across the front of my body and up toward my throat.

"And I'm willing to take the risk. I think we should get creative. It'll help us sleep."

3

I woke up after not nearly enough sleep to a muscular thigh wedged between my legs and Kostya's fiery skin warming the sheets. The morning air sweeping into the room and over my bared shoulder could only be described as alpine fresh and brisk. Sleepy-eyed, I eased out from the sleeping demon's possessive claim to my limbs and went to close the windows.

A golden-eyed harrier was perched on the ledge of our bathroom's window. And on the sill at my elbow was a gnarled crabapple and a small dead vole. The raptor nattered at me. Though I didn't understand what the handsome creature was saying, I understood the gesture. I picked up the fruit by the stem and the rodent by the tail and thanked the bird. It fluffed out its wing feathers and took off into the shadows cast by the eaves.

"Looks like you have an admirer, Miss Beryl."

"Looks like I'm calling Uncle Mal and Tía Mari," I said, walking nearer to the bed to show Kostya my tribute.

"I think that's a good idea. What're you going to do with that mouse?"

"It's not a mouse, it's a vole, and I can't throw it away. That'd be rude."

"Put it in the bathroom. I'll deal with it. Or maybe the castle has a cat."

I set the harrier's gifts into the woven basket under the oaken washing table. Aromatic hand soap got rid of the faintly gamey smell, and once I'd peed and brushed my teeth, I was ready to crawl back under the covers. Kostya took his turn in the bathroom while I straightened the sheets and blankets in the hope that would keep me vertical.

"I think the others are awake," he said, pressing his ear against the door to the hall.

"You need to put some clothes on before you go out there." He glanced down his front, and mine, and suggested I do the same.

"Do you think we're required to dress like them?" I asked, rifling through the rustic, farmhouse-style armoire. One shelf held stacks of towels, and the other shelves held an assortment of the same drawstring pants, rough wool sweaters, and felted slippers we'd seen the night host and others wearing.

"I think it's a good idea. We'll blend in better."

"Clementine and I will blend in better. You and Laszlo will never blend in here, even if you do cloak your wings and your horns."

Kostya needed my help getting the neck of the largest sweater I could find over his horns.

"What, you don't think we could pass for druids?"

I snorted. "See if you can find some pants that will accommodate your thighs and let's go. I hear knocking." I was ready before him. Mostly. I had a slipper in my left hand and in my right, one of the boots I'd worn through the tunnels. I held up both for Kostya's opinion. "Slippers or boots?"

"Boots. We're in battle mode, babe. Got to be ready to head back into the fray at a moment's notice."

"Yes, but before I go into battle mode, I have to go into supplication mode. I've never visited a crone before, and I don't know the protocol."

"Clean clothes. A submissive demeanor. And a bottle of wine should do it."

I swatted Kostya's butt and unrolled handknit socks over my cold toes. Boots on, curls dampened and slicked behind my ears, and wand in the pants' handy side pocket, I was ready. I was about to lead Kostya into the hallway when he reached for my elbow and pulled me back into the room.

"Beryl? Before we go anywhere or do anything, I want to acknowledge what a big thing it was for you to tell me about what happened to you and how it's affected your magic."

"Thanks," I said, wrapping my arms around him and resting my forehead on his chest. "It was time."

"We're going to figure this out. I promise."

I squeezed him extra hard before letting go. "Let's see what madness is in store for us today."

He reached behind me and opened our door inward. Clementine and Laszlo were standing there, poised to knock.

"You ready to visit the Crone?" my sister asked.

"As ready as I can be on four hours of sleep. Though something caffeinated would help me string words together better. Oh, and Kostya suggested we bring her a gift, like a bottle of wine. What do you think?"

"Let's see if we can find anything edible for us and suitable for her down there," she said, pointing to the end of the hall. "The guy who showed us to our rooms did say they always put out food and drinks."

We straggled into the sitting room. My eyes lit up at the morning's simple spread and the view to the mountains beyond the windows. Kostya poured cups of coffee and passed them around. Needing more in my belly, I broke open a seeded roll and slathered on unsalted butter that tasted like it had been made that morning. Clementine copied me, sliding a plate under my roll and adding a generous dollop of strawberry jam. We agreed it was one of the best breakfasts we'd ever had and prepared second rolls.

Laz filled his plate and wandered around the room, poking into the backs of shelves and cupboards. He found a stash of dusty, unopened bottles of brandy and suggested one would be a suitable libation for an elder of any race.

I wiped the dust off with a cloth napkin, tucked the bottle in the crook of my elbow, and finger waved to Kostya. Nerves had me wanting to be first through the door and down the stairs so we could get this requested meeting over with and get on to the business of planning the next act. Clementine kissed Laszlo and followed me out of the sitting room.

"Wait up, Beryl. I need to grab another sweater or something from my room. Aren't you cold?"

This far from Kostya, I realized how much his heat kept me from noticing it was November in the Alps—in a château that lacked central heating.

"I am, actually."

"Wait here." Clementine ducked into her room and came out with two lightweight blankets, cream-colored wool with light blue stripes at either end. She draped one over my shoulders and followed me down the hall. "We've gone from hardly seeing each other since Mom died, to picking up the pieces she left behind. Kinda wild, huh?"

"Kinda wild, Sissy," I said. "Kind of *very* wild." I threaded the fingers of my free hand through hers when we got to the bottom of the tower's precariously narrow stairs. I pulled Clementine closer. Losing our mother seven years ago was a shock I still wasn't over. The recent loss of our father had a whole other tone to it. I knew I would be experiencing a more profound and immediate grief if he and I'd had more of a relationship. But we didn't—we hadn't—and there had been no time to mourn in the days since he been killed.

I chose instead to hang on to the love I had for Clementine and Alderose and hope that, once we were back in Northampton, we'd think long and hard about what to do with the tangible and intangible aspects of our legacy.

"Is this the orchard?" My sister must have paid much better attention to Tanner's instructions as Laszlo relayed them during our breakfast. Once we exited the main building, I'd had my eyes to the ground, mulling over my conversation with Kostya while keeping track of where I was stepping. When I looked up, fruit trees heading into dormancy dotted the uneven meadows to either side and low clouds blocked the view to the mountains.

"Mm-hmm. And I think *that's* where the Crone lives." Clementine paused as we neared a squat, ancient hut. Spindly tree branches reached up and out of what was left of the timber roof. The walls of the round building leaned in slightly. "Because Laz did say we were to walk to the end of the path cutting through the orchard and look for the old building with a tree sticking out the top."

A mounded knee wall circled what we could see of the hut. Up close, the fairytale entrance with its chipped, dark red trim felt small, even for me. I raised my hand to knock.

"The door is always open for those with a gift." A raspy voice with a thick French accent sounded from behind the door. Clementine and I darted glances at one another. She took hold of the metal latch, pressed down, and pushed.

"Hello?"

"The door is always closed on those whose eyes would spy." Once we crossed the threshold, the door shut of its own accord and the latch clicked into place. Up close, the tree wasn't all that large, just curvier than usual through the middle. Light filtered down into the room through jagged holes made by the branches, and the air was redolent of overripe apples, dried lavender, and the passage of time.

"Welcome, daughters of Moira, and thank you for accepting my invitation. Please, sit. What have you brought? Your mother always gifted me the prettiest bugs." The voice seemed to be coming from behind the tree. While waiting for the Crone to appear, I turned in a circle. There was no place to sit, other than on the packed dirt floor, and no sign of a working kitchen or a bathroom or even a bed.

"We brought you a bottle of brandy, Madame du Blanc."

The tree's branches quivered. "*That* appellation belongs to my daughter, who seems to have forgotten I continue to live and breathe, and that I have eyes and ears, rootlets and buds, and am able to see and to *listen*," she hissed. The tree shook again and gave a long sigh.

"Call me Grisette. Or la Crone if you insist on something more formal."

"Where would you like us to put the brandy, Grisette?"

One of the lower branches slowly unbent and reached toward us. My sister and I watched, wide-eyed and incredulous, as the bark on the branch crackled and split, revealing an older woman's sun-weathered arm, all the way to her shoulder. Burnished gold bracelets lay flush with her skin.

"Would you uncork the bottle first?"

"Did you bring a knife?" Clementine whispered, tipping the neck of the bottle in my direction.

"No." I patted my pockets anyway. I could do a lot with my wand but making a fine cut through the red wax covering the cork would be more in line with Alderose's skill set.

"You will find a knife in the wall by the door. It has been

there since the last time my daughter visited, and I have lost track of when that might have been. It was probably when she needed something, and I wouldn't give it to her. C'est la vie..."

I hung the blanket now slipping off my shoulders on a peg sticking out of the wall. Firing up the tip of my wand, I swept its light across the shadowed entrance. There really was a short-bladed knife embedded there at head height. I had to hand my wand to Clementine and grab the knife handle with both hands in order to pull it free of the wattle and daub construction.

"What's she doing stabbing walls?" I asked, not expecting Grisette to answer. I wiped the rust off the blade before handing it to my sister and taking back my wand.

"I believe a modern healer would say Ni'eve has anger management issues," the Crone said. In a lower voice, she added, "Amongst other things."

Clementine shuffled closer to the tree and pressed the long neck of the bottle into the Crone's hand. As we watched, the narrow part of the trunk past the shoulder morphed into a neck and jaw and an upper chest. A cluster of what I thought were knots in the wood became an elegant, patrician face with pale blue eyes framed by silvery eyebrows. The same gold inlay circled her neck and the curve of her ear.

Grisette smiled and pulled more of her human form, including long strands of thick gray hair, out of the tree. She grimaced, exhaled, and took a long swig of the brandy, not at all fazed by the alcohol's burn.

"Thank you. That was a particularly fine Calvados. The apples used in its blending were grown by some of our sweetest Keepers. Now, what may I do for you?"

"Tanner said—"

"Ach, Tanner Marechal, un bel homme avec une belle âme. Tell me, what did that dear boy say?" She tucked our gift against a curve in the bark where her chest would be.

"He said you knew our mother and that you might have something to" –I swallowed to clear a tickle in my throat– "to tell us about her."

"How long do you have?" Grisette asked, holding up the brown glass bottle to the light. "Over the years, your mother and I shared many glasses of brandy and many stories and many hours of silence."

"Not long, at least not today," I said. "We're leaving soon to go back through the tunnels to Lionel Vigne's fortress and rescue the rest of the Magicals he's been holding captive."

"As your mother did before you."

"Yes."

"Will you visit with me when you have completed your mission?"

Clementine reached for the sleeve of my sweater and tugged. "Sure."

"There *is* one thing you should see which will provide you a little insight into your mother and the time we spent together. Here, please put this somewhere." Grisette handed the bottle back to Clementine, then pressed her lips together tight.

"This used to be so much easier," she said, "back in the day when my daughter and the other Keepers sought my council with regularity and thought my wisdom was a thing to be treasured, not trashed." She grimaced, and a creaking sound erupted from where her trunk met the packed soil of the floor.

"See that board? Lift it off and go down the ladder. Follow in your mother's footsteps. Better use your wand, little witch, unless you can see in the dark."

A crack in the dirt revealed the outline of a square trapdoor. I stuck my finger in the knothole, lifted, and set the door against Grisette's trunk. "*Lucerna lumen,*" I whispered, holding my antler-tipped wand at arm's length as I stuck my leg into the hole and felt for the promised ladder.

"Go all the way until the ladder ends."

I lowered the intensity of the glow, stuck the wand's handle between my teeth, and began to descend. Clementine waited until I was well on my way before I felt the vibration of her foot testing the uppermost rungs.

I continued down. And down even more. Until I stubbed my toe on packed dirt. I held tight to the sides of the ladder, felt around with my foot, and let Clementine know I'd made it to the bottom.

"The bottom of what?" she asked. Her voice was muffled by the shaft's constricted walls.

"The bottom of the Hole to Nowhere," I joked, making my voice scary. I held my wand out and turned in a slow circle. The tip lit candle after candle as it passed, all of them beeswax and all pulled from molds of flying bugs and butterflies.

"I think this is where Mom worked, or maybe where she stayed, when she was passing through here."

I shuffled to the side and gave Clementine room to stand next to me. She thwacked my shoulder and begged me to stop teasing her about dark places.

"Sorry, Sissy."

The room was roughly the same shape and size as the one above ground, with a lower ceiling. A narrow cot with folded bedding at one end was wedged against a wall. A steamer trunk on its side hunkered underneath the frame. The three other walls supported a worktable and two freestanding sets of shelves. Each piece of furniture was old—very old—and crafted from hand-hewn wood aged to a rich, dark brown. Miraculously, there wasn't a speck of dust or even a spider's web.

"Look, Beryl, all of these little drawers are labelled." Clementine lifted a candle shaped as a damselfly and started to read. "Dream Ease. Blood Cease. Loss Abatement. Fear Release." She opened one of the narrow, oblong drawers and withdrew a handful of items that looked like something you'd insert into your ears or nose. "These were labelled 'Breath Boost'. Do you think Mom wore them when she was in the tunnels?"

"That's entirely possible," I said, peering over her shoulder. "She was bringing out Magicals who'd been through trauma. She had to keep them breathing, keep them moving, as she got them here. Do you think Grisette helped her? Or Ni'eve?"

"I have no idea, only a bajillion questions. Some of which we can get answers to when we come back." She turned and let me see what was in her palm. "What about bringing these to share? It couldn't hurt to have something to help us breathe. We have no idea what going into the tunnels will be like this time. The fae know we're here. They might have set traps."

I picked what looked like a nose plug out of the pile and slid it over the cartilage at the front of my nostrils. "It's like one of those pinching things we used to wear at the town pool during swimming lessons," I said, inhaling. "How do I look?" I crossed my eyes for an added dollop of sultriness.

"Goofy. But I say we bring—"

Clementine pointed at my face. I felt the material crumble and the thing fall off my nose.

"Oops, I think those are past their expiration date," she said

"Anything else look like it would be helpful for today?" I swept my wand overhead, illuminating the uneven ceiling and aimed the light into the corners by the bed.

"Beryl. Look." She slid a thin notebook out from one of the shelves. Handwritten across the front was a date.

"Open it." I noticed my hand was shaking. I would have been fourteen when Mom wrote those numbers. Right around the time I turned Micah to stone and got fitted for my first corset.

"The notebook looks like the kind you use," she said, tucking an errant hank of hair behind her ear. She slid the side of her thumb in between the cover and the first page, gingerly opened the notebook, and began to scan the lines.

"What's it say?" I asked.

"So...it looks like it's information about the Magicals she was looking for. Name of victim. Their race and type of magic. Physical description. Who reported them missing. When they were last seen, and where. What they were wearing." Clementine scanned the next couple of pages. "Basically, Mom took on clients whose family member or friend went missing. I don't think any money changed hands—and look, this one was found. But not here."

"Let's take all the notebooks and read through them later. If we leave them in our rooms, it means we'll have to make it back, right?" I collected the other four tucked into the one cubbyhole and held them close to my heart, then opened the drawer labelled *Fear Release* and felt around inside. Whatever had filled it was gone.

"We should go."

I didn't want to leave the underground room. We were getting a glimpse into our mother's world, the one she inhabited when she left us at home. "It's like she was living two, three different lives. When did Mom come here, any guess?"

"I have no idea, and I'm not sure Grisette would be any help. It doesn't seem like she has a firm grasp on linear time," Clementine said. She held her hair away from her face and blew out the candles one by one.

We climbed the ladder in complete darkness and set the trapdoor. Grisette had her eyes closed, at least the one eye we could see. The other side of her face had become more tree-like and her human arm was resting against her trunk. The bottle of brandy dangled from her fingers

"Grisette?" I said, lightly touching her bark. "We're going now."

"Did you find anything that could be useful?" she asked, keeping her eyes closed and her arm limp. Clementine crouched, worked the bottle free, and set it near the trapdoor.

"Notebooks. Her supplies were either out of stock or too old."

"Hmm. I guess it has been a while since she was last here. Visit me when you return. I will prepare tea. And may the Goddess go with you. You're going to need her help."

Clementine and I didn't speak as we draped our blankets over us and drew the door closed. Turning to make our way back through the orchard, we both gasped at the view.

"Those are the Alps," she said. "I kind of forgot where we were."

During our time with Grisette, sunlight had burned off most of the clouds, giving us a panoramic view of craggy, snow-capped mountains. In the distance, the pale stone and white plaster walls of the château gleamed. Beyond, on the other side of the valley, the Vigne fortress hunkered against the side of a mountain currently cloaked in shade.

"That's today's destination," Clementine noted, giving an exaggerated shiver. Once we'd done enough gawking and stepped onto the wider gravel path, she curled her fingers through mine.

"C'mon," she said, planting a kiss on my cheek. "There'll be plenty of time to marvel at all this beauty later. Lots of frightened Magicals need our help. Starting with our sister."

4

———

WHILE WE VISITED THE CRONE, ALDEROSE HAD BEEN MOVED FROM a private room to the communal recovery room within the château's treatment wing. Clementine and I entered together. Kostya and Laszlo paused a few steps from the doorway set into the thick wall to speak with each other. I snuck a glance back at Laszlo's near-black wings and pictured his brother sporting a pair with similarly epic proportions.

My hand went to my belly. I really had to get my corset fixed. I was not cut out to have a solely platonic relationship with the man who was, and had been, my one and only lover.

Uff.

Inside the austere room, a row of hospital cots was set against the pale blue outer wall. The head of each metal bed frame was placed directly underneath a narrow window. Mattresses were made tidy with white sheets and charcoal-gray blankets. Patients could get a little privacy by shifting moveable panels of white curtains and trifold screens, while belongings were relegated to bedside tables with a single drawer and a single shelf.

"I thought a place of healing run by druids would be a lot

more, I don't know...organic," Clementine whispered. "This feels sterile."

I agreed, then nudged her with my shoulder. "There's Rosey."

Four beds away, our sister had a second wool blanket folded across her chest, an extra pillow propping up her head and shoulders, and a phone to her ear. Tears were streaming down her haggard face. There had to be a story in those watery tracks. My older sister had a limited emotional range, and usually any crying that happened around her was because of something she'd said or done.

When she finished listening, she pressed the phone to her chest, wiped her face with a fistful of sheet, and announced her feet were tingling.

"I think my magic's coming back," she added, shaking her feet back and forth underneath the covers.

The hope flickering in her eyes almost started *me* crying. I waited for Clementine, or one of the druids tending to the patients, to tell her no, her magic wasn't coming back. Not this morning. Not without expert help we didn't have inside the high walls and hallowed halls of Château du Blanc. As far as I knew, this place and its inhabitants were not dedicated to witchcraft and whatever other type of magic was used to insert metal *inside* my sister's body, not simply bond her magic to it.

"Rosey?" I said, when no one else stepped forward. "That tingling you're feeling is a phenomenon similar to phantom limb syndrome."

"But my toes are intact. I saw them when the healer was examining me." Alderose scrabbled unsuccessfully to kick off her covers, bouncing her gaze back and forth between me and Clementine and the silent caregivers moving among the beds. I stepped closer to her cot. Uncrossed my arms. Softened my expression as I made myself sit.

"What I mean is that the loss of your magic is so recent your body and mind haven't fully registered or accepted the implications."

Alderose grabbed hold of the metal frame sticking out on either side of the mattress. Her knuckles whitened as she squeezed.

"You're right," she whispered, rattling the springs. "You're right. This is just...iron and steel. Now what do I do?"

"I don't know, sis. You've never shared with us how metal became your thing. If we don't know how it was put into you in the first place, or who those white-robed women were who took it, we're going to have to wait until we can get you to Tía Mari and Uncle Mal. I'm *positive* one of them will know what to do."

I wanted to be sure they would know, I really did. My mother's siblings had fast become the go-to experts in the family. Alderose's cheeks drained of what little color was left, leaving pale purplish half-moons underneath her eyes.

"I was only supposed to go through that once," she whispered, still gripping the bars. I gave her admission a respectful pause, then asked who she had been talking to on her phone.

"I was listening to a message from Sid. Sidan. My girlfriend. She's...she's alive. She's healing. Only she didn't say where she was."

"That is the *best news*, Rosey," Clementine said, dropping onto the opposite edge of the cot and gathering our sister into a hug. She caught my eye and subtly shook her head while we had Alderose wedged between us. *What happened to her?* she mouthed. I raised my eyebrows and blinked. I was out of explanations.

"Were any of you guys the ones who, you know, who found her?" Alderose asked. She had gone limp and seemed unable to support herself. Clementine eased her back against the pillows, and I fussed with her blanket.

I really didn't want to describe what I'd seen in New York. While I debated how much to tell her, two of the caregivers rushed out of the room. The door stayed open long enough for the sounds of raised voices to filter in. One of the druids tending the handful of patients dropped a metal bowl. Alderose flinched.

"Well, were you?" she repeated.

"Kostya and I were sent to your apartment building. When we got there, your door was open. There was a lot of blood on the hall floor and one wall." That stop would have been a lot harder to describe if we'd found a body.

Alderose wobbled her head in a nod. "Cat and Jake's people must have helped Sid. Cat said she would send in a team. They should have dealt with the blood." She closed her eyes and scratched at the back of her head. I tried to smooth the tangles out of her raging case of bedhead, but she winced and pushed my arm away.

The door opened again. The noise in the hall had lessened. Kostya walked in first and came right over to where I was seated.

"Hey, Rosey. Lookin' good. Did Beryl tell you we met Jake when we were in the Facility rescuing you?"

"No. But I'm glad you helped him too. Is he here? Can I see him?"

"He elected to stay inside the tower." Laz took up a stance behind Clementine. "We were able to free Sheenah, the jaguar shifter. Iván escorted her back to the Reformed Realm. She's shaken, but she's with her daughter and her father-in-law. Sheenah's going to be okay."

Alderose got agitated. "That's great, that's great but wait, go back to Jake. You *left* him with Lionel?"

Without warning, the commotion that had been building in the hallway spilled in through the door. Startled by the cluster of solemn, white-robed figures lined up and waiting to enter, I rolled to my feet and stepped away from the cot. Clementine stood too and the moment her weight was off the thin mattress, Alderose let out a ragged scream and hurled a blade she must have concealed under her covers at the intruders. The lead figure caught the weapon's grip, bent her elbow, and threw the blade overhand. It landed in the wall above Alderose's head with a dull thud and a steady *twang-g-g.*

"*You* did this! She—*she* did this! Beryl, Clementine, that's her, *that's* the one who took my metal, took my magic, took my—" My sister choked on a long guttural scream and scrambled to untangle herself from the bedsheets. Clemmie and I reacted in tandem. We sandwiched Alderose between us and yelled for Laszlo and Kostya to do something more than just stand there.

The blade thrower tilted her head to the side and pushed back the deep hood covering her features. Glossy, straight black hair tumbled over her shoulders and down her back. She continued to the foot of Alderose's cot and stopped. Her ankle-length robes swayed and settled around her body, and her face radiated a familial connection to Grisette. This had to be Ni'eve du Blanc.

"I had to take your metal," she said. Though she lifted her chin and looked down her nose, she spoke to Alderose in a somber tone that suggested she understood my sister's pain, she was sorry for the pain, and she had long ago accepted that pain was a part of life.

"You didn't have to do *anything*," Alderose spat out.

"Lionel Vigne has my daughter."

The woman crossed her arms. Her fingers were long and elegant and there wasn't a twitch or a quiver in sight. "Lionel Vigne was going to find out about your metal sooner rather than later. And because continuing to contain all that metal within your body would have rendered you ineligible to participate in his breeding program, he would have ripped it out of you using a far more brutal and barbaric method than mine simply for the pleasure watching you suffer would provide.

"He requires only your *body* to house the fetus," she continued, gripping the frame at the foot of the bed and leaning forward. "He does not need your *mind*."

The druidess waited a beat before releasing the bedframe and calling for Tanner to be brought in.

"Before I'm accused of forgetting my manners, my name is Ni'eve du Blanc. Welcome to my home. May all the rules and comforts of the Guest be given."

I didn't know what to say or how to respond—or even what part of her performance I was supposed to respond to. Alderose was shaking and whimpering from deep within her being. She pushed against me and Clementine with the little strength she had and said she needed to lie down. I turned my back to Ni'eve and tried to make my sister comfortable. She tapped the phone against her chest and stared at the ceiling.

"What did you do with my metal?" she finally asked.

"I have your metal right here."

That swiveled my head. Ni'eve slipped her hand into her robe's side pocket and withdrew a ruby pink crystal box. "All of it. I extracted it, and I have kept it safe and contained for the time when you are ready to have it re-enter your body."

"I'm ready. Right now."

"Are you?" Ni'eve asked, arching one dark eyebrow. At Alderose's silence, she nodded. "Then I shall make it so. The Keepers shall bathe the witch and bring her to the ritual garden." Clementine and I protested. Another raised eyebrow silenced us before the druidess left the room, her white-robed followers close behind.

"Rosey, how can you—"

"Will you two stay with me?" Alderose asked. Her knuckles

had gone white. I covered her hand with mine and tried to warm her up.

"Always."

"Yes."

"This changes our plans." Laszlo returned to Clementine's side. "If you two can stay with Alderose while she is made ready, Kostya and I will find Tanner and meet you at the ritual space."

"I'll stay if you want, though," Kostya said, crouching beside the cot. He rubbed Alderose's bony shoulder and let his touch linger on her arm. She didn't push him away. "You can do this, Rosey. I know you can. I'll heat the metal for you, if that helps."

Alderose bit her bottom lip and smiled weakly. "I would appreciate that. And I get that I can't just borrow Beryl's wand and magic the metal back. And I get that I can't fight against Lionel without it. Makes me too much of a liability."

I touched her gently on the shoulder. "Oh Rosey, I wouldn't say—"

"Of course you wouldn't say that, Beryl," she said, switching her gaze from Kostya to me. "Dad taught me how to fight without using any magic at all. Most days I can use my fists and my feet and my blades when I'm powered down. But I've never, *ever*, been drained like this. I can hardy lift my arms and legs without help. And we all know that's no way for me to go into battle. My skill is in my hands."

"Got it." Now was not the time to argue with Alderose Brodeur.

The demon brothers left. Four figures in moss-green robes entered the room and helped each other draw back the hoods covering their faces and neaten the stray hairs coming loose from their braids. All four were young women. The resemblances ended with their uniform clothing. They gestured with their hands until Clementine and I understood we were to step aside and make room for them to tend to our sister.

One went to the bank of sinks at the far end of the room and returned with a bowl of water topped with floating herbs and flower petals. She set it on the bedside table. Two others helped Alderose to sit while they stripped the bedding with practiced efficiency and replaced the sheets and blanket with layers of towels. The fourth young woman took her place at the foot of the bed, turned her palms skyward, and began a chant.

Clementine and I moved away from the Keepers and their ministrations, after first taking Alderose's phone, and watched as tender attention was lavished on our sister. First, they removed the druid-issued muslin nightdress and undergarments and washed every inch of Alderose's skin. After she was patted dry, one of the young women shook out a heavily embellished robe lined with fluffy white sheepskin and held it open. Alderose needed a moment to steady herself once she got to her feet.

I rushed in to help. I hadn't been at my sister's first metal ceremony. In hindsight, I couldn't recall any mention of it. But she needed me now, and I needed to help her. I propped her up as the robe was draped over her body. I only stepped away so one of her attendants could tie the warm garment closed in front.

"Want me to brush your hair?" I whispered. Alderose nodded. I smiled. My offer was a trick I employed when I was much younger and wanted to bask in her older-sister presence. When I asked for a brush, the Keeper who had brought over the bowl of water handed me a wide-toothed comb.

The four young women gathered in front of Alderose, bowed, and repositioned their hoods on their heads. Another druid entered the room and presented similar dark green robes to me and Clementine. I recognized the French word for snow as they fluttered their fingers in the air.

"Do you need shoes, Rosey?" I asked, drawing the comb through the ends of her hair. One of the Keepers shook her head and said, *Non*, then drew another Keeper to her side and gestured for Alderose to walk behind them. The remaining two Keepers moved me and Clementine behind Rosey, then gathered behind us.

Low voices began a simple song. Together, we passed out of the room, down the hall, and across the spacious entrance hall. We exited through a different door, one that opened onto a courtyard lined with cracked pots of overgrown trees. I didn't get the sense the château had been neglected, just that it was wild at its heart. Maybe a stronger or more attentive hand was needed to spruce it up—if that was even a concern.

Snowflakes drifted down. They didn't last once they were on the ground. We passed underneath a heavy stone arch and followed a pathway around the main part of the château. The Keepers led us through an elaborate, rusted gate and into an area protected by high walls and even higher, vine-choked trees.

Ni'eve was standing at the head of a waist-high altar. Warming torches had been placed in a wide circle around the altar and lit. Tanner stood opposite the druidess. His wavy hair was loose and fell to his shoulders, and he was barefoot. As we proceeded closer, I noticed his goddess-blessed blades were housed in their leather sheaths and strapped to his outer thighs.

Kostya and Laszlo stood to either side of the altar's chiseled, pale gray stone. Their hair was also loose. They had been given robes similar to ours. Together, the four Keepers, Clementine, and I continued to escort Alderose forward at a measured pace.

Up close, I could see a thick layer of translucent, silvery ice coating the top of the massive slab. I took the place next to Kostya. Clementine stopped when she got to Laszlo, and Alderose was brought to Tanner. The Keepers turned and took up places in between the torches and continued to sing.

At a signal from Ni'eve, Tanner hoisted my sister up by the waist and set her bundled body on the slab. I could see the vulnerability in her eyes, the wishing that she could do this part of the ritual on her own. Or maybe that was just me imagining how difficult it would be for me to be this vulnerable in front of strangers.

Tanner gently positioned her until her legs extended toward him and her head was close to Ni'eve.

"Do you remember how to execute the Breath of Acceptance, Alderose Brodeur?" the druidess asked.

"I remember."

"Clementine, Beryl, please assist with the removal of your sister's outer garment."

I had to coax Alderose's arms to straighten enough to slide the sleeves off. Removing the warmth and protection of the sheepskin in the cold air might have been harder than making my confession to Kostya. Ni'eve waited for me and Clementine to resume our places at the sides of the altar, then raised the crystal box high above Alderose's naked chest.

"The fire demon shall keep the surface of the witch's skin warm, thus keeping the metal in its liquid state. The ice demon is charged with keeping the altar cold. The ice will numb the surface of her body, allowing an abatement from the pain when the metal penetrates her outermost layers."

"I can help feed the ice," Clementine said. I'd seen her rest her hand on Laszlo's forearm and witnessed the resulting flash intensify the lines from his wrists to his elbows.

"What else may I do?" I asked.

"Your sister will need something to focus on. Stand close. Let her see your face, your eyes. Do not allow your gaze to waver. And do not touch her body until the absorption is complete."

In the background, the four Keepers continued to sing, adding percussive beats using their hands and small drums and rattles they must have stashed in pockets of their robes.

Carried deeper into the space of sacred ritual on the rhythm,

I found my sister's dark brown eyes. I created a connection between us based on the bonds of sisterhood and shared history. I discovered a smattering of brilliant red hairs threading through her mostly brunette waves. And the moment Ni'eve lifted the lid on the crystal box, I slid a finger between my corset and my skin and reopened the tear.

Beguilement, eager to be released, hovered near my ribs. I began to feed my magic to Alderose as Ni'eve poured a dense, silvery liquid onto my sister's sternum. I fed out more threads of pink-hued magic as my sister's jaw clenched against the onslaught of heated metal and frigid cold. I invited her to hold my wrist and nearly rescinded the invitation when bone met bone in her crushing grip.

I widened my peripheral vision in an attempt to observe what else was happening. Tanner had his palms pressed to Alderose's feet. The tendons on his neck and arms were taut, and his hair was sprouting vines adorned with tiny white leaves.

Kostya had shed his robe and activated the demon lines on his bared arms. Sweat rolled down the sides of his face as he waved his forearms above Alderose and murmured to the coating of living fire licking at his skin. The metal branching across her torso in ever smaller rivulets was kept in motion by his efforts.

Across from him, working in tandem, Laszlo and Clementine coaxed nerve-numbing ice into forming up the sides of my sister's limbs. Where ice met fire, drops of water hissed and spat. I returned my full attention to Alderose. Her eyes were closed. It was time for me to ramp up my efforts.

I poured more of my Beguilement into her, morphing the desire to belong to me into the desire to reunite with her magic. I pulled the tiniest hint of magic from the metal, blended it with the Beguilement, and pushed the combination through my sister's torso and out toward her fingertips and her toes, readying her body for the act of acceptance. There was nothing I could do about the pain that would accompany that embrace.

What I *could* give her entire being was the knowledge that this pain had meaning.

This pain had *power*.

And that accepting every pinch and pinprick and stab of sensation would lead to her regaining the thing she valued the most. And that the pain would end.

"Step away." Ni'eve's voice broke into my awareness. "Everyone. Slowly."

The Keepers quieted their instruments and voices. Kostya and Laszlo tempered their magics, though they didn't shut down the flow through their demon lines completely. Tanner drew his hands away from my sister's feet as Ni'eve emptied the last drops of liquid metal in an arrow-straight line from Alderose's navel to her pubic bone.

My sister—and the entire block of stone—were encased in blue-tinged ice with only a narrow strip of pale brown skin overlaid with a network of silvery lines. None of us could touch her. The next step, as Ni'eve quietly explained, involved inviting the metal inside.

Alderose was required to do that step all by herself. Her breath was leaving her body in short, hard exhales. Her belly muscles tensed from the effort. Fingers of frost reached over the curves of her waist and hips, searching for the metal. My sister stared at the sky, stiffened her spine and set her resolve, and inhaled.

She paused...and exhaled a piercing scream.

The high-pitched frequency burst the liquid metal into thousands of the thinnest, needle-sized slivers. Alderose sucked in a breath and drew the slivers into her body. Every last piece entered on that singular, prolonged inhalation. Pinpricks of ruby-red blood were left behind to sparkle for a moment before evaporating.

One more exaggerated breath and Alderose's chest and belly were coated in a dusting of fine, dark red powder. At Ni'eve's signal, Kostya swept his fire-coated arms up and down Alderose's length, freeing her of the ice. It took every ounce of restraint I had to not rush in and offer comfort.

Next, the four Keepers stepped forward and wrapped her in the sheepskin cloak. They lifted my sister's limp body with reverence, placed her onto a board with handles cut out on either side, and took her away through the spruce trees, in the opposite direction of the castle.

5

———

"Where are they taking Alderose?" I asked. My heart was pounding so hard I could hear it in my ears. Low branches swished back into place as the cortège carrying her passed out of sight.

"She's off to be buried," Ni'eve said.

"I want to witness."

Ni'eve turned her head, with its long, slightly hooked and noble nose toward me. "You have not been blessed."

"We're her *sisters.*" I stifled the urge to stomp my foot. Ni'eve had to understand I wasn't going away and even though Clementine hadn't said a thing, I knew she felt the same.

"Very well. You and whomever else would like to witness the symbolic death and rebirth of the witch, Alderose Brodeur, are welcome to follow her. My role in this ritual is finished, and Alderose is now in my debt. We will break our fast in the common dining hall at eleven. I shall hear your plan to rescue my daughter at that time."

Kostya slid his fingers through mine and made no move to leave until Ni'eve was gone. Once her rigid back disappeared beyond the gate, he led the way off the wide stone path onto a narrower one. The moss was finer here and denser underfoot, and these spruce trees were compact and gnarled.

"Why'd you hold us back?" I asked, pulling the wool blanket tighter around my shoulders.

"This is my first time in Chamonix," he said, shoving his arms into his borrowed robe's wide sleeves. "My first time at Château du Blanc. My first up-close experience with druids, surrounded by druidic magic. I'm not sure where we stand in regard to Ni'eve du Blanc, and I don't at all like that she removed something so vital to Alderose just to get us to rescue her daughter and now she's saying that Alderose is somehow in her debt. She's an arrogant ass, and that's fucked up."

"That bugs me too. She could have just asked," I said. Though I suspected Ni'eve wasn't the ask-nicely type. I hugged Kostya close and accepted the kiss he dropped on my head. "Thanks for staying alert."

"And thank you for saying exactly what I was thinking, brother," Laszlo said.

Kostya grunted. "C'mon, I suspect there's an overgrown labyrinth between us and Alderose."

There was, and the deeper we went and the more turns we made, the shorter and denser the bordering trees became. I had to use my robe to shield my face. Laszlo hopped on to a random slab of marble and said he could see a clearing, as well as the four women carrying Alderose.

"Can we please run?" Clementine asked. "I don't like being this far from her."

"As soon as we're out of this part of the labyrinth." A few strides later, Kostya paused to hold aside the overgrown branches blocking our exit.

Side-by-side, the four of us strode over crunchy, snow-dusted meadow grasses toward the Keepers. They disappeared into the ground, then reappeared one at a time to take positions at the corners of what turned out to be an entrance. As we got closer, I could see a set of narrow steps leading below.

"Someone should stand guard," Laszlo said. He peered into the hole, stretched out his wings, and glanced to each of the Keepers.

The tallest one, who appeared to be their spokesperson, spoke. "Would you like us to continue guarding the cardinal directions while you wait?"

"Is that an essential part of the ritual?" Clementine asked.

"Standing guard is more of a symbolic gesture. Not everyone does well with the underground segment of these rituals."

"How long before Alderose is able to arise?"

The Keeper pressed her hands to her chest and dropped her gaze. She seemed to be counting, or tracking, or listening.

"If she has not risen on her own power within another three hundred or so breaths, you may descend."

Kostya, Laszlo, Clementine, and I took up positions close to the opening. I found myself counting my breaths, and then losing track before I got to fifty.

"May I ask why you are called Keepers?"

She smoothed her robes and checked in with the other three. They nodded and returned their attention to the gaping hole in front of us.

"The mission of the Keepers began long ago, in another place and another time, and was bestowed upon our earliest sisters by the Goddess Idunn, she who keeps the apples of immortality. Myth tells us Idunn was once kidnapped by Loki, the trickster. Though Idunn was returned, safeguards had to be put into place to ensure, should she be kidnapped again—or worse—the gods of Asgard would always have access to the apples."

The Keeper telling the story paused, pressed her hands to

her chest again, and went quiet. She picked up her story many breaths later and spoke more slowly than before.

"The earliest caretakers of the seeds of Idunn's apples were culled from her female followers. In return for safekeeping the lineage of the fruit, this group of thirteen were gifted with the ability to change their form. One of the forms they may take is that of the apple tree.

"Most of the early safekeepers chose to make that change just once, as their human lives were ending. While one of the Keepers was in the lengthy process of making her final change, a younger one was beginning her initiation into their ways. This allowed the thirteen to stay at a constant number.

"Within a few generations, the Keepers had to look farther and farther for women willing to commit to the rigors and responsibilities of their role. A handful of the younger ones decided to experiment with changing back and forth while they were still in their fertile years.

"They discovered that as long as they bled monthly, they could shift between human and tree, thereby keeping a semblance of a normal, human life. But even with this development, they could not bear children and their numbers dwindled until only three of these women were left."

She took a deep breath in, let it out slowly, and paused. "Together, the three agreed to experiment with their own mortality by eating the sacred apples—which they were warned never to do. They began to morph into a hybrid of human and tree at the cellular level. Which meant they could bear human children. And some of those children carried the capacity to bear the apples of immortality.

"Grisette is one of these women. Ni'eve is her only child. And the four of us here, plus Jessamyne, are all granddaughters of those three. There are more Keepers, and most of them are in our orchards settling into their wintersleep.

"None of us had any choice but to grow up in the Keeper tradition. That is our story, and that is why Ni'eve is so intent on getting the Apple Witch back.

"And if my count is correct, your sister's three hundred breaths are complete."

She and the three others bowed toward the opening in the ground, turned, and left, the hems of their robes whispering across the clumps of wild grasses. Clementine, Laszlo, Kostya, and I stepped into their places. I was ready to retrieve my sister, and I wanted a moment to absorb the Keeper's story.

"That was...intense," I said.

"I'll say. To have no choice about your path? No wonder Jessamyne's trying so hard to break away." Clementine shook off her blanket, folded it, and placed it on the stone threshold. I handed her the one I was wearing, and she folded it too.

"Let's get Rosey. Got light, Beryl?"

As long as I had my fingers, I had light. Though that was another thing I had been keeping from my sisters—and from Kostya. To activate most aspects of my magic, the acknowledgment of intent, the uttering of a spell, and a simple flick of my fingers was sufficient.

I decided to stop pretending I needed a wand for something as mundane as creating light. Once we descended enough the weak sunlight no longer penetrated, I lifted my hand, pictured a bright yellow flame, and uttered *lucerna lumen*.

The light coming from the end of my fingertips intensified the darker it got. Crumbling stones walls weeping with moisture were hungry. My light was the toll we paid for safe passage. I didn't need a Keeper or a directional sign to fill me in on the appetites of the local magic. Here, underground, it was palpable, and I wanted Alderose out.

"How did they get her all the way down here and back up so fast?"

"You read my mind," Kostya said. "You sure you're okay going first?"

I growled at him and continued. We weren't that deep into the crypt, the magic was minding its manners, and I could sense a bigger space waiting ahead. A few more steps and I could see my sister lying prone on an altar much like the one in the château's ritual garden.

Only here, Alderose was convulsing so hard the sheepskin cloak had fallen away from her body. I raised my arm with the lit fingers, scooped my other arm underneath her shoulders, and brought her closer to my chest.

"Sissy, Kostya, she's...*leaking*." Crimson droplets littered the front of Alderose's belly, concentrating in the half-moon dip between her hip bones. Kostya rushed forward and stopped just short of pushing me out of the way and scooping Alderose into his arms.

"She's dropped a lot of weight too," he observed, touching her gently. "Fat and muscle mass, from when we grabbed her at the Facility to now. That's less than twenty-four hours. What the fuck's going on?"

"Look at her closely. Either of you see a more obvious wound?" I rolled her toward me and waved the light across her back. Kostya shook his head.

"Rosey. Rosey, wake up." The ground below and around us shook. "Is that coming from her?" Clementine fumbled for the handle of the board Alderose had been carried in on and shielded her legs with her body.

Kostya pointed to the low ceiling and the tangle of rootlets keeping the larger pebbles and bits of dirt from landing on our heads. "That rhythm sounds like a horse. Let's get Alderose out of here and back to the infirmary. Or maybe we should bypass the druids and just call Malvyn or Maritza."

"I like *that* plan," I said. I took a fistful of the sheepskin and pulled it over my sister's exposed hip and shoulder. Clementine did the same on the other side, tied the sash as best she could, then stepped away so Kostya could bundle Alderose into his arms.

"Lead the way, my witch."

We were through the room and halfway up the crumbling, uneven stairs when we heard Laszlo yell for someone to halt. He yelled again, louder and more stridently, before adding his own thunderous stride to the shaking ground. I doused my flames, sited Laszlo's location, and turned to guide Kostya over the raised lip of the crypt. Clementine scrambled out from behind him and went right into a crouch.

Wings arched and legs pumping, Laszlo was chasing a white horse and gaining rapidly. Whatever large thing was draped over the saddle flapped in the air as the beast galloped through a tight turn and headed straight for us.

"Fuck." Kostya set Alderose on the ground and threw off his robe. He motioned for me and Clementine to sit with her, then joined his brother in the chase. If my sister hadn't been in such a wasted condition, I might have enjoyed the live-action fantasy of watching two well-muscled demons giving chase to a white horse with a flowing tail and mane. But these weren't normal times, and I had been drained of my belief in fairy tales and happy endings the day I turned Micah to stone.

Alderose moaned. Clementine managed to get her arm underneath her head and lift it enough that she could bite off the corner of the scarab eater's treat she'd thought to bring.

"Water," Alderose croaked.

"We forgot to bring water, Rosey," I said. "We're taking you back to the druid's infirmary. You're still bleeding."

She collapsed against Clementine, closed her eyes, and chewed. She even opened her mouth when she finished, like a little bird hungrily requesting another bite. In the field, Laszlo and Kostya double-teamed the horse and were able to get it to slow down to a walk. The poor thing's sides were heaving, and it was freaking out at Laszlo's wings. Laz handed the reins to Kostya and ran toward the three of us.

Blood flecked the front of his robe, shirt, and pants. He pressed his finger to his lips, shook his head, and gestured for us to stand.

"I'll carry Alderose," he said, jerking his head in the direction of the castle. "You two walk in front of us. Make a straight line for the opening in the trees and then hoof it. We've got a life or death situation and we need the healers."

Clementine and I knew when to follow orders. Whatever else Laszlo wasn't saying had to be bad. We gathered up the blankets, and I found myself running for the second time in one day. This time I had no desire to complain. I looked back to see Alderose's head bouncing against Laz's chest, and powered forward at his grim nod. Right before Clementine and I had to stop to hold the trees apart to let Laszlo onto the path, I looked back again.

Alderose had climbed half out of the sheepskin cloak and was elbowing Laszlo in the face. Her naked backside was streaked with blood and I couldn't help wishing that Laz's introduction to the oldest Brodeur sister had come with less... commotion.

"Whoa, Rosey, stop," I yelled. "He's helping you. We're helping you." I ran back, jumped, and grabbed for her arm. It was like closing my fingers around a metal tube. "*Goddess*, you're strong."

"Help him," she said, slurring her words. "Help. *Him*." She managed to wiggle out of the sheepskin enough she was now propped on Laszlo's shoulder, facing back toward Kostya and the white horse and whatever it was on its back.

"Who's *him*, Alderose?"

"It's Guillaume," she said, pointing frantically.

I turned to look, and that's when I put a face I barely remembered to the body on the horse. Guillaume. Lionel Vigne's indentured vampire.

Laszlo had to put Alderose down to see to the vampire before she would agree to enter the tree-lined labyrinth. She insisted we blindfold the horse and cover Guillaume's body with her sheepskin cloak to protect him from the branches.

I ignored her orders and suggested Kostya use the robe the Keepers had loaned him on Guillaume. I didn't have the heart to say there wasn't much left of him to protect. Alderose accepted my suggestion then insisted she was the only one who could lead the horse.

When Rosey insisted, humans and Magicals alike followed. And so we emerged from the mystical labyrinth onto the grounds of Château du Blanc: two witches of below average height, fully clothed; a winged demon with long, silvery white hair and blood splattered clothing; another witch, also short and also covered with blood, leading a glittering, skittish horse with an awful burden; and another demon, eyes on fire, bringing up the rear.

"Who the fuck does that to another being?" Kostya whispered as we gathered at the same side entrance we'd emerged from only a couple hours ago. He stepped away from our group, lifted his face skyward as he scanned the high walls, and yelled for Tanner.

The wide, double doors in front of us opened, and a handful of castle inhabitants streamed out. Tanner rounded the corner of the building and started barking out orders on the run.

"Stable Master, Ni'eve's horse has returned."

He stopped, lifted the robe off Guillaume, and made a fast assessment. "Healers, we have a flayed man, a vampire. Keepers, alert Ni'eve."

"I'm going with Guillaume," Alderose said, extending her arm and waving me closer. "I need more scarab medicine. What you gave me helped. Give me the rest."

"Clementine has the crackers, Rosey. You need water, you need to get checked out, and you need to eat and bathe. Let their healers take care of the vampire."

"I can't leave him, Beryl. I won't leave him. I need revenge on Vigne. Revenge for what he made Guillaume do to you and for what he's now done to him."

I swallowed everything I wanted to say. Leaving my sister to her heroics, I entered the castle and, by some miracle, made it to the room Kostya and I shared without getting lost. I wanted out of the gore-flecked clothes and into another bath.

I dropped the blanket and stripped off my boots and the loaner pants. By the time I was naked, my demon was already in the bathroom, warming the water filling the copper tub.

"My sister is a...a...*uff.*"

Kostya wisely kept his mouth shut and turned up the flames lining his arms and legs.

"She's going to lead us into a fight before we're ready, isn't she? Just like *that.*" I snapped my fingers for added emphasis.

Kostya gave a small shrug. "She's doing exactly what she would do if it had been any one of us on that horse."

"Since when does the vampire who almost killed *me* get the VIP treatment?"

I glared at the demon as I stepped into the tub and lowered my butt onto the slatted seat. I felt like a character in an illustrated kid's book, all ready for my adventure on the open sea. All I was missing was a tricorn hat and a wooden sword.

I placed a hand over the now slightly larger tear in my corset and stared belligerently into Kostya's eyes. Within moments I surrendered my frustration to his more measured and understanding point of view.

"You have this amazing ability to melt away all my righteous indignation with a look," I said, accepting the bar of soap he held out.

"Noted. Now, tell me what's going on with that?" He waggled his finger at my midsection. "You did something to your corset before Ni'eve poured the liquid metal on Alderose."

"You saw me?"

"I did."

I rolled the soap between my hands, working up a lather and releasing the scent, thinking that I wasn't at my best when I was angry. I was already regretting my outburst.

"There's a lot Alderose has never shared with me and Clementine, especially about her relationship with our father and how he nurtured her magic. She's never talked about what they had to do to get her body to accept the metal the first time. She and my dad are both Unbinders. Did you know that?"

He said he did.

"Well," I said. "I feel like Clementine and I are just beginning to piece together who Alderose is. What she was trained for. What she's capable of.

"When she said that thing about feeling tingly, like her magic was coming back, I knew it wasn't. She was lying there looking so helpless and so damn hopeful. And I could sense the complete lack of, of every quality I normally associate with her."

I spread the fragrant lather over my arms and around my breasts. "It messed my sister up to see Ni'eve walk in, and that's the moment I decided I would try to ease Rosey's pain any way I could, because her pain isn't just physical.

"It's...I think it might be existential, something she was born with, something she will always have to carry." I shrugged and started to rinse the soap off my skin. "My solution was to pull out the smallest thread of the metal's magic, bind it to mine, and infuse that combination throughout Rosey's body. I wanted her to know the pain that was coming had a purpose, to accept it, not fight it."

"That doesn't seem like such a bad thing," Kostya said, rising to shake out a towel. The floor was cold, and I had to dash into the bigger room and paw through the standing closet for another set of druid-made clothes.

"It was an *untested* thing, Kos. I hadn't tried it on anyone, and before today, no one Magical, no one situation, has made me think *combining* another magic with mine would be a good idea." I left out the part about what I'd discovered when I was a kid, about *borrowing* other Magicals' abilities. I'd leave that for another time.

Kostya leaned against the open closet and watched me hop from foot to foot to avoid the cold floor as I dressed. His gaze was deeply appreciative.

"You listening?" I asked.

"Always. I watched the whole thing, Beryl. I saw your sister's fear become something else and I assumed it was her accepting fate? But to know that your desire was to help, and that your instinct was to use your unique magic as a kind of...flux? That was brilliant."

6

As I made my way from our room to the ground floor, it seemed like the mood in the castle had shifted. When we first arrived, there was a kind of curiosity about the witches and demons who were here to run a rescue mission. Now, a palpable tension surrounded everyone I passed on my walk through the main hall.

My shoulders relaxed when I entered the dining hall and saw Maritza, Alabastair, and Malvyn seated at the head table with Ni'eve. Parked on the floor behind my aunt and her lover was the same assortment of luggage I recognized from their recent visit to Northampton.

Which meant the elders of my family had come prepared to wield magic.

That was a relief. I hugged the newest arrivals and breathed in the scent of family. I wanted my aunt's opinion on mending the corset. I needed to ask if either she or my uncle had heard of other instances where the Demesne had become entangled with the primary magic of any of our ancestors. Ni'eve's tight lips suggested now was not the time for small talk.

Helpers exited the kitchen area and circled our table with trays. Kostya set a small, round baking dish on my plate along with a chocolate croissant. He knew I needed to have something savory like the baked eggs before I ate anything sweet, and that I always gravitated toward eating the sweet thing first.

Across from me, Alabastair was lavishing the same attention on Maritza, only her portions were smaller and there was a greater variety. We'd all become aware that once the two of them were united by the Demesne, the curse caused their magics to take from one to fill the other. Given that he was much taller and larger all around than my slender aunt, feeding her was his full-time side gig. I suspected the Portal Keeper carried some guilt about this aspect of their bond and wondered if my uncle was working on a piece of spelled jewelry or a trinket that could prevent the imbalance from happening.

"Beryl. We hear you've had quite a morning already." My aunt's amused gaze caught me about to shove a big piece of croissant into my mouth. I set it back on the plate.

"Mm-hmm, we have." I leaned forward and lowered my voice. "Do you think I could speak with you and Uncle Malvyn after we eat? Alone?"

She reached across the table and stroked the top of my hand lightly as she studied my face. "It's urgent, isn't it?"

"Very."

Ni'eve shoved her chair away from the table and cleared her throat as she stood. "My presence is required with the healers and the vampire. There is a classroom in the same wing as the infirmary. I will meet with all of you there as soon as I am able."

She gathered her robes in her hands and swished away from the table. Maritza whispered in Alabastair's ear. He glanced at me, reached for one of their suitcases, and withdrew two smaller cases. I recognized one held needles and the other held threads.

At my aunt's nod, he extricated himself from the communal bench, helped her to stand, and handed over the cases.

"Malvyn? Can you spare a quarter hour? Beryl has asked for our counsel."

My uncle hurriedly wiped his mouth, checked his watch, and excused himself.

"Shall we meet in my room?" he asked, joining us in the hall.

We followed him into the tower, up the stairs, and down the same hall as the other guest rooms. He placed a palm-sized metal disc on the center panel of his door, turned it right and left repeatedly and pushed the door open once a set of tumblers released whatever spell he'd set.

"Just a little something I do no matter where I stay. I'm afraid I can't offer either of you anything to drink."

"I don't need anything more to drink *or* eat, Uncle Mal," I said. "What I do need is your expertise." I shrugged out of the bulky sweater and placed it over the room's only chair. Drawing up the hem of my next layer, a soft cotton T-shirt, I kept my chest covered but exposed my belly.

"What do we have here?" Maritza asked, coaxing the little chair across the floorboards with a flick of her wrist and parking it in front of me. She sat, spread her fingers, and waved her hands slowly over my torso without once touching the invisible garment. My uncle watched her, then set down his briefcase, flicked the clasps, and drew on a pair of red-lensed glasses.

"No," he said, more to himself than to either my aunt or me. He chose another, more elaborate pair of exam-style glasses with multiple lenses and slid them on.

"What are those?" I asked, following Maritza's request that I turn in place.

"Interference lenses," Malvyn said. "They filter out all but the primary forces at play on the surface of a magical object or, as in your case, a body. When your aunt has finished, I would like you to step onto the chair. We'll first set it closer to the windows where there's better light."

"Let's get her up there now, Mal." Once on the chair, I held the T-shirt in place and studied the walls and the exposed beams. Everything was identical to the room I shared with Kostya. Even the sense that the beams and walls were alive.

"What do you two think of the magic in this place?" I asked.

"Well…" My aunt's voice trailed off for a moment. "One can feel that the original building materials were quarried and extracted from this land or harvested from plants and trees that grew here. You sense it, don't you, mija?"

"I'm aware of a presence," I said. "The magic feels very alive, like the beams could grow branches and snatch me."

My aunt caught my eye and grinned. "You have a beautiful imagination, Beryl. And your imagination's not all that far off. Druids cultivate a oneness with their surroundings, learning over the course of their initial training to join with the elements and with other living things. They even—*oh* dear."

She tapped her chin. "Malvyn, I see the problem."

"Mmm, I see it too," he said, coming closer to the chair. Absorbed in whatever it was he was observing through his special glasses, he pointed to the tear in the corset. "That is an extraordinary garment, Beryl, able to continue doing what it was created to do even as it heals the damage it sustained.

"That said, your magic is leaking, yet I see no reason to think you will suffer from a lack of power anytime soon."

"Look more closely, brother."

Malvyn and Maritza exchanged looks. He refocused the lenses on his glasses and returned to examining my front. Two minutes later, he sat on the edge of the nearest bed and echoed my aunt's, "Oh dear."

"Is there a problem?" I asked, knowing there had to be.

Malvyn removed the interference lenses. He folded in the

earpieces and nestled the glasses back in their special case before looking at me.

"Without further tests, I cannot say with absolute certainty what has occurred here, Beryl. But I can posit a theory. Mari, would you care to go first?"

"Let me get a needle threaded and seal up the last bit of that rip."

She opened one case, then the other, quickly chose a needle and a length of the palest pink thread and let go. The thread found its way through the eye of the needle, and with a flick of her fingers, the needle floated toward my belly. I felt the slightest sting when the point met the corset. Ten stings later, the needle backed away.

My aunt took my hand and helped me step down off the chair. She handed me the sweater I'd removed and while I put it on, she returned the needle to its case.

"Before I tell you what I think," she said, "I would like for you to share with us how it is you came to possess this garment."

For the second time in twenty-four hours, I explained both the sandbox incident and the greenhouse tragedy. I relayed what I knew of the sea witch who'd made the original garment, and who continued to send me a new one every year on my birthday. I hadn't met her in person since I was fitted for my first corset, I didn't know what she did with the used corsets, and I doubted I could pull her out of a line-up. I didn't leave out anything pertinent to the garment.

"Let me begin with what is clear, mija. Your base magic was that of Binder. As you know, your mother took her base magic, explored its possibilities, its desires, and decided that becoming a matchmaker provided the best application of her skills."

My aunt cleared her throat. "I assume you noticed I used the past tense when I spoke of your Binder magic. It is no longer viable in you. I am afraid the Demesne has met a similar end.

Though I can see where the Demesne once resided in you. It was strong, wild almost."

"I was going to say untamed," my uncle interjected, "though I imagine fourteen years of wearing that corset had a lot to do with what is there now."

"Malvyn, have you ever heard anyone in our family speak of the Demesne happening at age *seven*?"

"Never, Mari. And that is what's throwing a wrench into my theorizing."

"Mine too. But I'll put it on the table anyways. Beryl," she said, lowering herself onto the chair, "I think the garment became a crucible. That in doing its intended job, which was to suppress the Demesne, it gave no space for your natural magic to develop in the normal ways of most witches.

"By keeping everything confined and not allowing your Binder magic free rein, it forced it to bond with the Demesne, and in the process, something wholly new was created. And that something new is this thing you call Beguilement."

"Does that mean I have Binder magic, the Demesne, *and* the Beguilement?" I asked.

My aunt hesitated to respond. "Malvyn? What were you able to see with your glasses?"

"I'm afraid the Demesne is gone and what I can see of the Binder magic is merely a shadow."

I slipped my hands underneath the cotton shirt, felt for the boundaries of the corset, tried to absorb what my aunt and uncle were saying. And everything they weren't saying.

"I'll finish by agreeing with my sister's assessment, which is you have inadvertently become the creator of a new strain of magic. The closest I can relate your Beguilement to is that of the Siren's song and the succubus's lure."

I felt myself smirk before I could stop. "Except that I'm not trying to lure anyone to their death or drain them."

"Are you engaged in a regular practice with the Beguilement? Getting to know its potential and its limits?"

I shook my head. "Before this morning, when I used it to manipulate the magic within the metal before it went into Alderose? No. And I only did that so she could survive having the metal returned to her body. I've been terrified to work with the Beguilement. In fact—"

Just then someone knocked. Malvyn went to the door and opened it for Kostya. My chest swelled at the concern in my demon's eyes.

"Kostya, come in," Malvyn said. "And excuse me for getting right to the point. We're pressed for time. Have you felt any shift in Beryl's magic since you arrived in Northampton, what was it, two weeks ago now?"

"None at all in her magic. Though we did stop—I mean we haven't—" Kostya didn't usually fumble for words. "We hit the pause button on our physical relationship because of something happening in my body."

"Would you mind sharing more details?"

"Not at all." Kostya managed to pull his sweater over his head without snagging it on his horns and laid it on the end of the bed. He pulled his T-shirt forward and again over his head, exposing his muscled shoulders and the upper part of his back. Ridges under the skin and to either side of his spine gave evidence to the changes that started to take place when we were having sex in his walk-in closet.

"Come closer to the light, please," my aunt said. Malvyn again took out his interference lenses, made an adjustment, and examined Kostya's skin.

"I'm no expert on demon physiology," he said, "and I would certainly defer to the elders of your realm. From what I can see, the awakening of your wings is coming about because of the demonic imperative about the order of things once one's fated mate has appeared. This is happening because of a push coming from within you, not as a response to Beryl's external pull."

"So... that's good, right?" I asked.

My uncle removed his glasses and held them by the frame. "If Kostya's wings began to grow during moments of intimacy with you, Beryl, I imagine it's because his essence believes he has found his fated mate in you. And because you wear this imbued corset and have experienced some version of the Demesne twice before in your life—it was only the two times, correct?"

"Correct." I nodded hard. After seeing Micah turn to stone, I'd had no wish to date. Ever. Until Kostya Arkadi came into my life—as Alderose's sort-of boyfriend. "I've been encased in some version of the corset twenty-four hours a day since I was fourteen. I was wearing it when Kostya and I first met."

I had been twenty-one, freshly graduated from college, ready to embark on a career in retail marketing and merchandising. I was in my mother's shop when Kostya passed in front of the windows of Needle and Sins.

I didn't know he was on his way to meet my sister. He looked for all the world like a horned demigod surveying his lands. I had grabbed my phone off the counter and run out the door intending to get his picture, only to meet a solid wall of demon chest and Alderose's very amused expression.

"Beryl. *Beryl*." Maritza snapped her fingers in the air. I apologized. "What you have come to believe is that your leaking magic, combined with what happened in your past, means that Kostya's physical response is false?"

"Exactly," I agreed. In that moment, the strain of constant vigilance eased simply by being able to share my concern first with Kostya, and now with my aunt and uncle.

"Mija, with what my brother and I observed, the Demesne is no longer viable. The Demesne is gone. Your Binder magic is similarly gone. What you are left with is the magic that is the birthright of every witch—underdeveloped as it is—and this marvelous thing that is uniquely yours."

"You make it all sound perfectly rational. Now what do I do?"

"Well, that's up to you and Kostya." She turned to her brother. "Malvyn, would you check the garment for leakage one more time?"

My uncle willingly donned his glasses. "No more pretty pink magic leaking out. How is your spell casting functioning?"

"It's been fine," I said. With the corset repaired, I could channel power for the work ahead to flow out both arms and all ten fingers without having to worry about it coming loose from other places.

"Kostya, Beryl, can the two of you set aside your desire to explore what this news means for your personal relationship, until we have seen this mission through to completion?" my uncle asked. "It is my preference that we all hold our current focus until Lionel Vigne is in custody."

"I can and will," Kostya said.

"Me too." I agreed. Though I was giddy at the prospect of being given the okay to explore this thing my...body? my magic? had created.

"Who's putting together the plan for how we're going to do this?" I asked. "I've never been part of anything like trying to take down a criminal, but there's no way I'm standing on the sidelines. And you definitely don't want me assigned to the infirmary."

Kostya stiffened. Without him saying a thing, I knew he didn't embrace my eagerness to be inside the action. He had to understand, and accept, this had gotten personal for me starting with my abduction from the royal ball, and in the hours afterward when I woke up with donated bloods from half a dozen Magicals flowing through my body.

Malvyn gathered his things and offered my aunt his elbow. "I would like to hear what Ni'eve has to say, and I reserve the right to edit my current opinion of her."

"If anyone asks, Beryl and I will be down shortly." I wasn't expecting Kostya to steer me out of Malvyn's room, down the hall to the stairwell and out the door we'd passed through earlier. He didn't stop until we were close to the spruce trees bordering the labyrinth.

"Why the need for secrecy this time?" I asked.

He turned me to face him, slid his hands over my shoulders and down my arms until he was squeezing my fingers. I squeezed back and reminded him though I was short and mighty, he was the one with a crushing grip. Especially when he was worried. And my guy was worried.

"Beryl, there's nothing I can say to prevent you from volunteering to go to Lionel's, is there?"

"That's correct. Especially not after seeing the inside of the Facility. Sure, there weren't very many captives—at least not that we could see—and we left Jake inside because he insisted. But before there was you and me and everyone else who're trying to fix this situation, there was my mother."

I took a big breath and barreled forward. "In a way, this mission is *my* legacy, Kostya. Mine and Clementine's and Alderose's. I *have* to go in there. I have to witness. And even though I haven't asked my sisters, I know they feel the same way."

Kostya's brown eyes and long lashes captured my attention. "Will you promise me, Beryl, *promise* me, that you'll stick with me, that we'll only separate if it's the right thing to do from a tactical standpoint or if it will save your life?"

For whatever reason, Kostya had gone to his knees in front of me. I had to accept he wasn't down there because the Beguilement was forcing him to kneel. He was there, he was *here*, with *me*, because he wanted to be.

"I promise I will stick to you like white fuzz on a black sweater. In fact," I added, leaning over to kiss him, "I really like the idea of us fighting alongside each other."

"A good thing too," he said with a wry smile. "I would never want to find myself fighting opposite a Brodeur woman."

7

HELPFUL DRUIDS DIRECTED ME AND KOSTYA TO THE CLASSROOM where Ni'eve expected us to gather. My aunt and uncle followed us in. Alabastair, Clementine, Laszlo, and Tanner were already at a table covered with scratches and burn marks. Alabastair stood quickly and offered to make tea for everyone. He added a pointed reminder to my aunt that he'd seen an appetite stimulant among the herbal offerings and would she like two or three cookies with hers?

I poked Kostya and let him know I'd take a mug of peppermint tea with honey and two cookies would be fine. I got a kiss full on the lips before he went to help Alabastair.

I was still smiling to myself when Ni'eve strode in, her voluminous white robes flapping around her long legs. Her hair had been corralled into two whip-like braids that ended at her butt, and she hadn't bothered to take off the blood-splattered smock from her time in the infirmary. I gave her points for the dramatic entrance. Knowing more about her background from the Keepers, and her attendant responsibilities, I could understand why she seemed to require the spotlight.

Tanner rushed forward and drew out the heavy chair at the

head of the table. He waited for Ni'eve to sit before retaking his seat.

"Is there an update on Guillaume's condition?" he asked.

She glanced down, noticed what she was wearing, and slipped her arms out of the smock. One of her assistants materialized at her side and whisked the bloodied garment away. Another assistant waited by her chair with a bowl of water and a hand towel.

"The vampire will live," she said, immersing her arms up to her elbows in the bowl. "I have asked Maritza to apply her renowned needles and threads to his wounds."

My aunt pressed her lips together in a gesture I was starting to recognize as her annoyed face.

"I *volunteered* to attend to him the moment word of his injuries reached me, Ni'eve, as I would for any of my nieces' friends. If he is stable, I shall go to him right now."

"Finish your tea."

I found Ni'eve's treatment of my aunt to be off-putting. Alabastair wrapped his arm around the back of Maritza's chair and whispered into her ear. The smile she gave him assured me she was fine. Maybe me thinking my slender-boned aunt needed to be coddled was similar to the way others expected less of me in the magic department. Most times what they noticed were my manicures and custom-made dresses.

I took a page from Kostya's book. Never underestimate *any* of the Brodeur witches.

While I was tracking my aunt and Alabastair, and fussing inside my head, someone must have asked a question because Ni'eve raised a finger.

"Lest anyone become overly excited by the ease with which you accomplished what you did last night, know the Vignes are never, *ever* to be underestimated. Lionel Vigne was banished from fae lands close to three hundred years ago. Here, within the protective shadow of the Alps, he has gone to great lengths to protect what he feels is his."

"Even when what he considers *his* is an autonomous being?" I asked, unable to stop myself from butting in. "One whose wants and desires were never considered before he brought them to his fortress?"

I was able to stop myself from adding a comment along the lines of her being okay with what Lionel was doing, as long as he wasn't poaching Keepers from her. Ni'eve ignored me and asked for more tea.

"Help us get inside Lionel's head," my aunt said, sitting taller in her chair. I mimicked the move. "It almost sounds as though you consider him a friend."

"I would not call him a friend, Maritza, though Lionel and I have always made an effort to get along. Considering the length of our lives, it's a prudent approach. Otherwise—" She shrugged one shoulder and examined her nails.

"Then what moved him to take your daughter? Surely he would have known such an act sends a very aggressive signal."

Ni'eve drummed her fingers on the table. I admired my aunt for continuing to push for clarity.

"I don't know why he took my daughter. Jessamyne had returned to me, to this place, at the end of the summer after a long sojourn. She'd barely resettled herself into our schedule when she disappeared."

Malvyn asked Ni'eve how she discovered that Jessamyne ended up in the Facility.

"Four of the druids who live here year-round accepted vulture as their air animal form. They monitor the entire valley, alerting me when they spot anything out of the ordinary. Their surveillance routine includes regular fly-bys of Lionel's new tower, the Facility. The topmost floor has mostly glass walls, and one of the birds noticed a tree inside with a chain around its trunk. On closer look, the birds determined the tree's shape resembled that of those found in our sacred orchards and reported their findings to me."

Ni'eve shook her head and sighed. "Jessamyne has something of a reputation. Through decades of experimentation, she has turned herself into a unique Magical, one that can take human form, tree form, other forms—and still bear offspring. Human offspring. She is known as the Apple Witch."

"One can see how Lionel Vigne might find that irresistible," Malvyn said.

"Oh, yes. Yet prior to her return, he never showed any interest in her, at least none that I noticed. The Vignes and I have maintained a peaceful truce for decades and have stayed out of each other's businesses. Through Jessamyne's abduction, I have been made aware of what Lionel and Linette have been up to. It horrifies me to think I never knew what was happening right across our property line. And it mortifies me that I shared Jessamyne's accomplishments with Lionel out of maternal pride."

I wasn't completely buying this contrite, uninformed version of Ni'eve. Her excuse, her entire tone of voice, lacked sincerity.

"Were you not aware that my mother, Moira, had been coming here for *years* to rescue those Magicals?" I asked. "She used the same tunnels we used to go in and get Alderose. She even had a place to stay underneath your mother's house. Clementine and I saw it this morning."

Ni'eve flared her nostrils. "The Crone has been out of her mind for decades. You can't trust a quarter of what she says."

"She seemed pretty sharp to us," Clementine said.

"Frankly, I can't remember the last time I saw or spoke with my mother."

Malvyn, who had been mostly silent, cleared his throat.

"Before Maritza leaves to help Guillaume I would like to know why you did what you did to Alderose."

Ni'eve had already explained to Alderose why she removed her metal. I was curious to see how she would spin her actions for my uncle, whom she probably viewed as more her equal.

"The Vignes had my daughter, Malvyn, and the only way I could guarantee Jessamyne's continued safety was to perform the Ritual of Removal when Lionel asked. They suspected Alderose had magic at her disposal that prevented them from using her body for reproductive purposes. I had every intention of putting her metal back when the time was right."

"What you did goes against Magical Law."

"What I *did*, any parent would have done to save the life of their child."

"One could argue it has been a long time since Jessamyne was a child, Ni'eve," Malvyn countered.

Alderose entered the classroom during Ni'eve and Malvyn's standoff. Her face was drawn and pale except for two bright red patches on her cheeks. She focused her attention on her sweater's overly long sleeves.

"I saw Jessamyne when I was being given a tour of the Facility, Ni'eve. Lionel's exact words were, *We have one of the druidess's tree witches in our possession*. After he said that, I put my hands on her trunk—at the time, I didn't know the tree was your daughter—and I felt a great deal of compassion for whomever was trapped there. Because Lionel said something else I found unsettling, and I couldn't tell if he was speaking the truth or simply bragging."

"And what did he say?" Ni'eve's voice dripped with disdain.

"According to him, Jessamyne practically begged them to take her." Alderose paused. "And according to him, he's the preferred match to father a child with her."

If Alderose was hoping to get a reaction out of our host, it worked. Ni'eve shoved her chair away from the table and shot to standing. Her braids whipped around her arms and her robes parted in front. The movements reminded me of Rémy and the way the mage could manipulate water and wind to terrifying effect. I half expected a snow squall to come tearing through the room.

Ni'eve pressed her hand against Tanner's chest when he tried to come closer. "Jessamyne would *never*—"

"Ni'eve, stop," Tanner said, circling his fingers around her wrist and forcing her arm down. "It's time you faced the truth. Jessamyne's only priority is Jessamyne. We both know she was only going through the motions while she was here, and she knows *exactly* what to say to manipulate your bond. She convinced you she didn't need restraints, magical or otherwise. Believe me, I know how hard it is to refuse her. She capitalized on my feelings for her for years, long after she'd killed any chance of us being together permanently."

I caught Clementine's startled gaze and the *Ooh, intrigue!* look that flickered across her face. It seemed that not even the upright druids were immune to relationship drama.

"I will not have her reputation dragged down any further, Tanner."

"Jessamyne's reputation can't *get* any lower, Ni'eve. Yours can. Her actions call your leadership into question, and if you continue to refuse to see that clearly, you owe it to everyone assembled here to turn this mission over to someone who can see the way forward without a major block in their vision.

"I give you my word, I will do everything I can to get Jessamyne out of the Facility. I want *your* promise that when she's back, you'll agree to the intervention I prepared for her a year ago."

The druidess was not at all happy about being put on the spot in front of a table full of guests. The only other one amongst us, it seemed, who could relate to the parental bond thing was my uncle. I breathed easier when he went to Ni'eve and drew her into an alcove. Heads together, she seemed to be listening.

Her cheeks were aflame when she returned to the table.

"If what Alderose says is true, my daughter has slid further down her twisted path than I have been able to admit to myself —and I truly did think I could handle her. Enforcer Brodeur has offered to create a mollifying collar. I have asked him to manufacture as many as there is time for, with the hope that whichever one of you reaches her first will be able to get the collar on and return her to me, safely."

"Hold on. How are we supposed to get a collar on her if she's in her tree form?" Alderose asked. "They have her rooted in this massive ceramic pot and she's already wearing one set of shackles."

My sister described a circle around a foot and a half across with her arms.

"She'll have to shift." Ni'eve and Tanner shared a glance that begged interpretation. He shoved his shoulder-length hair out of his face and tied it back with a bit of string he pulled from his pocket.

"What can she shift into?" Alderose asked.

I was thinking the same thing and had to mask my reaction when Tanner said, "A hellion." Then he took a deep breath. "A woman in her early-thirties if we're lucky."

Ni'eve directed one of her assistants to escort Malvyn to the château's foundry. At Laszlo's request, a map was brought in and unrolled on top of the table. He wanted Tanner to explain the tunnel system and include details like the interior height and material composition of each one.

I wanted to listen in on their discussion. Ni'eve smoothed the fronts of her robes and approached my aunt. "Maritza, if you are ready, we could use you in the infirmary. Please."

"I am ready, and I think the sooner we set to repairing the unfortunate Guillaume, the better. Alabastair, could you hand me the case with medical grade needles and threads?"

"Do you require my help?" he asked, sliding the box she requested into a stylish handbag. He nestled the strap on her shoulder.

"I've got this, darling."

Alabastair saw my aunt to the door, then returned to the table. He joined us in studying the map. Laszlo was attempting to draw information from Alderose.

"Is there anything you can add to our knowledge of the castle's interior, the number of employees, etcetera?"

"What I saw was limited to my cell and the hallway connecting that section of the castle with another section that had a rotunda," she said, surveying the second map. This one was a close-up of the valley, with the druids' sprawling holdings on one side, and the Vignes' walled fortress on the other.

The Vigne castle was shaped like a cross, with the longer section running parallel to the mountainside. I could see a large circle near the head of the cross, with rooms branching off it in regular intervals. Alderose used a silver teaspoon to direct our attention.

"I was taken from the cell at this end to a formal dining room, an informal salon, and a breakfast room in this circular section. I only saw the rooms on the one floor, but if I were asked to make an educated guess, I would say this is where the Vignes live.

"The other end of the hall with the cells had a door that opened onto a courtyard with a portal tree. It seemed like everyone had forgotten the courtyard and the tree existed. Cat,

Jake's assistant, was able to send her familiar in and out through that door. And here, at the opposite end of the castle?" She pointed to a boxy area off the large circle and traced a line to a rendering of a tower in the valley below the castle. "That's where they installed the mechanism that moves the aerial tram. Lionel's son, Arnaud, told me this was the only way in and out of the Facility."

My sister studied the raised pattern on the handle of the spoon. "I think we can surmise by the state of Guillaume's back that Lionel was displeased we found another way in."

"Tía's going to fix him, Rosey," Clementine said, throwing her arms around her. Alderose let herself be touched for a count of three.

"Have any of you contacted Cat?" she asked. "She told me she was staying in a chalet. Should we relocate her here? She's got surveillance equipment with her, and according to Jake, she has access to more gear. And more help."

Kostya had Cat's number in his phone from earlier in the week. I could feel his relief at having an actionable task. He dialed, and I heard, *Talk to me, Fireball.* My demon chuckled. He got the toe of my boot delivered to the side of his shin.

"Hey Cat, we're here at the druids' castle. Consensus is it would be better all-around if you were here with us. You and your toys and your cat." He listened and nodded. "Yeah, Château du Blanc. You sure you don't want an escort?" he asked, before signing off and ending the call.

"Cat's on her way. She's bringing Oscar."

Someone else's phone buzzed. Alderose pulled hers out and glanced at the text. "Guillaume wants to see me. Let me do that before Cat gets here."

My sister didn't wait for anyone's permission to leave. That left Kostya, Laszlo, Clementine, and me at the table.

"We owe the two of you a night on the town," Laszlo said, pulling Clementine onto his lap.

"Yes, you do." I leaned against Kostya. "I never got to sample any of those amazing desserts when we were at the ball."

"Anyone have any thoughts they want to share while it's just the four of us?" Clementine had read my mind, and I loved her all the more for it. "Because I for one find Ni'eve very annoying. I'm also concerned with what feels like a lack of urgency. Or maybe I'm still buzzing from what we accomplished yesterday, and I want to go and do it all over again."

"I'm concerned about Jake," Laszlo said. "Lionel's got to have active surveillance throughout the castle *and* the Facility and would have seen the dragon talking to us."

"I want to know how we're all supposed to work together," I said, "and how we're supposed to communicate. I mean, Clemmie and Rosey and I have our sisterly psychic network, but we haven't tried to coordinate our channels since we were little girls and goofing around." Clementine nodded and gave me an amen when I added I needed a plan, a flow chart, options, and code words—all the spy stuff.

Kostya cracked a wide smile at his brother. "Laz, we need Iván and his set-up."

"What's his set-up?" I asked.

"Back when we were wee demons, we got our hands on human-made devices and adapted them to work within the Reformed Realm's slightly different electro-magnetic field. Thus was Arkadi Communications born. Laz and I left it behind with our childhoods. Iván ran with it, only he's a concept guy. He found other Magicals to design the actual hardware and software and adapt the devices to different types of magic."

Kostya fiddled with his phone while he was talking and turned the screen so we could see. "There are models for daywear and nightwear, models for underwater work. You name it, he and his designers have created it. They also do custom pieces."

"Anything with opals and pearls?" I asked, taking the phone from him. "I'm still hoping to get back that bracelet and head-piece I wore to the ball." I tapped on the dropdown menu's evening wear tab and sucked in my breath.

"Sissy, look."

Clementine snuggled next to me while Kostya and Laszlo reminisced about escapades they'd had in their twenties.

"I'm getting ideas," I whispered.

"Me too."

"We get Iván to throw a few bracelets in with all the smart watches and earpieces—"

"No. Uh-uh. Absolutely not," Kostya said, reaching for his phone. I shoved it down the front of my sweater.

"Absolutely not *what*?"

"Whatever it is you two are planning."

"Hear us out," I said, pressing my hand against my chest so he couldn't take the phone. "There could be an advantage to having a couple of gorgeous witches enter the Vigne castle through the *front* door—"

"And cause a distraction, perhaps?" Clementine added. "Lionel has to be expecting us to retaliate for what he did to Guillaume, and he's got to know we're coming after the rest of the Magicals. I doubt he expects us to knock."

"Or to be wearing dresses. Your tailor, what was his name... Joconde? He has our measurements. Ask Iván to ask Joconde for two dresses. Gowns. And remember to tell him we'll need shoes we can run in."

I was so caught up in my vision of what my sister and I could accomplish armed with gorgeous clothes, oodles of jewels, and secret spy gear that I must have missed the part where the two demons decided Clementine and I had lost our minds.

8

KOSTYA'S PHONE BUZZED. I LET IT DROP INTO MY LAP AND GLANCED at the screen. "Your new best friend says she's here." I showed my sister the photo of Cat standing at the front gate to Château du Blanc. She'd taken a selfie with snowcapped Alps in the background.

I couldn't tell how tall the Black woman grinning at her phone was, but already I liked her style. She looked like an in-the-know European tourist in casual winter resort attire, from her après-ski boots to her quilted, pale gold overalls and long-sleeved T-shirt. An Hérmes cat carrier was strapped to her back, and I could see two pieces of luggage leaning against her leg.

"Let's all go greet her," Clementine said. "Is that a vintage *McQueen* she's wearing?"

"Maybe Jake gives his assistants a clothing budget."

We were a few steps into the hall when I heard Alderose calling from behind us to wait. Tears streaked her face and she accepted fast hugs when she caught up.

"Where are you going?" she asked.

"Cat's here. At the gate. We're her welcoming committee. She brought her spy goodies. Laszlo and Kostya are calling in their brother Iván. He's got spy goodies too."

"I like goodies." Alderose sniffled and pressed her face into the crook of her elbow. "I've never seen anyone in as bad a shape as Guill," she whispered. "The healers are doing what they can, but he needs so much blood."

I kept walking, putting some distance between me and my older sister. I'd barely gotten enough blood back into my own body, and I didn't want to hear her ask for my help. Plus, seeing Alderose in tears twice in twenty-four hours messed with my head. I spun on my heel and offered an alternative.

"Have Iván add bags of that synthetic blood product to the list of things we're asking him to bring."

"That's a really good idea, Beryl. The base formula was created for use by all Magicals with venous systems," Laszlo said over his shoulder. "Variations were made as other races seeking help arrived in the realm for treatments. I'll call Iván right now. Have him add some synth-skin too." He waved us forward and said he would catch up.

Alderose tackled me with uncharacteristic enthusiasm and thanked me for sharing my idea.

"Let's not throw a party until after Guillaume's been treated," I said, letting my heart thaw a little.

"Beryl. *Here.* He had this in his hand." Alderose stuck out her arm. My wand—*my favorite wand*, the one I'd taken to the ball and lost in the Barrenwood—was clenched in her fist. She uncurled her fingers and turned the handle in my direction.

"Please tell me you washed this thoroughly." Gemstones were embedded in the smooth handle, all of them varieties of the stone I was named for. "What was he doing with my wand? And what's the story with you two?"

"He took it from you when he left you in the Barrenwood." We passed through the front doors to the castle, the ones that were big enough to drive a cart and two horses through and stepped onto the crushed gravel turnaround. "He returned it to me when I was in the cell in the castle. I left it underneath the mattress. As to what's happening between us? I don't know. I'm confused."

"Do you think it's the Demesne? Did you go to your knees?" I asked, stopping to let Clementine and Kostya get ahead of us. I held Alderose's upper arms and turned her to face me.

"No, it's not the Demesne," she said. "Neither of us went to our knees. When we met, Guillaume warned me that my stay would go easier if I cooperated with whatever Lionel wanted. My first night in the castle, Lionel ordered me to dress up for dinner. He'd found a corset in my backpack and—"

"A corset?" I said. "Since when do you wear lingerie?"

"I took it off one of Mom's mannequins. Lionel liked it, told me to wear it, and after dinner, he commanded Guill to bite me. I'd never been bitten by a vamp."

"I'd never been bitten by a vamp either, Rosey."

She dropped her gaze. "*Don't*, Beryl."

"I'm sorry. I'm having a hard time equating you having twisted feelings for someone who almost ended my life."

"My feelings aren't *twisted*, Beryl. They're confused. And Guillaume never would have gone that far."

"I'm fine with dropping this part of the conversation, Rosey. Let's move forward. Tell me more about that night."

"Lionel said it would be thrilling to watch me being bitten for the first time."

"Thrilling?"

"As in sexually arousing."

"Oh."

Behind me I could hear Kostya putting a lot of muscle into opening the massive gate. I allowed myself a moment to admire the muscles in his arms and thighs straining against his clothes.

"Was it?" I asked. This insight into Lionel Vigne could prove helpful.

Alderose blushed. "Yes, it was arousing, and under the circumstances of my being a captive, troubling. And another thing happened. When I met Jake, he spontaneously shifted into his dragon form. When he was back in his human form and could talk, he admitted an uncontrolled shift like that hadn't happened to him before."

"Rosey, I want to hear more. I really do." I wasn't going to share my own experiences with the Demesne in fifteen second segments. But it would be worth a future conversation to explore the mounting evidence that my sisters and I might share the potential to self-create unique magics. "I've had some weird stuff happen to me too. We should talk."

"Yeah," she said. "I really wish I understood what was going on." She broke into a jog, waving her arm and calling for Cat.

While we had been talking, a wind had picked up, cold and biting. We walked Cat through the gate and closed it behind her and her bags. After a round of introductions, Kostya expressed his interest in seeing the gear she'd brought. Alderose said she wanted to have a reunion with Oscar, the cat that was Cat's familiar. As Cat was shrugging the wide straps of the carrier off her shoulders, another boom sounded from deep in the ground.

"You all blowing stuff up in here without me?" she asked, grinning.

"Not us," Alderose said, as Kostya darted a glance at his watch.

"Beryl? Was it about two hours ago that we brought Rosey out of the crypt and caught the horse?"

"Yes. Why?"

"Because two hours prior to that we heard a similar boom when we were upstairs in our room, remember?"

I yipped as another tremor rolled across the courtyard and

up my legs. Kostya grabbed Cat's gear, and we all ran toward the château, the wind at our backs. A third boom came from behind us, near the front gate, along with the sound of wood being splintered, ripped, and torn. A *lot* of wood. We stopped, spun around, and headed back. The gate was falling inward from the weight of the tree leaning against it from the other side.

"What the—" Cat tightened the belt of the cat carrier around her waist and stopped, arms akimbo. "That tree was not there when I arrived, just a long, steep, winding road."

Laszlo and Tanner tore up behind us. With Kostya's help they started to pull away whatever they could get their hands on without getting injured. The bare, skinny branches of the tree wobbled and shook against the upper part of the gate's arched frame. As the three men unbent the metal bars, freed up the lock, and pulled the doors open as far as they could, the branches and the rest of the tree fell forward.

Tanner spun around, wild-eyed. "Alderose, do you have any weapons on you?"

"I've got nothing," she said, patting her pockets and thighs.

"All of you, try to hold him upright while I get my blades."

Tanner tore off for the castle. Searching the gate, I couldn't see a body, a *him*, just a tree that looked like it had been hit by lightning and split from the top down.

Laszlo and Kostya were clearing what debris they could, and Laz was yelling that he wasn't going to make it. Cat had her gear bag opened and was pulling out knives. She tossed one to Alderose and turned to me and Clementine.

"Want one?"

"I'm good." I pulled my wand out from between my breasts and ran for Kostya. He was standing there, slightly shell-shocked. I wasn't sure how I could help, until I got close enough to the tree to see who Tanner thought was worth saving, and who Laszlo doubted was going to make it.

"Is that *Larch*?" I asked.

The faun had turned up in Northampton when Alabastair retrieved him from Chamonix so we could interrogate him about Alderose's whereabouts. Now, he was tied to the tree. Thick ropes bound his chest, arms, and thighs to the trunk and as the tree had splintered, long shards of fresh wood had pierced his legs and torso. Though his neck and head were unscathed, I didn't see how he could possibly be alive.

"We've got to get him off the tree. Cat, can you wedge yourself against the stone wall there and prop up the trunk?"

She got to it.

"Clementine, feed me your magic. I'm going to flash freeze Larch's legs, try to stop the hemorrhaging then pull him straight off." While my sister stepped forward to hold one of Laz's arms, Kostya rolled a boulder under the base of the tree to help Cat keep it from crushing Larch's mangled limbs.

"Kostya," I said, waving my wand as I walked closer to the tree. "We can burn him out too."

"Fire's too dangerous. We don't want him to catch fire and—"

"He won't burn. Trust me." I zeroed in on one of Larch's legs, and from there to where the section protruding through his thigh originated. I aimed my wand at the split in the tree and waved Kostya closer.

"Give me your fire," I said. "Feed it right to me. Don't let it spread all over your skin."

"But we've never practiced that, and how do you even know—"

"Trust me."

I held Kostya's wrist tighter with my left hand and began the incantation I thought would work best, a call to fire to direct its power in a pulsing stream. I could tell more was happening around me—Tanner might even have arrived with his special blades, and Clementine and Laszlo were working together in a similar way.

My sole focus was on pulling fuel from the depths of Kostya's being and sending it along my arm to my wand and beyond. Getting the thin stream of concentrated flame through moisture-filled cellulose was tough. I drew closer, mentally closed off every stray thought, and kept pulling and directing. Then it happened.

"Oh my goddess, *Beryl!*"

Alderose had read my intention and waited, crouched on the gravel in front of Larch. She pressed her hand to his thigh and caught his leg as it swung free of the tree.

"Start on the other leg," she said. "I can hold him while Clemmie and Laz work on that big splinter in his chest."

I couldn't bear to look at the tangle of bloodied limbs and shredded wood any more than I already was. Kostya and I shifted positions until we were slightly behind the faun and started to cut through the thick splinter piercing his calf.

"Stay focused, babe. I'm sending you more fire." Kostya's internal hum increased. He steadied the side of my waist with his hand, giving me something to lean against as I pushed more power out my arm and wand. I'd never stayed in a prolonged outburst like that before, not ever, not even during secret practice sessions.

I was able to cut through the second piece faster. Tanner tossed his blades to Cat, caught Larch as the last bits of wood holding the faun to the tree were cut, and ran him toward the castle. The druid was halted within a few steps; a team from the infirmary had arrived with a stretcher.

I relaxed my exhausted arm, shook out my wrist, and stared at my wand. Gemstones, cut and set to my specifications, winked back at me as if to say, *You did it.*

"What the hell was that, Beryl?" Alderose grabbed my forearm and brought my wand close to her face.

"*That*," I said, "was a little something I've been practicing for most of my life."

"Kostya, help me drag what's left of the portal tree across the gate. It won't stop the fae but it'll—" Laszlo swiped his hand across his forehead. "Fuck it. We have to try to save the tree for Larch's sake. Once they commit to being a portal guide and choose their tree, they become somewhat interdependent. We need more druids because fuck if I know how to save his tree on my own."

"You might want to look some place other than here," Cat said, swiping her arms across her forehead. "This castle isn't secure, Laszlo, not physically, electronically, or magically. If you want, I can have people here within a few hours. Same folks who cleaned up Alderose's apartment in New York City."

Cat turned to my sister and patted her shoulder. "Your friend doing okay? I had my crew bring her to the only place we knew of that treats injured fae."

"I haven't spoken with her, not yet, but she left a message for me and...and, I can't thank you enough, Cat."

"It's in my job description, Rosey." She picked up her cat's carrier again and raised it in the direction of the main castle building. "Can someone show me to my room? I have equipment to set up and my boss to rescue. There's a bonus coming if I can get him out before the end of the day."

THE INSIDE of the castle was no longer the serene place we'd arrived at. Druids who lived, worked, and studied there were visibly shaken. Ni'eve had changed into cream-colored jodhpurs and a fitted riding jacket. Her skin was almost as pale as her clothes, and her gaze lifted as a nickering came from the courtyard.

"Where are you going?" Tanner ran after her and held her elbow until she stopped. "Ni'eve, talk to me."

She looked him up and down and didn't ask why he was covered in blood and wood chips.

"I am going to get my daughter," she said. "I am getting on my horse, I am going to ride to Lionel's castle, and I am going to insist that he see me. I gave you permission to use my castle in order to rescue the witch. I did *not* give you permission to stay and cause the death of my friends."

"Larch may pull through."

"He may pull through, but what about his *tree*?" Ni'eve pressed the heels of her hands against her forehead and stifled a scream. When she looked up, her face was splotchy and red. "I want all of you gone by nightfall. *Gone.* This is your fault, and if that tree dies, there will be consequences."

She stomped off, her bare feet impervious to the gravel pathway. The stable master handed her the reins to the massive beast and gave Ni'eve a leg up. She rode bareback, and like she was born to be on a horse.

Fuck. I barely knew Tanner, but he was more okay in my book than Ni'eve. The castle staff didn't seem in any hurry to shoo us out. If anything, they look terrified at what was happening and in need of clear direction.

Malvyn, Maritza, and Alabastair ran from the castle's front entrance. My uncle had his sleeves rolled up and a cluster of roughed-out metal collars draped over his arm. My aunt looked stronger and more filled out than I had seen her in a while, and Alabastair had traded in his capes and fine clothes for a pair of snug black jeans and a black crewneck sweater.

The necromancer waved us over and asked that someone close the big double doors to the courtyard.

"Here's what we can surmise," he said. "Lionel Vigne is upset that Alderose was removed out from under his nose, and he's taking it out on those he knows or suspects have a relationship to someone in our group." Alabastair looked at Cat. "I cannot venture to guess where that places your friend Jake in Lionel's hierarchy."

"Jake can fend for himself," she said.

"I don't think Ni'eve can be trusted to negotiate with Lionel in good faith. I don't think everyone living and studying here with her can be trusted. Therefore, at Tanner's request, I am off to fetch three men he trusts with his life. They are ready and waiting. Expect me back here in thirty minutes. I shall look for you in the section of the castle with the infirmary and the class-room. If something happens and you must shelter elsewhere, get a message to me."

Alabastair dashed out the smaller door set within the big doors. My aunt raised her arm and spoke. "What Alabastair did not add is his—our—feeling that Lionel Vigne smells blood. And like a shark, he is in the midst of a feeding frenzy. The sooner we can organize ourselves and get to the Facility, the better for us and for every one of those souls trapped over there. Let's everyone gather what you need from your rooms and regroup in the classroom. Cat, come with us. We'll see that you're situated."

Malvyn and Maritza guided Cat to the stairwell in the tower. She left her gear bags with us. Kostya, Laszlo, and my sisters and I didn't move.

"Is Larch going to make it?" Clementine asked Laszlo.

"There's powerful healing magic on these grounds. If his tree hadn't been so severely damaged, I would say yes."

"Then maybe we *should* try to save the tree," I said.

"Let's leave that to the druids. I want my blades and my

leathers, and I want to get going. I'll meet you all back here like Bas and Tía said." Alderose jogged off.

"You two coming?" Laszlo asked, leading Clementine in the same direction as Alderose.

Kostya put his hand on my waist and pulled me to him.

"Yes," I said. "We're coming."

Jogging was the new walking, and I was sweaty by the time we made it to the top of the curving stairs and into our room.

"I can't wear these clothes, Kos." I plucked at the bulky sweater and the loose pants. "These aren't appropriate or helpful for running through tunnels."

"I've got you covered," he said. "Iván's bringing things for you and Clementine to wear. Not dresses!" he added when my face lit up. "Pants. Shirts. Tactical gear that'll deflect certain classes of weapons. Boots you can actually run in."

"I'll take it." I dropped onto our makeshift double bed and closed my eyes. Kostya bumped my knee with his.

"You going to tell me what that was all about?"

"What was—"

"Beryl Brodeur. You had a trick up your sleeve, and it was one of the coolest tricks I've ever seen, and I want to know how you did it."

I grinned, still on my back and still with my eyes closed. "Give me a minute."

9

"Help me get these boots off?" I waggled my foot in the air. I was slightly giddy from the magic I'd channeled, while still fending off the raw images of the faun's torn skin and muscles and shattered bones. Kostya leaned into the sole of my raised boot and held my ankle.

"Beryl?" he whispered. "You okay?"

I draped my arm over my eyes. "Honestly, I'm having a hard time managing the adrenaline rushes. The idea of rescuing captured Magicals is exciting, Kostya. Getting your fire to travel across my body and down my wand was exciting. Doing this incredibly important thing, that's exciting.

"But the reality is what we're doing could get us killed. Or get those poor Magicals killed." I sat up suddenly, wedging my elbows firmly into the mattress. "So far today we've witnessed Alderose getting her metal put back into her body, which was excruciating for her. The same vampire who almost killed me was mutilated and delivered to the castle on the back of a horse. And someone, some *giant* or some *force*, tossed a tree up a hill where it landed so hard it split, turning the faun strapped to its trunk into *shish kebab*."

By the time I was done with the litany of everything that'd happened since breakfast, I was on the verge of hyperventilating.

"Beryl, sit up. Put your head between your knees. Breathe."

"I think I'm a better soldier than general, Kostya," I said, speaking to my feet.

"Am I correct in assuming that Alderose is the only one of you who's had hands-on weapons training?"

I nodded, and slowly raised my head. "I've trained myself in one thing. No, two things, but they're related." I looked up and brushed the damp curls off my cheeks. "Promise you won't hate me."

"Babe." Kostya slid to his knees on the floor in front of me and cupped the backs of my calves. "I could never hate you."

Outside the sanctuary of our little room, I could hear a commotion coming down the hall. I willed it to stay away long enough for me to make a confession.

"After the foxes stopped visiting me, I got mad at my mom, and in case you didn't know it before, you know it now—when I get mad, I get even. My mom had let me have a half-sized wand to practice my spells, and she'd make me sit near her when she was in the kitchen or in her shop. She could monitor my progress while also doing her own work.

"One day, I went to pull this thread that was hanging off my mother's sleeve and a trail of magic followed. I tried it again, using my finger to touch her then drawing my finger through the air. And once I could feel my mother's magic in my hand, I would practice passing it to my other hand and all the way down my wand to the tip. That's how I discovered I could siphon off her magic.

"When I got braver, I practiced using her magic to do spells. And whenever I applied the magic I'd captured from my mom to my own spellwork, everything was bigger, better, and brighter." I showed my empty palms to Kostya. "I'm a Binder. *Was* a Binder. Where my mom excelled at binding people in lasting relationships—or so we've been told—I can bind other Magical's magic to me and use it as though it was mine. Though...wait. Technically, I can't call it binding. Maybe it never *was* binding?"

"To me, it looked and felt more like borrowing, or channeling," Kostya said. "I never saw my fire go *through* you, babe. It went *across* you and right to your wand."

I thought about Kostya's perspective and agreed. "When I added your fire to my wand today, that was the most concentrated and powerful thing I've ever borrowed."

"You're using your body as a conduit and your wand as a tool to funnel and direct the magic."

"That makes it sound very reasonable and rational."

"Were you playing with your mother's magic when you pointed your wand at that kid and turned him to stone?"

Leave it to Kostya to figure that out fast. "Yes. I was fourteen and I had a social life. I was tired of having to drop my plans and go foraging with her or accompany her to places like the greenhouse. I felt like I was outgrowing that job, and I didn't understand why she wasn't taking Clementine with her. At the same time, Mom seemed to be holding me closer.

"That day, while I was racing around the pathway, I was balancing this tiny, crackling ball of her magic on the tip of my wand. I was embarrassed at being caught, and I forgot to drop the ball before I uttered a spell I thought would simply turn him away."

For more than fifteen years I had been trying to find Micah. My mom had never given me his mother's contact information, or their last name. If I was lucky, I'd find it in her papers back home in Northampton. And I really, really hoped I was going to get that kind of lucky.

"I don't suppose you have any more confessions to make,

something about another Magical getting blamed for something you did when you used their magic?"

"That's exactly what almost happened. I made sure to take the blame, and I'll tell you that story another time. I've admitted to enough of my magical wrongdoings for one day. Though I should have explained what I was going to do and gotten your consent before I took your fire."

"There wasn't time, Beryl, and you did the right thing. You have my permission to take my fire and use it for the good of Magickind and humankind without asking. But maybe we should agree on a code word before you grab and go."

"How about *fuego*?" I said. "And are you sure? When I took your fire today, I was doing more than scooping it off your skin. I was—I was going into your core." I tapped the center of his chest and heard the thud within the hollow bit of his sternum. "One of the storerooms for your fire magic is right here."

"You're right. It is. And I have been led to believe that my supply of fire is endless." Kostya rolled up to standing and offered me his hand. "Now c'mon, it's time for us to get ready."

THE SCENE in the hall outside the classroom where we'd met earlier was one of controlled chaos. Tanner was speaking with a crew of four teens armed with shovels. He sent them off to dig a new hole for the shattered portal tree and specified a location within the protective confines of the ritual garden where Alderose had received her metal. When asked, a shake of his head said he had no update for us on Larch's condition.

Inside the classroom, Laszlo and Cat were staring at the map. Alderose was nearby, playing affectionately with a large, striped tabby. The cat was equipped with a special harness loaded with miniature electronics.

Over at another rectangular table, my uncle was working

with the slender collars he'd roughed out in the foundry from a thin, flexible metal. My aunt had her cases of needles and threads in her lap and was smiling to herself and humming.

Tanner re-entered, followed by Iván. The druid was carrying a large backpack and the youngest Arkadi brother was hauling two huge, stuffed gear bags behind him. He set them on the floor near Maritza and Malvyn and waved us over.

"Kostya, Beryl, Clementine, can you three bring another table over here? I want to lay out all the gear so we can see what fits whom."

We set another long table end to end with Malvyn's and exchanged hugs and greetings. Iván broke away and introduced himself to Cat. I overheard him explaining his husband hadn't come with him because now that their surrogate was pregnant with twins, their agreement was that only one at a time could be off doing dangerous things.

"Can we help you unpack?" I asked. I was dying to get my hands on something other than scratchy, hand-loomed and knitted clothing that wouldn't stop a mosquito from biting, let alone fae blades from slicing and dicing.

"Help yourself, Beryl. It would be great if you could empty out the bags and stack everything on the table and one of the benches. All of the black and gunmetal gray items were made from fabric spelled to deflect many kinds of attacks. The stretchy pieces, those *there*" –he pointed to a clear, zippered bag stuffed with what looked like wide headbands– "you wear over your flexi-armor. They'll shrink or expand to fit and repel most of the finger blades the fae equip themselves with.

"Given what you've been through, I'd suggest wearing one of the wider bands around your neck. Other places I like to wear them are on the forearms, elbows, knees, and ankles."

I thanked Iván for his suggestions and started to go through the gear. This clothing was definitely more to my fashion liking.

I dropped my drawstring pants right there and stuffed myself into a pair of leggings textured like fish scales and reinforced in places I'd never considered needing extra padding. I lifted my knees high, one at a time, to get the leggings to sit right around my butt and thighs and through the crotch.

"What about boots, Iván? Did you have room for those?"

"Check the other duffel. I threw boots and socks in there, along with more of the communications gear."

Alderose stuck the cat back in its carrier and came over to check out the pants. "Those fit you great," she said. "Tía made a vest for me that has iron filigree on it. I'll wear that, though now that I see this stuff, I think I'll grab a jacket to wear over the vest."

She held up a form-fitting anorak, with a big pocket in the front of the chest and a snug hood. I opened the second duffel and started to pull out sets of boots. I found a pair that fit, and socks, and put them on, then got a little shy about what I was going to wear on top. I wasn't about to strip down in front of everyone. I grabbed an anorak and tied the arms around my waist. Tanner walked over with nothing on his feet. I was beginning to realize it was a druid thing.

"Everyone? Can you come over here?" he asked.

"We have an inadvertent diversion in the form of Ni'eve and her decision to ride her horse up to the front entrance of Lionel's castle and demand to parlay with him. Why she thought that would accomplish...anything." He threw up his arms, then tugged at his hair. "Honestly, I don't know how that will go. I can only hope he doesn't decide to harm her and that she can distract him long enough for us to get into the Facility and get out.

"Cat and I have been discussing the need for a secondary diversion. I'd like to set up that one at the front of Lionel's castle too. Cat's brought a handful of drones with her. We have the four resident druids who can take vulture form and they're all willing to work with us. They can be in the air within minutes." Tanner locked gazes with Cat. "Does that give you enough time to make something up?"

"I am the queen of making shit up as I go," she said. "If the vultures are willing to share airspace with the drones, then I think we can do this. We'll need at least one person on the ground with master access to the drones, which will allow them to fire whatever you want them to fire at the fae."

She switched her focus from Tanner to my uncle. "Malvyn? Do you think you and Alabastair can handle that job? I've got stun pellets. Fog. If you can manage the drones, help them keep up a steady stream of distraction at the front of the castle, then I can be in the first wave moving into the Facility. I've got Jake's gear and the sooner we get him suited up the faster this will go. For everyone."

Malvyn agreed to do his best and said he'd confer with Alabastair as soon as he was back from fetching Tanner's friends. Cat turned the floor back over to Tanner.

"Every piece of intelligence we have, plus what we gathered going in after Alderose, says the captives have all been moved to the Facility. I think we should use tunnels again, only this time, use different ones. There's a system that's older, and slightly shorter and steeper, and I believe there's very little chance the fae know about it."

"What about the aerial tram that connects the Facility to the castle?" Alderose asked.

"One of the teams will be tasked with securing it and shutting down the castle's ability to work it as soon as we're inside. Next step is assigning teams."

"We're here now, Tanner, and ready to serve. And you know how we love tight spaces." A trio of men, two redheads and one salt-and-pepper, all built like wrestlers and shorter than the demons, entered the classroom. Alabastair followed them a moment later.

Tanner smiled for the first time all day. "Everyone, I'd like to introduce you to Wessel Foxwhelp, Kazimir Wickson, and River de Benauge. All three are druids, all three can take river otter form, and all three have a working knowledge of the tunnels that are directly accessible from the château's grounds. We'll put one of them on each team. They'll shift and go through the tunnels first."

The newest arrivals shook hands with everyone and sat on the bench opposite Malvyn and Maritza. The way my aunt and uncle greeted the three men, they had to be well acquainted. Tanner waved his arm. "Cat? Iván? Do either you have explosives?"

Cat and Iván looked at each other and grinned, which made Tanner grin again.

"I take it that's a *yes*. Would you see that Wes, River, and Kaz are equipped to create a diversion should it be needed. Make it something that won't collapse an entire tunnel."

Tanner glanced down at the map. "I have two blades that will cut through fae magic. Ideally, I'd grab some of yours and have them blessed, but we're out of time. I'll keep one blade with me. I'd like someone else to have the other if—"

"Alderose." Clementine and I volunteered our sister at the same time. I glanced at Clemmie. It seemed like we both had more we wanted to say. She let me go first. I stopped pulling gear out of the duffel bags.

"I know we've got to get moving," I said. "But there's something that needs acknowledging. When Clementine and I first entered the tunnels what, twelve, fifteen hours ago on our way to get Alderose, we shared the same thought with each other. This mission to put an end to Lionel Vigne's terrible actions started out as our mother's mission. Even though we don't know when she first found out about Lionel and what he was doing, and we don't know how many times she travelled to France or how many Magicals she rescued, we—" I started to choke up a little.

Clementine finished the thought for me. "We want to see this through. Personally. Giving our sister that blade is one of the smartest decisions you'll make today, Tanner."

"Alderose, do you wish to carry a goddess-blessed blade?" Tanner asked. "They are known to have a mind of their own."

"I would be honored." She wiped her hands on her pants, and went to stand in front of Tanner. He undid one blade's holster and placed it on her turned palms.

"The short sword is rather beautifully balanced. Give it a moment to find you and connect with your magic. If I could give you only one piece of advice, it would be allow the blade to guide you. There are reasons why the magic in these seek the wrongdoers amongst the fae."

"Got it." Alderose smiled and hugged the blade to her chest. She immediately buckled the holster's belt around her hips and secured the thigh strap.

"The groups will be number one, Wes, Kostya, Beryl, and myself. Group two is River, Alderose, Laszlo, and Clementine." Tanner looked up from the map and the markings he'd made. "I assume it's okay for two of the sisters to be in the same group?"

Alderose and Clementine looked to each other, then to me.

"We're good," Rosey said.

"Group three is Kazimir, Iván, and Cat. According to Cat's plans, you'll go right to Jake and get him geared up?"

Cat nodded. Tanner addressed my uncle. "Malvyn, did you get the answer you were looking for?"

"I did. And I'm afraid it's not in our favor. Lionel created loophole after loophole and the Board of Magical Governance has no jurisdiction over the Vigne holdings. Though Lionel is prohibited from returning to fae lands, he is not a wanted man because the fae were happy to pay the local French council for the right to plant their flag.

"Bring Lionel off his property, and I can take him into custody and portal him to the Board's North American headquarters in Toronto. Alabastair's mapped out a special route for Lionel and anyone else we capture alongside him and can speed us through."

"Then we shall do our best to bring him to you," Tanner said. "Kostya, you and I will carry extra packs with weapons, first aid supplies, and tactical clothing for the captives. Beryl, what do you need for spellcasting?"

"Nothing. Any spells I cast are boosted if I can pull magic from others in my proximity. I've never tried to pull from fae, but I see no reason why I couldn't. That said, I would feel very weird about pulling from the Magicals who've been held captive."

I completely forgot that only Kostya knew the full extent of what I was talking about. The faces staring at me demanded an explanation. I dropped the short version.

"I can pull your magic off you and use it to enhance my spells without making it pass through me first. Kostya, can you help me show them?"

"Sure, babe." He rolled up his sleeve, fired up his demon lines, and raised his arm. I drew out my wand, held it aloft, and circled Kostya's wrist with my other hand. I whispered an abbreviated version of the chant I used at the tree and within seconds a stream of fire was flowing out the tip of my wand and across the room toward the wall.

"That's a mild show," I explained, releasing Kostya's wrist and dowsing the flame. "I used a very focused beam of fire to cut the big splinters that were keeping Larch pinned to the tree's trunk. Took only a couple minutes to burn through and free him.

"I can't change the nature of your magic," I added. "Like, I couldn't tap into Laszlo's ice magic and hope to create a stream of fire like I did with Kostya's."

"Could you manipulate my metal?" Alderose asked.

I had to pause and think about how to answer her question. Because in a way, I had already manipulated her metal, only that was before it had re-entered her body.

"I don't think I would want to. Whereas most magic is pure energy, yours is inside you in a solid form. I'd rather stick with what I know, which is energy I can pull and direct."

"I'm convinced," Wes said. "Druids connect to the natural elements, earth, air, fire water. Have at whatever you need, whenever you need it." River and Kaz nodded in agreement and I thanked them.

"Let's get suited up and armed. I'd like to be ready to go in ten minutes. If we're lucky, Ni'eve will continue to keep Lionel occupied, and we'll get this done before dinner."

"Oh, she's keeping him occupied alright," Cat said. She let Tanner know there was an update coming in over her headset. "The druids you suggested we use already shifted and made their first pass over the castle. They're coming back to have Malvyn and Alabastair get them up to date with the drones. I think ten minutes is fine. But let's see if we can do it in nine."

10

————

THE CHATTER IN THE ROOM DIED DOWN. I WASN'T PLANNING TO BE the one to dole out clothing and boots, but my rush to find ones for myself made me the expert. I ended up helping Tanner's friends, and my sisters.

Cat and Iván organized the gear they'd brought, and Tanner sent a couple of his younger cohorts out to gather as many hard-hats as they could find. They returned with armfuls of battered, narrow-brimmed hats.

"Those look like they've been around since the eighteen hundreds," I said.

"They probably have been. They're cuir bouilli, boiled leather." Tanner brushed dirt off the crown of one, rapped his knuckles on the leather, and declared it sound. "They're low-tech, and I'm not going to insist that everyone wears one, but I think they're a good idea."

Iván suggested headlamps, whether we chose to wear the hats or not. "Beryl? There's a box in one of the bags. Has a bright yellow logo. Lamps are in there. Should be enough for everyone."

The druid recruits cleaned the dirt off the hats. I found the box with the headlamps and tried each one's battery before handing them out. Cat reminded us to pack the weapons we'd feel most comfortable using and reiterated we'd be in close quarters. Malvyn gave out the collars for Ni'eve's daughter. He'd figured out a way to add hinges and had folded them so they fit into pockets.

The last bit of prep was happening so fast I didn't have time to do much beyond slide my recently reacquired favorite wand into a pocket on the outside of my thigh and duck into a bathroom to change into the anorak. Back at the table, Iván was holding a narrow, rectangular box.

"What's in there?" I asked. "I'm thinking...diamond bracelet?"

"Close. Open it up. It's yours if you want it."

I adored gifts. Gifts were my love language. One of my love languages. Food was another. I broke the seal on the box and lifted the lid. I was wrong. A wand could fit inside. A retractable wand. I lifted the matte gray metal handle out of the box and flicked my wrist. The wand went rigid with a *snap*.

"I like it!"

"Keep it. Try it out. Send us feedback. And look, there's even a wrist band." Iván rolled a piece of flexible material around my wrist. The ends went together with another *snap*. "You slide the wand in here and the moment you realize you need it, it's in your hand. When I saw what you did with Kostya's fire, I knew you had to be the first one to use it."

"Thanks, Iván. Anything I should know, any quirks?"

He shook his head. "We've developed a new metal. It bonds with its user over time. You can't share these wands, though we're running an experiment using the metal after its been recycled."

"I'll make notes." My enthusiasm was rewarded with kisses on the cheeks, followed by Cat handing me a comm set. I told her I didn't need it, that I wasn't planning to be more than an arm's length from Kostya, and I feared getting overwhelmed by everyone's chatter. She assured me there was no idle chatter on her missions, and that I'd be happy to have it if I got separated from the group. She even adjusted the earpiece and taped the mic to the side of my cheek. Alabastair came over to admire her technique.

"Did you get your monitoring station set up?" Cat asked.

He gave her one of his shy smiles and held up his phone. "Yes. Malvyn has it on his phone too. We'll both have eyes on you."

"Good. I've got Malvyn connected to a headset, and I left yours with him. Between the two of you monitoring the tunnels and Lionel's castle, we should be covered."

I sidled closer to Kostya. Cat and Alabastair's chatter was distracting, and I could see Tanner and Wes were ready.

"Are we taking separate tunnels from the ground level?" I asked. "Or are we all going together?"

Tanner retightened his ponytail and tried his helmet on again. "We'll head into the old cistern as a group and divide from there. I think the trio that's focused on finding Jake should take the ice tunnel route. It'll be faster, and it's less likely they'll encounter fae."

He patted my shoulder and whistled to the room. "Line up. Let's go."

We broke into our groups, checked each other's gear, and exited the main keep. The hat could have used a chin strap, especially as we picked up the pace as we neared the orchards, then veered away and down. The rutted path led to a circular, above-ground building that housed the château's water supply. Steps built into the interior of the cistern marked the first descent we'd make. Tanner propped the door open, reminded the last one in line to close it after them, and continued to lead the way.

"Lamps on," he said. Right hand pressed against the crumbling surface of the wall, I tapped the button on the side of my headlamp before we were swallowed by the dark. The entirety of my focus became stepping firmly onto the stone step ahead of me.

Conversation halted. Kostya kept his fingertips on the outside of my shoulder. I snorted softly. I should have been strapped into one of those contraptions rock climbers wore, which would give Kostya something to grab when I inevitably fell. Right after I had that idea, my foot dislodged a pebble and knocked it off the step. It landed with a distant *plop*.

We came to the entrance to the first tunnel before I convinced myself I wasn't going the way of that pebble. At least there was a wide ledge.

"Turn down your lamps and give your eyes time to adjust. We're not going forward until I get an okay from each of you," Tanner said, once we were all inside the tunnel. "Be on the alert for fae. Wes, River, Kaz, you three ready to shift?"

Wes was in front of me. I'd never seen a druid take another form, and I wouldn't be seeing it today. My view was blocked by taller, wider bodies. I did get to feel two large, furry otters pass between the wall and my legs.

"Iván and Cat, you'll see the ice tunnel as we get closer. It glows pale blue. May the Goddess go with you."

"May the Goddess go with you" was repeated over and over as we began the steep descent within the tunnel. Lots of loose rocks waited to turn ankles and stub toes. I mentally reviewed my new gear and pulled my magic forward. This was it. And in a few minutes, as we neared the blue light Tanner had mentioned, Cat, Iván, and a large otter peeled off and went half-sliding, half-scrambling down what Tanner said was the steepest section of the ice tunnel.

"We're taking a different route from last night," Tanner said, drawing us to a stop a few minutes later at a bend in the tunnel. It had taken all of my concentration to stay upright. I could feel cool, fresh air coming in from somewhere below us.

"Was that air moving through here the last time?" Kostya asked.

"No, which is why we're stopping. I was hoping we wouldn't have to use this particular tunnel, but I'm not getting a good feeling about what might be ahead."

The remaining two otters ran in a circle around Tanner's legs and headed off in the direction of the incoming air. Tanner held up his palm before pressing his finger to his lips. I heard the faintest rustling sound as the otters bounded away, then returned. They managed to communicate with Tanner, who waved Alderose forward and asked if she was prepared to take out a fae patrol.

Her face was serious as she gazed at the druid and raised the blade he'd loaned her. Tanner nodded and gestured for my sister to follow. One of the otters went with them; the other stayed behind. I leaned against the tunnel wall and tugged Kostya's arm to get him to come up close behind me.

"You okay?" he whispered.

"I'm good," I said. "I'm—"

I didn't have time to finish my sentence. The sounds echoing up through the tunnel choked off whatever inconsequential comment I was about to make. Grunts as bodies absorbed blows, and metal hit metal, and then...quiet. The first fight was much shorter than I imagined it was going to be. Clementine slid her hand into mine and squeezed.

"I'm wearing Mom's mascara," she whispered. "I didn't want to say anything before, but I'm terrified of hurting someone who doesn't deserve it. If I can see their stories, I think I can know if they're bad or not so bad."

I turned my head so my mouth was close to her ear. "I feel the same. And I also feel bad that I'm willing to let Kostya and Laszlo and the others do any physical fighting."

"Yeah," she said, "but I already told Laz my priority is getting to the captives and getting them out. We don't know how many are in there or if they've kept any in the castle."

I squeezed her hand and let go. Chuffing sounded from around the bend in front of us and I was never so happy to see Alderose in my life. She raised her arm and shook the short sword. Tanner came up behind her and drew everyone in as close as he could.

"Two fae. A patrol. They're alive and down and very out. We'll pick them up on our way out of the Facility. And change of plan. We're staying together until we make it inside. We'll disperse from there. Everyone ready?"

At our group *Ready*, and his terse *Go*, we went. Tanner set the pace. I concentrated on not tripping or falling as the walls gradually closed in and the ceiling lowered.

"No talking."

Quiet settled around me. Pitch black darkness slammed me in the face. The weight of hundreds of feet of stone tower settled on my shoulders. As Tanner explained when the maps were in front of him back at the château, the base of the Facility sat a full two stories below ground. We had arrived at that base. Our next step was to pass through it and into the sub-basement.

"Lamps on. Let your eyes adjust. Move when you're ready."

The ground had flattened out. We shuffled forward as one and were met by a wall and a large metal door, the kind you'd see on freight elevators. Aside from boots on dirt and our breathing, there was no sound. Tanner clicked his flashlight on. The two massive otters went to the double door and started scrabbling back and forth, sniffing along the bottom. Tanner crouched and traced a thin beam of light where the door met ground.

"I don't want to use explosives to take this down if we don't have to. Suggestions?"

Laszlo came forward. He motioned everyone to the sides and against the walls, fired up his demon lines, and touched all ten fingertips to the door. Ice spread across the surface. Alderose came up next to him and whispered something. At his nod, she tapped the ice with the pommel of the short sword and the entire door shattered. Falling pieces made tinkling sounds as they fell to the ground.

"Watch for metal shards and *go*."

I stuck next to Kostya. There was another door in front of us. Laszlo again called for quiet. Within seconds all I heard was Kostya breathing and the echo of my heartbeat in my ears—and a chuffing, snuffling sound from the other side of wall, accompanied by a high-pitched whimper. I turned up my headlamp and watched as the door in front of us bulged into the anteroom.

Kostya tucked me behind him and urged me to keep my back to the wall. Others drew weapons as they got into place. Between Laszlo's bright demon lines, and Tanner's and Alderose's goddess-blessed blades, the squarish anteroom was coated in an icy, blue glow.

I flicked my wrist, welcomed my extendable wand into my hand, and held on to the back of Kostya's jacket. In under three seconds, I could be directing a stream of fire at whomever, or whatever, was on the other side of that door.

The snuffling and banging stopped. I held my breath—and the beast rammed the door hard. On the second try it crashed through, tearing and bending two layers of metal and went straight to Alderose.

"Jake." She dropped to her knees and wrapped an arm around one of his necks. "What are you *doing*?"

The licking and quivering that followed was definitely out of affection, not an attack. We all got to witness my sister getting mauled by a three-headed, wingless, stubby-legged dragon. Cat and Iván were next through the busted door and into the anteroom.

"For Goddess-sake, boss. Chill. *Out*." Cat straddled the armored beast, smacked its center head, and grabbed hold of the collar circling that neck. Alderose scrabbled onto her feet, let him lick her face once more, then suggested now would be a good time for Jake to appear. Like a well-trained pup, he did, landing on his hands and knees in front of her and shaking his head.

"Wow. Sorry about that, Rosey."

"It's okay," she said. "Cat's got stuff for you to wear. Unless you want to go back to dragon form?"

Cat released her hold on the collar. Jake let it slip over his head before he stood. Dirt was ground into his knees and hands —and he was very naked. I noted I was beginning to get much more comfortable with other Magicals' nakedness.

"If someone could hand me a pair of pants, I'd like to introduce myself to the family. If there's time."

"Thought you'd never ask," Cat muttered, shrugging off her duffel bag-style backpack and loosening the drawstring at the top. She handed over a pair of boxer briefs and we all got to watch Jake adjust himself, beg for big boy pants, and pull those and a long-sleeved Henley on. Cat handed him one more item.

"What's this?"

"Wipes. No one wants to shake your hands after seeing where they've been."

Jake chuckled. Others followed. I was fascinated at the sight of the formerly three-headed dragon staring at Alderose. He finished cleaning his hands, tucking in his shirt, and apologized for deviating from the plan.

"Tell us what you found," Tanner said. Cat continued to pull out socks and boots and knives for Jake. Jake continued to only have eyes for my sister.

"We made it through the ice tunnel," Iván began. "It ended where you said, and we were able to enter the Facility through a service door that opened to a stairwell that led to the mechanism that houses the aerial tram. From there, we located the main stairwell. We encountered two fae and were able to stun, silence, and bind them without raising any alarms—at least not that we could see or hear. We stashed them in the smaller stairwell. I assume we'll haul those two and any others out once we've found all the captives and seen to them first."

"What's the report from Jake's floor?" Alderose asked. "I remember it being like an underground zoo. There were a lot of Magicals caged in there."

"We're not sure. We came straight through."

"Then here's how we'll run the next phase," Tanner said. "Wes, River, Kaz. The three of you dismantle the tram, but don't break it. We may need it later. When you finish, find us.

"Cat, Jake, Iván, Alderose, Clementine, and Laszlo. You six will work your way up. We know one floor has a laboratory. Another floor's set up like a hospital ward. Clear them of fae. Stun, bind. Kill only in self-defense. Highest capture priority goes to Lionel Vigne and his sister Linette. Questions?"

"What do we do if we come across a captive who's injured?"

"You each have trackers. Affix one to their ankle, or wrist, or behind an ear, and we'll set up teams to go back and retrieve them." Tanner scanned the group. "Okay. Kostya, Beryl, and I will head directly to the top floor. Alderose confirmed she saw Jessamyne there. I'll work on freeing her. If she's *not* there, the three of us will work our way down until we meet up the six of you. We'll regroup, check in with Malvyn and Alabastair and see where we are with the vultures and Ni'eve. Everyone ready?"

At his *go*, I followed Tanner. Kostya managed to keep his fingertips on me, and I used that constant touch to open a channel to his magic. We made it to the main stairwell and started a steady jog up. It took everything I had to not beg for a ride.

"Blow out hard, babe," Kostya said. "Makes room for more oxygen to get in."

We passed the windowless zoo level, and my sisters peeled off with their group. We got to the laboratory and tram station level, and Tanner's friends snuck through the barely opened door as otters.

"Two more floors," Tanner said, keeping his voice low. "You okay?"

I gave him a thumbs up and moved at a pace I knew I could sustain. The stairwell had one wall of windows, from the ground floor to the top floor. I couldn't see anything unusual in the side of the mountain visible beyond. Tanner had us stop at the final landing to catch our breath and to let my legs recover. He and Kostya were breathing like they ran stairs three times a day. I wasn't about to swear that I would find my way back to my gym or hire a personal trainer, but if I was going to continue with this search-and-rescue spy business, I was going to have to do something.

"Babe, you ready?"

"Ready."

I really wasn't ready. Especially when it became obvious the room we stepped into was intended to be one big play area for little Magicals bred in captivity. I had to let that sink in before I walked any farther than the colorful, flower-shaped welcome mat.

There were all sizes of balls to roll, blocks to stack or play on, and places for creatures with wings and fangs and claws to play. There were even two rectangular kiddie pools made out of cinderblocks. And to ensure that playtime didn't get out of hand, close-set, coiled chains were placed neatly on the floor at intervals of about six feet. One end of each chain was attached to thick metal rings embedded in the walls.

I would gladly participate in the room's destruction later. Our trio's first goal was to free Jessamyne. I could see a tree was right where Alderose said it would be, at the opposite end of the room. Assuming it was our target, I removed the leather headgear and my headlamp, and set them on the rug.

"Kostya, would you keep watch at the door? Alert us if there's activity in the stairwell. Beryl, come with me."

Tanner strode down the center of the room. I had to take three steps for every two of his. We passed double-paned windows interspersed with undecorated concrete walls, and painted murals. A wide, outdoor walkway ringed the entire room. Kids wanting to play outside would have been kept safe by the poles and protective metal mesh found in playgrounds all over the world. The mesh looked like it curved over the walkway, preventing anything with wings from flying away.

Tanner shortened his stride and motioned for me to remain somewhat behind him. We were close enough we could see where the metal ring had chafed at the tree's bark and exposed the paler underlayer. One end of a section of heavy chain was welded to the big ring. The other end was attached to yet another one of the rings in the wall.

I'd seen chains like this in barns with big animals or coiled in the back of flatbed trucks. This method of restraint seemed like overkill for a slender apple tree.

Tanner stopped. From where I stood, slightly behind and to his left, I sensed him make the effort to slow his breath and his heartbeat and neutralize his emotions. He was the picture of calm, cool, collected, with his feet grounded to the floor and his gazed homed in on the tree.

He reached across his body with his right arm and withdrew his special blade. Running the sharpened edge along his palm gave the blade a taste of his blood. The druid brought the metal close to his lips, whispered, and softened his knees. As he guided the short sword through the air in a series of figure eights, a high-pitched whine rose from the metal. He kept up with the movement and drew closer to the tree.

Dropping to one knee, he smoothly took the blade's grip in both hands and sliced through the chain in one clean stroke. The chain hit the rim of the clay pot, cracking it. More chain and sections of the pot dropped to the floor with thuds that reverberated up my legs. Tanner slid the flat side of the blade underneath the ring circling the tree's trunk.

"Beryl, come over to my right side. I want you to place your hands on the grip without moving the dagger at all. When I say *Go*, you will turn the blade ninety degrees so either of the sharpened edges meets the metal ring and apply continuous upward pressure. The blade will do the heavy work."

I sent my wand back into its sheath with a gentle tap. Keeping his voice quiet and calm, Tanner explained how he thought I should go to one knee for the most secure stance and brace my other leg against the outer part of the ceramic planter. I did, and once I was in place, I grasped the dagger's grip with both hands as instructed.

Oh, the power.

"This is intense," I whispered, sending my gaze down my arms and up the length of the blade to where it met the metal ring. "Almost makes a girl want a goddess-blessed sword of her own." I felt Tanner grin before he returned to assessing the angle of the blade.

From my slightly lower vantage point, I thought I could see a youthful version of Grisette's face in the handful of knots scattered across the higher section of the trunk, right above where the branches split.

"Got it?" Tanner asked, and when I said yes, he let go of the grip and stepped away.

I heard him strip off his clothes and say *Go*. I rotated the blade, began to apply steady upward pressure, and waited.

An animal whimpered behind me. It padded into my sideview enough I could see Tanner had shifted into a wolf. A big, white wolf with magic crackling off the tips of his fur. White-ringed blue eyes acknowledged me before the wolf dipped his head and shook his thick ruff.

He sidestepped into facing the tree, lifted his snout, and howled. The mournful wolf-words shoved my heart against my ribs, and I almost lost my grip. I glanced back, to where we'd entered the room. Kostya waved from his post in the doorway and I reapplied the pressure I'd let waver. Tanner finished his short song, trotted closer to the broken pot, and rested his front paws against the base of the tree.

A younger version of Ni'eve and Grisette wavered and formed underneath the topmost layer of bark. I had to stand as she grew taller, to keep the blade in place and the pressure consistent. Within ten seconds, the dormant apple tree became the infamous Jessamyne, with Tanner's blade pressed between the curve of her lush, naked hips and the girdling metal ring.

The wolf leapt back and barked a series of short *yip-yips*.

"Can't you hurry?" Jessamyne struck a pose. Lifted her arms to stretch and draw her long wavy hair away from her face. Her voice was raspy, dry, and her gaze tracked the wolf's movements. "My little wolf has finally come to his senses, and I don't want to waste a second of my fertile time."

Though I kept up the pressure and could feel the metal beginning to give, the Apple Witch made it obvious she was frustrated with the pace of her approaching freedom. She twisted her torso, managing to seize the grip and wrench the blade away from me. Her feet and legs were stuck in the soil in the pot midway up her calves, making her selfish move clumsy. She bent more at the waist and knees and tried again to push me away.

For someone who'd been a tree, she was strong. I fell, arms flailing like a broken windmill, onto my back.

With the goddess-blessed blade in her hands, Jessamyne sheared through the rest of her chains then swung the sword down at me in a gleaming arc, slicing clean through my anorak, my T-shirt, *and* the corset. Grinning, she dropped the weapon and leapt, spraying dirt and chunks of metal.

I grabbed for the sword's grip, rolled to my belly, and watched her run after the wolf.

11

STINGING PAIN LACED ACROSS MY RIBS. DROPS OF BLOOD LEFT A dark red line on the industrial carpeting. I sat back on my heels and surveyed the damage. The dagger had cut through my clothes, my magical protection, and my skin. I set the weapon between my thighs and fumbled to tie the two halves of the T-shirt across my belly.

Rumbling sounded from one of the floors below and shook the walls. I glanced toward the main entrance.

Tanner had shifted and was zipping his pants. He and Jessamyne were talking *at* each other and it didn't sound like pillow talk. Kostya kept trying to hand her a shirt and she kept batting his arm away. I had zero desire to get close enough to hear what they were saying.

Jessamyne turned up the volume anyway and started to yell.

"No, I won't go. You're the only thing I need, Tanner. I swear. I. *Swear*."

Tanner shoved his arms through the pullover shirt Kostya handed to him and stepped closer to the Apple Witch. She grabbed his neck and forced a kiss, and I saw the moment

Tanner gave in. He wrapped one arm around her back and the other around her neck, molded his body to hers, and kissed her.

I saw him wave his hand. Kostya stabbed something against Jessamyne's bared butt. She tried to twist out of Tanner's embrace and couldn't and as her knees went soft, Kostya grabbed her.

Tanner let her go and took a step back. For one frozen moment it looked like the two men were arguing over a naked woman. The moment broke. Jessamyne spun within the circle of Kostya's arms and grabbed a fistful of his shirt. And then she lifted her heels, leaned into his chest, and kissed *him* full on the lips.

I counted to four-one-thousand, five-one-thousand before Tanner shook off his stupor, grabbed something from the floor, and jabbed it, as Kostya had, into his former lover's thigh. She started to collapse more heavily against Kostya. He guided her to the floor slowly, laid her on her side, and pulled something from the nearby gear bag and covered her with it.

The tranquilizer shots Iván had insisted we pack had come in handy. And maybe weren't as strong as he thought. Or the Apple Witch packed the kind of magical power that wasn't diluted by spending days and weeks as a potted tree.

I waited for Tanner and Kostya to finish getting pants and a T-shirt on Jessamyne. I knew Kostya wouldn't have kissed her like that willingly. Not in front of me. Not after promising me— *uff*.

I returned my attention to my wound. I didn't have anything to wipe the blood off the blade, or the carpet. I wished Cat had tucked packets of wipes into everyone's pockets.

I could deal. I'd figure out something. Kostya jogged over to me.

"I'm good, I'm good," I said, pointing to my belly area and

pre-empting any attempt to explain away the kiss I'd witnessed. "Just a little accident with the blade."

He made me stand, untie the T-shirt, and hold the jacket open.

"You're bleeding. I've got butterfly bandages and antibacterial ointment. Can you hang on, or do you want to go back to the castle?"

"I'm fine, Kostya. Those little bandages are meant for deeper cuts. So. What's it like to be kissed by Tree Girl?" So much for waiting for a more opportune time.

"Jessamyne has it bad for Tanner. We had to tranq her twice, and Tanner's using at least two sets of restraints, plus the collar. Even with that, I'm concerned she's got the strength to bust out if she puts her mind to it. And the bullheaded determination of obsessive love. Tanner filled me in just a little bit on their history." He rolled his eyes.

I rolled *my* eyes and tapped him on the chest. "I saw her kiss Tanner. I saw her kiss you too, and I'd like to know what you think that was about."

"I don't know *what* that was about. One moment I was following Tanner's instructions, which were to wait for his signal then tranq Jessamyne anywhere I could. I saw the signal, I got her tranq'd, and then..." He shrugged and examined his palms. "And then she was in my arms and we were kissing, and if it helps my defense at all I could swear it wasn't me kissing her."

"I'm not sure what that means."

"It was her thinking she was still kissing Tanner, it was..." He shrugged again and this time he looked at me. I could swear I saw a streak of color on the side of his upper lip. "It was nothing, Beryl."

"I hope it was nothing. What's our next step?"

"Let's go—" He pressed a fingertip to his ear. "Laz? That you? Report."

There had to be something wrong with my earbud. I wasn't hearing anything. Kostya's face went blank. He interspersed nods with *uh-huhs* and *oh shits* and tapped his ear again.

"The floors below us are completely emptied out and clear of captives. They're assuming everyone was brought to the castle after we rescued Alderose and Sheenah." He pivoted toward the front of the room. "Tanner, did you hear that?"

"I did," he said, "and I think Laz's suggestion we retreat from the Facility in stages is sound. Would you two stay here with Jessamyne while I help transport the fae we captured to Malvyn?"

I picked up Tanner's sword. Kostya and I hustled to meet up with the druid. He'd gotten Jessamyne's head propped on a cushion, one of Malvyn's collars around her neck, her ankles tied together, and her wrists secured behind her back.

"I'm surprised you don't want to take her over first," I said, tapping my ear the way Kostya had. Silence.

Tanner crouched by Jessamyne's head and covered her ears with his hands. "I'm in a relationship with someone I hope to spend the rest of my life with. Jessamyne will never accept that I could love someone else. I have an intervention team on standby at a hotel in Chamonix. I'll make the call to them the moment I'm at the château. I want Jessamyne out of here before Ni'eve has a chance to talk to her, which is why leaving her here with you two would be ideal."

"Is she down and out?" I asked.

"She is," Tanner assured us.

"Then we're good," Kostya said. "Keep us in the loop."

Tanner checked Jessamyne's restraints one more time, shoved his short sword into its sheath, and rode the railing down the first flight of stairs. I suggested to Kostya that we move Jessamyne closer to the door and find something heavy to keep it propped open. I felt exposed this high up, and not fully comfortable with the job of babysitting Ni'eve's wild child. I was going to ask Kostya for his thoughts when he staggered away from me and dropped to his knees.

Now was not the time for my guy to be doing *anything* on his knees.

"Kostya, what's going on?"

"I—I don't know. Help me get my jacket off," he said, struggling to get his feet under him. Coming from behind, I grabbed the end of one sleeve and held it down while he worked his arm out. We repeated that on the other arm. I folded his jacket in half out of habit and dropped it on the floor.

"Shirt too."

His stretchy tactical shirt should have come off easily, only when I pulled it up his back and over his shoulders, I almost hit the floor beside him. Sections of Kostya's barely formed wings were moving underneath his skin. Joints were flexing and bones were growing and the skin to either side of his spine was splitting in vertical lines.

Goddess, not here. Not now.

"Shit, babe, what can I do?" Fainting was not an option.

"Can you make ice with your wand?" he asked, pressing his hand to his thighs and panting.

"I—" I had to think about that for a second. "No, I can't. Let's get you into one of the pools. Can you walk?"

"I can—no, I can't." He followed me on hands and knees to the closest of the two pools. This one had solid concrete sides and was blessedly cold. I had Kostya haul himself up and sit on the edge so I could untie and remove his boots and peel down his pants. He tossed his comm set to the floor and started to let out a garbled scream before I was done. I gave him a gentle nudge and encouraged him to lie back in the water.

While he floated, I scoured the walls for a first-aid kit, for anything I could use to bandage his skin. There was nothing, not even a curtain I could tear up, or a bathroom.

"Does that help?" I asked, once he'd been in there a couple of minutes. At his nod, I dashed to Jessamyne and checked her restraints and her breathing. She appeared to be as out as ever, and as tightly bound. Back at the pool, Kostya had a death grip on the tiled edge. His eyes were squeezed shut and he'd pulled his chest and head under the surface of the water.

Clouds of blood bloomed to either side of his body. I could see bits of cartilage and membrane beginning to float out from behind both shoulders. His wings were happening in real time, and they weren't happening at all how I'd fantasized since hearing Clementine explain what it had been like for her and Laszlo.

I had no idea why Kostya's wings had chosen this inopportune moment to show themselves. A trickle of wet on my belly reminded me I'd been cut.

Fuck. I needed help. Not with the cut, with Kostya. I tapped him on the chest. He drew himself up enough his face was out of the water. His horns were changing too and his lips were bloodless.

"I want to talk to Laz and let him know what's happening to you," I said, "but my headset's not working."

"Use my device. Stick it in your ear. Tap it twice. That'll get you right on the main channel. Tell Laz and Iván I can hold on, but if they've got anything for the pain, I'll take it."

"What if all they have is crude jokes?" I asked. Teasing was my back-up when there were no painkillers to be had.

"Tell 'em to fuck off and I'll hatch these myself."

"I'll see what I can do." I kissed his forehead, found his earbud, and got it positioned in my ear. Tapping twice dumped me right into a flurry of terse questions and commands.

Not knowing earpiece protocol, I spoke. "Laz. Laz. LAZ."

« Yes? Who is that? »

"It's Beryl. I'm using Kostya's earpiece," I said. Keeping my eyes on the demon in the kiddie pool, I walked backward toward Jessamyne. My witchy senses were twitching.

The sensation got worse when I noticed she was a good foot or so closer to the door, from where I'd left her.

"Oh no you don't." I flicked my wrist. New wand secure in my palm, I crouched by Jessamyne's feet and placed my free hand on her ankle. Within seconds, I had tapped into her magic. The sensation almost bowled me over. I held steady. Persistent.

Until inside the cacophony of tangled magics at her core I found one dark orange thread, strong and thick, deceit braided with wicked intent. I pulled it toward me with exquisite stealth, drew it up my arm, across my chest, and down my other arm to the wand. The moment there was a connection, I split and multiplied the dark orange thread into restraints that circled and looped her ankles and wrists.

There was no way Jessamyne could free herself of the tangle of knotted cords based on her own magic.

"Gotcha," I whispered. Her eyelids didn't even flutter. Goddess, she was good.

« Got who? » Laszlo asked, coming back on the channel.

"We've got a situation, Laz."

"Beryl!" Kostya hauled himself out of the tub, sending waves of water over the sides of the shallow pool. "Fire, I need the fire, not the water."

Water streamed down his front. He began to speak in Demonish, firing up the demon lines on his forearms and inner thighs and chest, the same ones he'd used to heat the copper tub. Standing with his legs spread, he stretched his fingers, then closed his hands into fists, and repeated that over and over.

Laszlo's voice startled me. « Talk to me. What's going on? »

"It's Kostya. His wings are coming in and I—"

« Beryl, what the *hell* were you two doing in the middle of a rescue mi— »

"Laszlo. *Goddess*. We weren't doing *anything*. Tanner left a couple of minutes ago to help bring the fae they captured back to the château, then he's coming back to the Facility. I'm trying to guard Jessamyne, who might have done something to Kostya. And Kostya is now standing in front of me completely on fire and in pain. A *lot* of pain, okay?"

Laz had *really* pissed me off.

« I'm sorry I jumped to conclusions. Let me see if Iván has any advice. Because I don't, other than to let it happen, let Kostya's instincts come through. We lived through it, he'll live through it too. »

"Yeah, but you guys were at least getting some pleasure mixed in with your pain. You owe me, Laz. And I'll pass your advice on to your brother." I let the channel stay open, in case Iván came on, and knelt by Jessamyne. She was tied as tight as she'd been five minutes ago, and I was satisfied the magic I'd manipulated was holding.

Kostya was near the middle of the room, completely on fire from his toes to his fingertips to the ends of his horns. He'd disappeared into the chant-like sounds he was making and the Demonic magic he was experiencing. I couldn't think of anything to do except be his witness.

I sat on the edge of the kiddie pool and slowly undid the knotted halves of my T-shirt. Dried blood lined the cut on my belly, and it looked like it was healing. The cut ends of my corset were drying up and shriveling as it lost its purpose. In the past, my mother had taken away the old corset as soon as the new one was on and sent it back to the sea witch.

I shrugged out of the pieces of the anorak. Stripping off the T-shirt, I immersed it in the pool water, wrung out the excess, and cleaned the area around my wound. The corset was damaged enough I finished peeling it off, folded it, and stuffed it into the undamaged pocket on the back of the anorak. Naked from the waist up, I closed my eyes to run an assessment of where my magic was in my body, where it was thinned out, where it was pooling or accumulating, nothing out of the ordinary flashed or pinged.

Maybe I *could* believe what Maritza and Malvyn said to me earlier, that what was happening with Kostya's wings had nothing whatsoever to do with my busted, and now completely ineffectual, magical garment.

And maybe I had to consider that the reason his wings were bursting from his body right now, right here, was because Jessamyne had done something when she kissed him. It could have been deliberate. She could have thought she was still kissing Tanner.

I shivered, put the anorak back on, and crossed and tied the front pieces. Kostya's wings were continuing to grow.

I wished—selfishly, unrealistically—that something as intense was happening for me.

Clementine had talked about what it was like for her and Laszlo when he got his wings and she got her own demon lines. Their coupling including orgasms and ice-forged diamonds and a marriage proposal.

I wanted that for me and Kostya. I wanted passion that burned hot, burnt us up, created something like diamonds in the process. Him popping out wings here, in this place...fuck, there was nothing romantic in it, and now I was feeling guilty for even wishing his transformation had the power to sweep both of us away.

I checked on Jessamyne again, stuck my head into the stairwell, and walked back to Kostya. It felt like he'd gone deeper within and even further away. His wings were unfurling ever so slowly, showing a gorgeous shade of chestnut brown with darker bones. He didn't seem to need me.

I told him I loved him and continued exploring the ambit of the room.

Testing the handles on the doors and windows, I found they were all unlocked. I grabbed a couple of the toy blocks, used them to prop open the door closest to Kostya, and blew him a kiss. I wasn't expecting a response, and I didn't get one.

I paused on the threshold to the walkway. Voices were coming in through the earpiece. All of the captured fae were either at the château or in transit, and Ni'eve and Lionel had retreated inside his castle. Tanner had enlisted Alabastair's help bringing the intervention crew from the hotel to us using a temporary portal.

Good, that meant they would be here soon to take Jessamyne away.

From where I stood, I could see the Vigne fortress hunkered alongside a desolate, shadowed section of the mountainside. Smooth, imposing curtain walls began to flare outward about halfway up. None of us were getting in from those sloping walls, not unless we could fly.

To my right and left, stone carvings perched on top of the stone corner posts. The backs of the beasts rounded in my direction and their tails curled around the posts. If the carved beasts could stand, they would be easily as big as the demon brothers. I stepped away from the wall to have a closer look, but rising winds knocked me back a step.

I decided to chance the wind and tried again. I wanted to see the entire valley up to the fortress and across to the druids' holdings. I held onto the metal chain-link and proceeded clockwise.

The fencing ended a couple inches before the first corner post and its statue and picked up again just after. I was able to snug myself between the stone post and the creature's muscular haunches and clawed toes. Lifting my heels gave me a dizzying view down the face of the four-story tower, and to the flight path of a pair of hawks. Two wings dipped in my direction before they swerved off and up toward the fortress.

"Their names are Coco and Pepito."

Whipping around, expecting to see someone standing behind me, I jumped so hard I nearly lost my footing. "Who said that?"

"I did." The voice was coming from inside the beast beside me. The stone beast. I slid my arm off its bent knee. That leg cracked free and the winged beast sprang away. It landed on the roof and shook out its legs and tail, spraying bits of stone conglomerate.

« Beryl? Are you there? » Iván's voice crackled in my ear.

"I'm here," I said.

The beast's black eyes stared at me. It gripped the gutter and peered through the holes in the mesh.

« I'm coming to help. I've got the salve Kostya's going to need. I'll be there in five. »

I kept my back to the windows and my eyes on the gargoyle. It tracked me all the way to the doorway. I had to stop worrying about what it wanted, what it might do, and focus on Kostya and his flame-covered body. His wings were fully out and open and pulsing with life—and tears were streaming down my beloved demon's face. I closed the door, bolted it, and circled the room, throwing the locks on all of the windows. Clawed feet scrabbled across the roof, following my route.

The only other door was the main one. I rolled Jessamyne out of the way and onto her back and shut and bolted that door too.

"Iván's coming," I said to Kostya. I glanced from him to the ceiling. The gargoyle had settled right above me. "He's bringing a salve to help with the pain."

———

12

I DIDN'T LIKE THE RANDOM SCRAPES AND SCRATCHES COMING from over my head. And I didn't like that the Apple Witch was beginning to mumble and twitch. I was on the verge of drawing on more of Jessamyne's own magic to further bind her when heavy boots and a hard knock announced a visitor. I tensed.

"Beryl, it's Iván. Can you let me in?"

I rolled to my feet, undid the bolt, and opened the door. I was relieved to see him and ready to hear anything he had to say about what he thought was happening to Kostya.

"I take it that's Ni'eve's daughter?" He glanced at Jessamyne as he stepped over her and immediately switched his attention to his brother. I'd been afraid to touch Kostya; Iván loosened the straps on his backpack and let it slide to the floor before embracing Kostya, flames and all.

"That's her," I said. "It took him and Tanner and two tranq shots to get her" –I waved my arm in her direction– "under? Out?"

"Is that your magic in her bindings?"

"It is." I showed Iván my wristband and demonstrated how

quickly the wand responded to me. "This is really easy to use, and it directs my magic very effectively."

"Good," he said. "Pinpoint accuracy is something the witches we've been working with have asked for." While we chatted, he walked around Kostya, always with a hand in contact with his arm, shoulder, back, or chest.

"Brother, can you hear me?"

Kostya's normally warm brown eyes were reddish, irritated. Even the irises appeared to be affected by the fire and by what he was experiencing. The entire time he'd been standing, legs apart, arms out, his gaze had never settled on me for long. When Iván spoke, it took a few moments for him to respond. Finally, he nodded his head.

"Does your throat hurt?"

He nodded again. Iván directed me to the backpack he'd dropped by the door and asked for the water bottle in the side pocket. Going through the pack parked me closer to the Apple Witch and this time I was sure I was seeing signs the tranq was wearing off. I brought the thermos to Iván and whispered my concern.

"Tanner should be here soon," I said. "I suppose we could just wait it out. What do you think?"

"Let's wait. I can't imagine she'd be much of a match for you and me." Iván screwed off the bottle's cap. He held Kostya's jaw and asked if he was ready. Kostya blinked twice and tilted his head back, allowing Iván to slowly pour some of the contents of the bottle into his mouth.

"He's mine now, witch."

I spun on my boot's heel and stared at Jessamyne. Her loose, disheveled hair covered most of her face, except for one eye. She blinked. I crawled over to her, swiped her hair away, and asked her to say that again. Louder. I wanted Iván to hear. She mouthed a silent, *No.*

"Beryl? Can you come here?"

Helping Kostya meant more to me in that moment that trying to gag a witch using threads of her own magic. I threw Jessamyne's hair back over her face and stood.

The flames that had been flickering all over Kostya were gone. His eyes were a little clearer, a little more settled. And his arms were relaxed by his sides, not held stiffly away from his body.

"He's over the worst of it," Iván said. "Could you stand in front of him? I want him to hold onto something sturdy while I spread this salve on his back. If he's anything like me and Laz he'll heal quickly, but he'll tolerate this next part better if he's connected to someone he loves.

"And I know he loves you."

I rested my hands on Kostya's waist. I could be as strong and as sturdy as he needed me to be, for as long as it took Iván to do his thing. Kostya put his hands on my shoulders.

"Ready?" Iván asked.

"Ready."

Instead of staring straight ahead at my demon's sternum and the heart of his fire magic, I stared into his eyes. I admired the curve of his bone-colored horns and the collection of rose gold piercings he'd added to over the years I had known him. The longer I spent taking in the details of the face I already knew so well, the more I wished I could pull him close and kiss the pain away.

He might have read my thoughts, because he grinned. He winced right after, and sucked in his breath, but I took the grin as a win and smiled. When he opened his eyes, his gaze bounced over my shoulder and landed behind me.

Tanner and his group were at the door. I hadn't heard anyone coming up the stairs.

"I have to let them in," I said. "I'll be right back."

I undid the bolt. The door swung out, into the landing. Tanner was there, along with Alabastair. Both men had taken snug jackets from Iván's stash.

"This is Beryl," Tanner said, introducing me to the two witches who'd materialized from behind him. "Beryl, my friends have asked to remain nameless." We shook hands. Their eyes beamed warmth when they smiled and cooled as they entered and went to examine Jessamyne.

« Beryl? » I pressed my fingers to my ear and turned away. It was hard to hear Laszlo through the comm, even over the witches' muted conferring. I went to the window and leaned against the glass.

"Hey Laz. Iván's here, working on Kostya. Tanner's here too. He and Alabastair and a couple of witches are picking up Jessamyne now."

« Good. As soon as Iván thinks Kostya's ready, I'd like the three of you to return to the château, same way you got in. We're expecting Ni'eve back within the hour. »

A soft swishing sounded on the outside of the glass. I'd forgotten about the gargoyle. Apparently, it hadn't forgotten about me. Its glossy black tail with the triangular tip was waving back and forth right in front of my face. I stepped away from the window.

"I'm sorry, Laz. Would you repeat the last thing you said, the part about Ni'eve?"

« Sure. She should be here within the hour. I hope the three of you can get back before she arrives. »

"That sounds doable. I think they're ready to escort Jessamyne out."

Laz said goodbye and good luck, and I double-tapped the earpiece to disconnect.

I was right, and I was wrong. Tanner and the witches were ready to take Jessamyne away. Jessamyne was not ready to go.

The layers of restraints she'd been in were off and a simpler set was on. She could move her legs enough to walk, her arms were behind her back, and her hair had been pulled into a high ponytail. Her shapely neck was missing the collar I knew I had seen her wearing earlier.

However much the witches had done to make sure Jessamyne wouldn't escape while in transit, they neglected to fully shut down her magic—and what I could sense of her magic was rich and varied and very awake.

Jessamyne was pulling against the witch holding her from behind and heading toward me. I backed away and bumped into Kostya. His heart was pounding hard. I wanted to protect him, get him out of the way, and let Tanner handle his ex-lover.

Kostya gripped my shoulders and moved me to the side. I could see his wings were slick and folded against his back, and I could see he only had eyes for Jessamyne.

"Kostya?" I grabbed the waistband of his pants and jerked my arm.

Jessamyne was speaking to him. I recognized a few words I knew were Demonish. Iván spoke up, in the same language, his voice urgent. I definitely recognized the words, *No*, and *Brother*.

And I definitely recognized the kind of magic that resided within a witch's hair, strand by strand, always hidden in plain sight and always accessible. Thick, wavy locks of Jessamyne's hair floated away from her head. There was no wind moving through the room. I knew all of the windows and doors were closed and barred, except for the main door to the stairwell.

Kostya took another step closer to Jessamyne, raised his arms, and fired up the demon lines in his arms.

"Tanner, do you have your blade?" I asked.

"I do, and it's in my hand."

"Iván, may I take some of your ice?"

"Whatever you need, take, sister," he said, whispering into

my ear. He extended his arm and pulled his sleeve to his elbow. Icy lines decorated his arm. There was no time for me to interrogate him about his primary and secondary magics, because I could tell immediately his ice magic differed from Laszlo's. There was only enough time to grab his forearm, find the ice living in his collar bones and pull it to me, flick my wrist, and point.

"Freeze!"

I sent the first shot to Kostya's feet. The second, to his wings. The third, to Jessamyne's feet. Alabastair kept Kostya from stumbling, the two witches grabbed Jessamyne from either side, and Tanner pressed his goddess-blessed blade to the back of her head and sliced through the long ponytail hanging down her back.

She screamed and fainted. The witches guided her to the floor. Tanner crouched near her head and cut off the longer hairs near her face that first alerted me of her intentions.

I found Iván's arm again, tapped into his ice magic, and yelled *Freeze* twice more at the clumps of hair Tanner had flung away. It creeped me out to think of hair as being sentient, and I had to make sure it wasn't getting close enough to the Apple Witch that she could access what power might be left in its strands. One of the nameless witches gathered up the hair using their own wand and directed it into a drawstring bag.

"Fuck."

Tanner stroked Jessamyne's head. Choppy sections of what was left of her hair threaded through his fingers. He leaned forward, whispered an apology, and strode to one of the windows. He punched the glass and swallowed the pain and didn't turn around until Alabastair had left with the two witches and the unconscious Jessamyne.

"You three go," he said, his voice muffled against the glass. "I'll follow in a minute."

Iván, Kostya, and I let him be. I scooped up my helmet and the headlamp and trailed behind Kostya. The sound of our boots hitting the stairs rang hollowly through the four-story stairwell. Walls closed in on us as soon as we shut the sub-floor door and passed underneath the base of the Facility and into the tunnel that would take us to the château.

Kostya refused Iván's offer of help and apologized he couldn't offer me a ride on his back.

"The skin feels like it's burning and the wings are too delicate to handle much touch. The membrane will harden though. Just have to give it time."

I held Kostya's hand more firmly and quickened my pace. "I hope you can shower, or at least let me help wash you. I want to scrub every place Jessamyne touched you. Twice. Including your mouth. I think her kiss delivered something that got your wings to speed up their entrance."

"You got it, Beryl." Kostya drew me closer to his side.

"And my uncle has these special glasses that can see different kinds of magic on surfaces, including skin. I think he should examine you for any lingering external influences."

"Yes, dear," he said.

I smiled in the near dark at the gentle teasing in his voice.

KOSTYA'S BATHING session included a visit from Malvyn and Laszlo. Though I had to shoo Laz out. The smallness of the guestrooms combined with the tapered ceilings didn't make much room for one six-foot tall demon, let alone two of them *and* their wings *and* my uncle. Mal spent a half-hour examining Kostya. The only place he found lingering traces of magic that wasn't identifiable was the side of Kostya's mouth. I told my uncle I remembered seeing a smudge of color there, after Jessamyne had kissed Kostya.

"We could wait, and remove it la—"

"Now," Kostya said. "Do whatever you need to do. It can't hurt any worse than when the wings were coming through."

The furrow between Malvyn's eyebrows had a different opinion. My uncle had me hold his special glasses while he set up a test tube rack on the narrow windowsill. He placed two small, brown glass bottles in the rack and an empty vial between them. Next, he balanced a slender glass stirring stick in another empty slot and said *yes* when I asked if I could try the glasses on.

"As soon as the two compounds are mixed together, I will have thirty seconds to apply the antidote to Kostya. Have a look at the side of his mouth now, Beryl, then I will need to have the glasses back and the dials properly set. Speed and accuracy are critical. Otherwise it will have to be repeated."

I held the glasses up to my eyes. Kostya sat in the chair and lifted his face for a better angle. The curve of his full upper lip came into view, as did the contrast between the pinker skin of his lips. There, embedding themselves in the corner of his mouth, were tiny strands of the same dark orange magic I had pulled from Jessamyne in order to bind her arms and legs.

Deceit, which made Kostya's demon nature believe *she* was his fated mate.

And wicked intent, which guaranteed his wings would emerge in response to *her*, not to me.

"Whoa...these glasses are amazing, Uncle Mal." If I lingered too long on thoughts of fated mates and physiognomic responses and how the special occasion we'd been waiting for was now ruined, I was going to cry.

"If you would like a pair for yourself, put in your order. They take more than a year to complete, and I would be happy to make them for you."

I took a last look at the traces of Jessamyne's magic, returned the glasses to my uncle, and admitted I would love a pair of magic-detecting eyeglasses.

Then I hugged him.

"You'll have to be trained on how to use them properly," he added, patting my back.

"I think Kostya and I could handle a visit to see you and James and Leilani," I said.

WHILE MALVYN TENDED TO KOSTYA, I slid another T-shirt from the dwindling stack in the armoire and ducked into our bathroom. Cold water, soap, and the rough washcloth did a decent job of getting the dried blood off my skin.

Both of us patched and clean, we walked into the classroom together. Seeing Laszlo, the reality of Kostya's wings sunk in even more. Now there were two demons in the Reformed Realm with no intention of excising the extraordinary part of their anatomy every demon once had, and always kept. Kostya couldn't talk about what getting his wings had been like—a bandage covered one side of his face and most of his mouth. Nor could he tolerate being slapped on the back due to his wings' sensitivity to touch. He could, and did, accept handshakes and congratulations.

"Do we have an update on Ni'eve?" I asked.

Cat said, "She's on her high horse and heading back here."

When I snorted, she wagged a finger at me. "I'm serious. That beast is easily eighteen hands."

Tanner came over, looking haggard. He started going through the piles of gear on the table. "Did the drones have anything interesting to show us?"

"The glass used throughout the castle is that old stuff with lots of bubbles in it which makes it hard to see through. And the below-ground cells only have slits for windows. We were able to get a couple of drones and two birds on the ground. Everything they saw points to an increase in activity in that part of the castle."

"If the captives have been moved to the cells, then we can get in easily," Alderose said. "There's a portal tree less than fifty yards from the door, and I left one of Bas's portal stones inside my old cell. It's on the floor underneath the metal cot. The legs of the cot are bolted to the floor, so I doubt the stone has been found. Sign me up for portalling in."

Noises coming from farther down the hall announced Ni'eve's return. We all stopped talking and watched the door. When she crossed the wide threshold and entered the room, it was clear she had more than arrived. She had bathed, her hair was braided differently, and she'd changed back into her long, hooded robe and a pair of boots.

"I have made a deal with Lionel," she announced. "He has generously offered to return Jessamyne to me and release every other Magical staying at his castle. In exchange, he will take one of you. All you must do is decide who you are willing to trade."

Tanner stepped around the table. While we were talking, he'd been changing out of the clothes that marked him as one of the druids. Now, every part of his body, except for his head, hands and feet, was sheathed in the form-fitting garments Iván had provided. Tanner had even switched out his usual scarred, brown leather accessories. He made a slow production of sliding his goddess-blessed blades into the coal-black sheaths strapped to his outer thighs.

I would not want to be going up the usually laid-back druid.

"Ni'eve, Jessamyne has been removed from the Facility and is on her way to a rehabilitation program."

"She *what*?" Ni'eve spun on her heel and stormed toward Tanner. "Who removed her? On whose orders?"

"Jessamyne was escorted from the area by a team I trust.

They have expertise treating Magicals who have acquired an excess of magic. The extraction was done under my orders."

Ni'eve ignored Tanner's personal space and slapped him across both cheeks. He didn't flinch or react, other than to continue speaking.

"Every step of this has been my doing. I did not share my plan with you because I believed you would veto it. Past behavior predicts future actions, as you know."

Ni'eve raised her arm again, only this time she pointed in the direction of the château's courtyard.

"By taking this action, you have usurped my authority as Jessamyne's mother, as the leader of this order, and as the Keeper of the Keepers. We settle this now, Tanner Didier Marechal."

"We settle this now, Ni'eve Isabeau du Blanc."

Tanner bowed and followed Ni'eve out of the room.

13

ALDEROSE, CLEMENTINE, AND I SCRAMBLED OFF THE BENCH WE were sharing. I had a blessed moment of forgetting my own drama, it being eclipsed by the one unfolding in front of us. While Tanner and Ni'eve were facing off, his blades had begun to vibrate and glow.

We followed the same path and gathered in the same ritual garden where Ni'eve had returned Alderose's metal to her. There was nothing small or contained about the druidess as she strode across the stones, waved her arms in the air, and shouted a command.

At her words, the ground shuddered, swallowing the massive altar and sending pebbles tumbling in all directions across the frost-tipped grass. Once the block was flush with the other stones, Cat, Jake, Alderose, Wes, Kaz, and River formed a loose half-circle on the far side of the sacred space.

Kostya, Laszlo, Clementine, and I stood together. Ni'eve spun in place and yelled out another command. The ground trembled. Flat rocks embedded in the pathway shifted and lurched, which only seemed to irritate the druidess. She yelled again, this time directly at the ground. Nothing happened, earning a section of the grass a couple of kicks.

"Is this really worth it, Ni'eve?" Tanner asked. He stood opposite her, arms relaxed, completely at ease. "I have no wish to cut you down, but I am duty-bound to see to the health and well-being of this place and our tradition, and Jessamyne is bound only to Jessamyne. Surely even you see that."

"You went behind my back."

"Yes, I went behind your back," he said, keeping his stance relaxed and unthreatening. "With your mother's blessing."

"My *mother*? *Grisette*?" Ni'eve looked around wildly, as though she'd completely forgotten she had a mother and half expected the Crone to leap out of the surrounding spruce trees. "She gave up her right to lead us so long ago I cannot remember what century it was."

"She was *forced* out, Ni'eve. After all this time, can you not admit even that?"

The sun gave up trying to burn off the cloud cover. Dark gray clouds melded together, creating a gloomy canopy over our heads. I stepped closer to Kostya and snuggled into his side. Hearing sounds behind me, I turned. The Keepers who had bathed Alderose before her ritual and carried her to the crypt filed into the garden. Behind them were other druids, some I even recognized from my time inside the château. They slowly filled in the spaces until Ni'eve and Tanner were ringed by bodies, with a fair distance between the two of them—and us.

The Keepers and the druids joined hands. Cat, Jake, and Alderose accepted their silent invitations. We did too. When the circle was complete, circuits of magic lit up. One travelled through our arms in a rainbow of colors, and one through the ground below our feet. That circle glowed in shades of greens and browns.

And though no one's head touched anyone else's, some kind

of energy passed through and connected all of us there as well. I *felt*, more than saw, that circle.

While the assembled crowd connected, forming a fence of bodies, Tanner and Ni'eve had stood their respective ground— until Ni'eve attacked. She pulled strands of green light up and out of the ground, made a rolling movement with her hands, and directed a ball of tangled lines at Tanner. He deflected the ball with the broad side of his short sword.

"You would bring *those* blades into this circle and use them against *me*, Tanner?"

"I would. Though if you object, I shall hand them over."

"I object."

Tanner tossed the swords to River. Ni'eve immediately launched more balls, which he punched away with his hands, elbows, and knees in a flowing show of dexterity.

I felt the incoming presence of another Magical before I saw them enter the ritual garden. Everyone else felt it too. Ni'eve and Tanner stayed facing one another, and because his back was to the gate, I got to watch the druidess's face as she reacted to her mother's entrance.

"Ni'eve, this can't be what you want," Tanner said.

"Of course, this is not what she wants, Tanner." Grisette paused behind the barrier formed by two Keepers' joined hands. "Because the one she really wants to humiliate and do away with is me."

Those two Keepers moved apart, giving Grisette room to enter the circle. Her thick gray hair flowed away from her fore-head and down her back. The gold inlaid around her throat and up her ears glowed as if lit from within. Her long robe, pale green and embroidered with apples, was open down the front. Underneath, a simple, pale-gold dress clung to her slender legs.

The staff she carried was no ordinary walking stick. It too wore swirls of glowing, inlaid yellow gold.

"I never gave up my position, as head of our order, as Keeper of the Keepers, and no one knows that better than you and Jessamyne, Ni'eve," she said, planting the staff in the ground beside her as she came to a stop. "Today, my granddaughter was given her final chance to redeem herself. And today, I take back my robes and my stave. I would prefer to do it without a fight, but if I must force you to give up that which you stole, then I shall use every weapon in my arsenal."

Ni'eve cackled. Her hair started to unbraid itself as she lifted her arms away from her body and turned her palms to face the ground. Her fingernails sparked, one after the other, until miniature bolts of lightning danced between her fingers. Keeping her palms horizontal, she drew her arms in front of her body and slowly raised them to the height of her chest.

Her magic coaxed a stone sword, obsidian black, chiseled, and crackling with magic, into rising from the ground. As the pommel met her hands, she took hold of the grip, raised the sword, and yelled. A zigzag of bluish white light hit the tip then fizzled. Ni'eve yelled again, repeating the same single word command. The zigzag reappeared, slightly more committed to a show this time, but again quickly fizzled out.

Grisette had been raising her own magic. She strode forward, arms aloft, nothing frail or ancient in her gait. Wind whipped the layers of her robe and dress out and away from her body and lifted her hair too. She shot one arm skyward, pounded the stave against the earth, and lightning—big, sharp, loud—split the ground in a circle around Ni'eve. Thick vines shot out, wove themselves into a birdcage, and encased the furious druidess.

Her mother mimicked a bird in flight, and lifted her face to the sky. The largest raven I had ever seen swooped in, legs down and talons spread. Its feathers glimmered with iridescence, emerald green and midnight blue, in the muted, overcast light.

The raven's beating wings kicked up grit as it grabbed the top of the Ni'eve's cage. At a word from Grisette, the magnificent bird flew off. Ni'eve's curses rained down on our heads, along with a few feathers and the obsidian sword. Iván leapt forward, caught the blade by its grip, and dropped to one knee in front of Grisette.

The Crone was watching the bird's flight path. She waited until her daughter's invective faded before she set her stave on the ground, dusted off her hands, and placed them on the top of Iván's head.

"We have not met before," she said, smoothing the white streaks that shone against his long, black hair. "Our tradition holds that they who find the sword, may keep the sword. Do you wish to keep it?"

"Does it have a personality?" Iván asked, smiling up at the ancient druidess.

"It does. It will shine best from a strong hand, and it will leave you when your time with it is done."

"Then I shall gladly accept this sword, my—"

"My name is Grisette. I am but a simple keeper of apple trees who longs for simpler times." She grinned at the demon and turned to us. "Ni'eve invented the birdcage, you know. She was rather taken with the idea of a portable means of confinement. Seemed only fitting to use it on her. My daughter will be brought someplace safe, and I shall deal with her later."

The Crone checked the fastenings on her beautiful robe and stepped closer to the circle of ripped up stone and grass.

"Tanner, will you come here please?"

He went to kneel, and she swatted his shoulder.

"You never need to kneel before me, young man. Please stand. River, may I have one of those fancy swords?"

River bowed to Grisette and handed her a blade.

"A new season for les Druides du Blanc begins today," she

said. "And though the winter solstice draws closer and now is not the time for planting, a symbolic gesture is called for. I would have one of your goddess's precious seeds."

Tanner removed the high-tech jacket and the T-shirt underneath and turned, exposing his lower back to Grisette. We all moved in closer by one or two steps to get a better view of the tree tattooed on Tanner's hip. It's branches peeked out from the low-slung waistband of his pants. Interspersed with the delicately incised lines were raised spots the size of grains of rice.

The Crone pressed the tip of the blade against one of those spots and made a tiny cut. She twisted, drew the blade away, and showed the tip to Tanner.

"Tanner Marechal has been blessed with a task few of us would want. Let us celebrate his dedication to Idunn and plant an apple seed. Perhaps the Goddess will bless us with a tree."

Grisette knelt, stuck the tip of the dagger into the exposed soil, then handed the blade to Tanner. She crumbled chunks of dirt over the seed, murmured a blessing, and stood.

"Now, let us take down that wicked, wicked man once and for all."

Tanner offered her an arm, and Jake offered her another. The Crone seemed extremely pleased to be escorted into the castle by two dashing Magicals.

"Never a dull fucking moment," Cat muttered, passing me on the path. Clementine and Alderose slid their arms around my waist and shoulders.

"I'm amazed to see Grisette so...awake and alive."

"Me too. I liked her when we met, and now I really like her," Clementine said. "Do you two think we could talk?"

We were nearing the castle, and before either Alderose or I could give her an answer, she steered us away from the main entrance and toward what was clearly a barn. The interior smelled of hay, oats, corn, and molasses. Though I had never been a fan of horses, the soft nickers coming from the stalls were comforting.

Clementine made us haul a couple of bales of hay into a triangle and sit.

"Okay, first things first. That raven. It looked a *lot* like the one I saw in the story threads, when Mom conjured a bird and it flew her out the window of her workroom." She shook out her arms and shuddered.

"I was going to ask you about that, Clemmie." Alderose leaned forward and gave Clementine a quick hug.

"When this is over," I added, after giving her a hug too, "I think Grisette is going to be a bigger resource about our mother than we thought. And it makes me wonder even more about Ni'eve and her connection to the fae."

"I agree. And here's why I brought you two in here. You know that Laszlo and Kostya are going to do everything they can to ensure we're not in the front lines when we go to Lionel's castle, don't you? And with three-headed Jake, and Cat and Iván with all their fancy equipment, they're going to put us at the back of the line at best and make us stay here at worst."

"You speak the truth," I said. "What are you thinking?"

"The three of us are going to come up with a plan so brilliant that Laszlo and Kostya and the others aren't going to be able to say no."

Alderose snorted and kicked at the bale of hay I was sitting on. "If Tanner's willing to let me use one of his blades again, I *know* I'll be on that front line."

"And I'm asking you to at least *consider* working with us, Rosey. You heard what Ni'eve said. Lionel's willing to trade every one of his captives, for a single one of us. He's already met you, and he's already met me, but he's never really met Beryl. And I think Beryl might be the best weapon we have."

"Explain."

"Yeah, explain," I said. "Because I'm not sure what you're getting at, Clementine."

She reached into one of her pockets and took out a small, black tube. "I'm putting on the mascara. Rosey, sit there and enjoy the show. Ready, Beryl?"

I assumed Clementine meant the Beguilement, though I'd never told her about it. "Yes, I'm ready."

I drew from my heart's well and sent a stream of loyalty toward Alderose's center which, as I'd noted when Ni'eve was pouring liquid metal onto my sister's body, was situated below her navel.

"For Goddess sake, Beryl, what the *fuck* are you doing?" she asked. She dashed to the nearest stall, opened the chest-high door, and closed it behind her. "I'm ready to pledge my sword to whatever cause you want me to, no questions asked. Clementine, do you *feel* that?"

Clementine stumbled to her feet and reached her hands toward me. Her pupils had grown larger, her eyes less focused. "I think the mascara gives me an immunity to Beryl's magic. I was seeing these threads of sparkly pink mist hovering around the front of her body and I just knew they had a story to share."

I took hold of Clementine's hands. "You're seeing the magic I call *Beguilement*."

Alderose gave a low whistle from behind the stall door. "Do Clementine and I have that too?"

"Probably not." I guided Clementine back to her hay bale, drew in the Beguilement, and got myself situated. "It's safe to come out now, Rosey. Sit down and I'll tell you a story."

My sisters got to hear about the foxes, and that I was reason our childhood backyard got fenced in. They got to hear about the magic I learned to pull off our mother when I was seven, and how I was playing with that magic when I tossed the spell that turned a boy to stone when I was fourteen.

They heard about me getting fitted for my first corset soon after, and all of Mom's warnings, and my fears about dating and falling in love and having sex, and how Kostya was the only lover I ever had because for whatever reason, I trusted him.

They also got to hear about what Maritza and Malvyn discovered when they took a closer look at the tear in my corset. How I'd lost my Binder magic, and I'd lost the gift, or the curse, of the Demesne, but that I'd gained something uniquely *mine*.

"It's a lot to absorb, I know," I said, when I cut my story a little short in response to the banging on the door.

"Hey, hi," Cat said. "Alderose, good news. Your girlfriend's on her way here. I kinda didn't ask if you minded that I monitored Sidan while she was with those fae fixer-uppers, but I did and she's better, and she wants to help, so I said okay. That alright with you?"

"That's the best news. Get your ass in here. We need your help." Alderose gave Cat a full-body hug and made room for her on the hay bale.

Clementine and I filled Cat in on our magics; she already knew about Alderose and her metal. We explained that we wanted to send me in as the trade for the captives. She agreed the Arkadi brothers weren't going to be thrilled that their mates were willing and eager to put themselves in harm's way.

"There's a solid reason for sending *me* in as our trade," I said. "By using the Beguilement, I can get Lionel, and anyone else in his immediate vicinity, to want to be with me in a way that feels all-consuming and absolute. I don't have to dance, I don't have to sing, I just have to go in there without holding back anything. Once I'm in, I can use the Beguilement to get Lionel to do whatever it is we decide."

Clementine butted in. "I'll go as far as the castle. We'll insist that every one of the captives is brought out and given over to us, *before* we hand over Beryl. I'll be able to tell if they're lying, and if they've given us all the captives."

"And I'll be invisible," Alderose said. "Which means I actually *could* go in with Beryl. Or even before her and wait." Alderose smacked her forehead and grinned like she had the answer to every one of our problems. "Sid can make me invisible. It's a skill she developed for herself and she once told me she can extend her invisibility to me for a limited time if I'm right beside her. Laszlo and Kostya can object all they like, they won't have a leg to stand on, because Sid and I will be right there with Beryl, only no one will know."

"While I heartily approve thinking outside the box on this," Cat said, "I'm skeptical the other fae won't know there's a witch in their midst who's being cloaked by fae magic."

"Can you create another diversion, Cat? Or a series of diversions? All we need is enough time to do a full sweep of the castle to make sure the fae have given us everyone, and then get Beryl out too, with Lionel. Like Malvyn said, we've got to get him off his property in order for him to be taken into custody and charged."

"Between the vultures, the drones, and whatever else Jake and Tanner have up their sleeves, I think we can do this."

"Beryl, all you need is to wear the sexiest outfit we can find," Alderose added.

"In here?" I laughed. "Have you seen the clothes the druids wear? They washed the sexy out centuries ago."

"Tía brought her needles. She can whip out a sexy black dress. Believe me, I know Lionel's taste in women's clothing."

14

INSIDE THE CHÂTEAU, ALDEROSE AND CAT STAYED IN THE classroom to gather what we'd need from Cat's, Jake's, and Iván's duffel bags and backpacks. Clementine decided helping them organize would be more calming to her nerves than watching our aunt do her thing. I found Maritza resting in her room, outlined the plan we'd come up with, and waited for her to tell me what a crazy idea it was.

"I think that could work," she said, sitting up. "The right dress could make you absolutely irresistible to Lionel Vigne, and I think I have the perfect threads in one of my cases."

"What should I wear for shoes?" I asked. "I've only got black combat boots and those oversized felted slippers."

"We'll cut a pair of ballet flats from one of the capes I packed."

"One of Alabastair's capes? Won't he be upset?"

"We'll take it from the bottom. He'll never notice the loss of six inches," she said, "and if he does, he'll understand it was for a very good cause."

For this project, Maritza chose two sets of knitting needles and multiple spools of a thick but soft black thread. Her tools worked so fast that a lacy, body-hugging dress was soon taking shape in front of the window. She shook out the cape she mentioned, a simple black wool creation with no added bells or whistles and asked me to pass her the heavy shears.

"This will be perfect, mija. The cloth has been spelled to resist many kinds of magic. It will keep your feet safe, and I will use the scraps to create motifs that will add interest to the dress, as well as provide further armoring."

"Like pasties?" I teased.

"Like pasties, silly witch. Now go wash your hands. They smell like the barn."

Coming out of the bathroom, I paused to watch my aunt work. Her mastery was inspiring—and made me wonder what *my* mastery would be. My natural witch magic might blossom without the constant restraint of the corset. My ability to draw magic from others and use it as though it were my own, with their consent, was a skill I could use openly now.

And now that I understood the Beguilement more clearly, I didn't carry so much shame. I could make time to study and test it in controlled, non-stressful circumstances.

"Beryl, I would advise that you bring all of your focus and power to the task at hand. You are going to need it when you come face to face with Lionel Vigne. He is like no one you have ever known, and he will not go down easily. Always, *always* assume that he knows exactly what you are doing." My aunt shook her head as she stroked my cheeks. "You and your sisters are very brave, a little foolish, and I hope that by tomorrow's sunrise, this will have been resolved and we can be on our way home."

"Me too, Tía. Me too."

I ducked out to pace the hall, remembered the room at the end with its promise of around-the-clock snacks, and entered. Ni'eve's departure and Tanner and Grisette's coup must have sent the château's resident workers and trainees into chaos. The bread on the cutting board was stale and the sliced fruit had browned and gone mushy along the edges.

I popped the cork on a bottle of brandy, poured a fingerful into a teacup, and curled up in the window seat. Wood groaned underneath my elbow where I rested it on the windowsill, and that eerie feeling I'd gotten before, of the entire building being alive and somewhere on the magical spectrum, returned.

Perhaps it was welcoming Grisette into her rightful home.

I tapped the window's warped frame with my elbow. Cold air swept across my face like a call to pay attention. I did, reviewing what my aunt had said about Lionel, especially the part about him knowing exactly what we were doing. Which meant lives depended on me staying alert. I shifted onto my knees and reached out the window, teacup in hand.

Goddess, I thank you for your help in the coming hours. Keep my new friends safe, keep my loved ones safe, and watch over those we hope to help.

I poured out what was left of the brandy and heard it hit the ground. After I shut the window, I doused the light, and gasped when I opened the door to my aunt's room. The most gorgeous, bell-sleeved gossamer dress floated below one of the low beams. Scattered across the bodice in all the right places were delicate black butterflies. The bodies were stitched down, and the wings fluttered off the knitted fabric.

"How are you making them do that?" I asked, reaching out to touch one with my fingertip.

"Magic. Pure and simple, mija."

"Do you think I should put the dress on now and just show up in the classroom, ready to go?"

"Beryl, your magic is your weapon and your armor. This dress simply enhances what lives inside you and will make the viewer see only what you want them to see—which is you. Not your sister who will be reading the story lines and feeding you her impressions. Not your other sister, who will be hiding in plain sight.

"Those who would take issue with your magic being of the seductive kind can go take a walk around the château until they've cooled off and come to their senses."

"This might be my one and only chance to use the full power of the Beguilement on purpose, Tía."

"And what a noble purpose it is." She plucked the dress out of the air at its shoulder seams and held it in front of me. "Are you ready?"

WEARING such an exquisite garment without a fabulous pair of heels and a pair of sparkly drop earrings felt odd. I kept wanting to walk on the balls of my toes. Revel in what that did to the curve of my spine and the lift of my butt. Shake my head and feel the weight of jewels dangling from my earlobes.

Some other place, some other night.

I glanced down the front of the dress and noticed some of the butterflies had free rein to land wherever they wanted. I pictured my mother's third-floor workshop, her supplies for drafting patterns and making mock-ups of clothing and hats she would later imbue with magic. The big desk where she met with clients looking for their true love.

I realized that's what I wanted too. A place to grow my magic, to embrace my heritage and become a business-based witch. My familiarity with bespoke clothing suggested I should take over the couture arm of Mom's business. That would be sensible, logical, and practical.

I wanted something more than sensible, logical, and practical. I wanted to use my unique magic in service of helping Magicals find romantic partnership, companionship, and love.

Resolved to reach for the matchmaking stars, I gently lifted the sides of the dress with both hands and pushed the door to the classroom open with the side of my hip.

Kostya looked up from whatever he was fiddling with and swept his gaze down and up my attire.

"No. A thousand times *no*, Beryl. You are not going to Lionel's castle in a see-through dress."

Trembling inside, I let go of the skirt, raised my arms, and released a torrent of Beguilement, an unmeasured dose of everything I'd held back since my mother and the sea witch first wrapped the corset around my scrawny chest and damped my magic. I added a little spin. Let the dress lift away from my legs as I sent pulse, after pulse, of my magic into the room.

And pulled it back a few seconds later. If I was going to use my magic seriously, I was going to have to temper my responses.

"The plan is for me to walk through the front gate of the Vigne's castle," I said, to a room full of surprised faces, including the gargoyle I'd encountered on the roof of the Facility. "Before that, Clementine will read any and all the threads that she can. Alderose and Sidan will be there too. Invisible. My magic will be primed and ready. It's a sound plan. And if everyone will sit down and hear us out, I think you will not only agree" –I spun around once more, slowly this time, so I could look every single being in the room in the eyes– "you will see that this plan will work. There is room for each of us to bring our best."

Kostya frowned his displeasure. My belly quavered, and a moment later, Iván cuffed the side of his brother's head. Tanner came forward and took my hands.

"Beryl, Alderose and Clementine explained the plan you three came up with. I'm all for it, and I think your magic is a perfect foil for Lionel. We're just waiting for Alabastair to return with Sidan, and then we go," he said. "While you were upstairs, I made contact with Lionel. He said he is very much looking forward to seeing who we're bringing to him. He emphasized that he has a soft spot in his heart for witches—after I mentioned a witch is what he would be getting. He also said he never intended any harm when he invited Jessamyne to stay at the Facility as his guest and that having her gone and in her mother's care would be a blessing.

"He did not appear to know that Jessamyne had already left the building."

Tanner squeezed my hands before letting me go. "I think we all know that Lionel Vigne has absolutely no intention of freeing these Magicals he's been acquiring for years. He has no intention of shutting down the Facility or his research, and he has every intention of seeing that his program of forced breeding delivers results.

"So let's use everything we know about him and get this guy, shall we? Iván, do you have the sisters' earpieces ready?"

My tech-savvy future brother-in-law didn't wipe the grin off his face as he showed off a stunning pair of earrings sitting in a gunmetal gray box.

"You like?" he asked, and when I nodded, he said he thought I would. "I wanted something flashier for you, but then I thought too much sparkle would draw attention to them, and we want these to stay on you."

He gently clipped the drop part of each earring onto my earlobes, then slipped the cuff part on the upper curve of each ear. "The top pieces are your back-up."

"Thanks, Iván." He kissed my cheeks and went to give Clementine and Alderose sets of more utilitarian adornments. Alabastair came through the door, chatting with someone who could have been his twin brother—until the someone shimmered and shifted and turned into a tall, female fae, with lavender-blue skin, the usual pointed ears, and an unusually wide grin.

"Sidan!" Alderose ran to her girlfriend, grabbed her wrist, and hauled her out of the room. I stayed right where I was, waiting for the two of them to return. Most everyone in the room did too, including a slightly cranky Jake.

It struck me that transportation was one piece of the plan we hadn't covered, or that I'd missed hearing about. "Are we getting to the castle by portal or—"

"Limos," Cat said. "I hired two from a local car service. They're waiting outside the château."

Sid and Rosey snuck back in, and my sister brought her over to the table where Cat and Jake were sitting. Tanner waved his arms in the air and whistled for attention.

"All of us arriving at the same time, showing a united front, sends a message to Lionel. We make him believe we are following official protocol for this kind of exchange. We focus on giving Beryl room to work her magic. If she gets separated from the rest of us—which we know could happen—we don't react. Our job, in their eyes, is to remove the captives and deliver one witch.

"In addition to what I already covered, I think we can assume Lionel may have kept his most coveted acquisitions hidden within the castle, and that he intends to resume collecting once the attention is off him.

"If Lionel has the captives assembled and ready for us to take, we go with that. If the captives are inside the castle, we go in together. Alderose and Sidan, you'll be invisible the moment you get out of the vehicles. In the first scenario, you'll enter the castle as quickly as you can and get to work.

"In the second scenario, you'll enter with us and proceed from there. Beryl? I know it's a stretch, but if you can get Lionel into one of the limos right off the bat, the driver will bring you here. If you can get him to walk with you outside of the castle's

main gate, Alabastair and Malvyn will be there to take possession of him and portal him to Toronto.

"If Lionel insists on bringing you inside the castle, go with
him. You have your earpieces, you have Alderose and Sidan, and
you have the rest of us. There are a lot of moving pieces, and
there's a lot that could go sideways. Our objective is to free the
captives. Further, taking Lionel Vigne alive will allow Malvyn to
interrogate him about missing Magicals. Questions?"

I raised my arm and pointed to the gargoyle. "Who's that?"

The gargoyle let out a string of words. Laszlo, Kostya, and
Iván seemed to understand what he was saying.

"That's Phineas," Laszlo said. "Normally, he lives in Paris. He
came to Chamonix to explore the architecture. His first night on
the roof of one of the Vigne's towers, he saw things that
disturbed him. He's been making observations and taking notes
and was planning to file a report once he figured out who would
handle this kind of case."

Phineas hopped off the table and bowed. I was glad that
mystery was solved.

"Oh, and Phineas has offered to come with us and coach me
and Kostya through our first attempts at getting airborne."

"You're going to *fly*?" Clementine asked. The glances
exchanged between Phineas, Laszlo, and Kostya answered that
question. My younger sister did not look happy at her mate's
news. I declined forming an opinion about the timing of the
demon brothers' announcement.

"If there are no more questions, we should go." Tanner made
his way to the door as he spoke.

We filled both cars. The three Arkadi brothers, Jake, and
Phineas were in the bigger limo ahead of us. Kostya's discom-
fort with the plan was palpable, and I missed having him next
to me. There was very little talking between me, Clementine,
Alderose, and Sidan, especially once we hit the curving

sections of road with the hair-raising switchbacks—until Cat spoke.

"I'm bringing everyone in on this. We're almost there, and I want the details fresh in everyone's mind." Cat turned around from the middle seat. "Alderose, Jake, give us a head count from your time in the Facility. Don't over think it."

« I'm not going to be much help," Jake said. "I was at the farthest end of the sub-ground zoo, and I was drugged when they brought me in. Rosey? Hope your memory's better'n mine. »

My sister cleared her throat. "Top floor, the aerie. Vacant, except for the tree. Next floor down was called labor and delivery. Maybe three or four fae medical staff. I don't recall seeing any captives. Four of the rooms had aquariums. Oh! If you end up doing a sweep through there, don't breathe in the air. It's laced with something that does a number on your hormones.

"Laboratory level. I only saw—nope, I didn't see anyone. Zoo level, phew, okay." Alderose put her head in her hands. "All the captives were kept contained by invisible bars or—or *walls*, of fae magic. I saw set-ups that were just a bunch of big, flat rocks. Other sections had big branches, whole trees that had been cut up and were lying on their sides. Big nests. Shallow pools. A couple that were like jungles. Three of each habitat, no birds, so maybe a dozen, including Sheenah and Jake."

"Everyone make note, we are looking for Magicals that fly, crawl, swim, slither."

Silence. "Good. Flyboys, you can hop out any time now."

A minute later the monster-sized limo in front of us stopped. Jake, Laszlo, Kostya, and Phineas got out. I caught glimpses of the quartet as they jogged off the road and disappeared into the boulder-littered mountainside. They'd all stripped down to skintight clothing; all but Phineas had weaponry positioned flush against their arms and legs. I took my body's physical reac-

tion to seeing Kostya and his wings and wove that into the
waiting Beguilement. A witch had to use everything at her
disposal.

"Wait, did Tanner call them flyboys?" I asked. I had been so
intent on seeing that our plan was the chosen plan, I hadn't paid
attention to what Kostya and Laszlo might have been cook-
ing up.

"Yeah, flyboys. I take it Kostya didn't tell you? Well, he and
Laszlo took a little booster that Iván just happened to bring.
Couple that with encouragement from Phineas, and our boys
believe they can use their wings to get them up that wall and
into the castle."

There was nothing to say. I had assumed the flying lessons
were happening *after* this mission was over. Kostya's wings had
barely come in and in my humble opinion, he was in no way
ready to fly.

I let that go, and settled back against the plush seat. Tires
rolling over the paved section changed their song as the ground
gave way to broad stones. We slowed and came to a stop.

I opened my eyes. All I could see were shades and textures of
gray. Gray sky, gray rock, gray building stone. Drops of rain
splattered the windshield and the sunroof, and metal clanged as
the two halves of the gate swung open. Our driver put the car in
gear, eased it through the entrance, and glided to a stop.

Three fae in suits and holding black umbrellas stood in the
courtyard. Behind them were a few more, similarly attired,
standing under the covered entrance to the castle.

"Those outside are probably staff. I don't remember their
faces very clearly," Alderose said. "I see Lionel behind them.
He's in the dark silver suit. I think the head nurse, Nadège, is the
one in the white uniform."

Sidan leaned forward and peered intently. "We may have a

problem. The invisibility cloaking becomes reflective in the rain. Rosey and I will have to wait it out behind the car."

"Tanner's taking lead," Cat said. "I'm acting as his second in command. Ideally, we get all the captives loaded in before we hand Beryl over."

Two more vehicles pulled up behind our limo, blocking the exit. My heart sped up.

"Relax. Those are ours, Beryl. We'll use them to take the Magicals to the château."

Handles clicked, and the doors beside Tanner and Cat whooshed open.

"Clan Vigne welcomes you. If you will come with us?"

15

"LOCK THE DOORS WHEN WE GO," CAT SAID. "BERYL, DO NOT leave the car until Tanner or I give the okay."

They exited the limo. Sidan grabbed Alderose's hand. The two curled forward, shimmering into invisibility as they left their seat. Clementine sat closer to me, and Kaz and River took up watch on either side of the car.

If things went to plan, Laszlo, Kostya, Jake, and Phineas would already be scaling a nearby section of the wall, putting eyes on the exterior of the castle. Soon Alderose and Sidan would be finding a door or a window and putting eyes inside the castle.

Goddess watch over everyone. My offering is coming.

Rain splattered the exterior of the foggy windows. I wanted a better look at the Magicals Lionel had been obsessed with collecting. Wiping the windows from the inside would advertise my curiosity. I would see them later, at the château. Breathing into stillness, I began to send out the first wave of Beguilement on neutral feelers.

"Sissy," I said. "Are you reading anything from your threads yet?"

She opened her eyes wider and stared straight ahead, past the middle row of seats and the closed window sealing us off from the driver. "Threads are beginning to cluster. All I can see right now is that he is every bit as cunning as we've been told, and he has...he has a long history, Beryl, and many, many scars."

I squeezed her hand. I could see mouths moving and bodies adjusting. "Everyone's talking now. I'm going to try to listen in."

"I'm ready to help." Clementine extended her arm. I circled her wrist, closed my eyes, and felt for her magic.

Her threads were unlike anything I'd ever seen.

"Do you think your threads have been affected by your connection to Laszlo?" I asked, "because they're like...they're like filaments of ice. They look brittle, like they might break."

"Oh, they won't break," she said. "And no, I've never really stopped to think about what they look like inside of me. I'll pay more attention as I send them out."

"I'm drawing on them now," I said. "Let me know if you can feel it."

I coaxed her threads toward my hand, and just as I did with other magic, drew the threads up my arm and across my chest and down my other arm. This time, I used my hand rather than a wand to send them toward where Lionel and the others were clustered.

Lionel's voice came through clear as bells. "Tanner Marechal, our mutual friend Ni'eve alerted me you would be escorting my gift in exchange for taking these *guests* off my hands. Do you intend to hold to your end of our bargain?"

"Lionel, yes. Your gift is here. Before we complete our side, I would like to speak with each of your guests."

"Come, they await their new host. A word or two is acceptable. And I am beside myself with anticipation."

"See if you can keep Lionel talking," I said into the mic. "The more he talks, the more I learn about him and his magic." All the little holes in my knitted dress created a sieve for my *borrowing* magic, allowing it to flow out as Clementine's threads —searching, seeking, tasting, collecting—and flow back in like bees coming back to the hive loaded with pollen. Only these threads carried information.

Tanner remained in the freezing rain, keeping up a running conversation with Lionel, while Cat questioned each Magical before sending them to one of the cars behind us. Wes acted as escort. Once in a while I picked up a handful of Lionel's words, pouring them back and forth from hand to hand before letting let them slide through my fingers. It intrigued me that even while directing his conversation to Tanner and Cat and the other fae, his attention was primarily on the limousines. He wanted to know what was behind the mirrored windows.

I answered by beginning to make my presence known. I let go of Clementine's magic, and sent out the Beguilement on languid, diaphanous filaments. One caressed Lionel's cheek, its whisper following the elongated curve of his pointed ear and getting lost in his hair's tight waves. Another coiled around one of his ankles, then the other, like an affectionate cat, before returning to me. Others travelled up his sleeves; slipped between his top button to explore his neck; wound around each of his fingers and caressed the metal blades just beginning to slide out on top of his fingernails.

Lionel Vigne was becoming aroused in a way that was wholly unfamiliar to me. Though Alderose had given me fair warning. Another burst of thread magic told me his arousal included thoughts of watching, waiting, hurting, and hiding. It required constant effort on his part to not let his voice break, to not rush over and throw open the car doors. The moment I felt myself enjoying the overly voyeuristic aspect of this process, I pulled back. Delicately. There was information in the returning threads, and I would be more informed if I took this time to extract what I could and examine its usefulness.

Oh, Lionel Vigne, you have been a bad, bad man.

He'd come into possession of his land in the late seventeen hundreds through a lie, a terrible lie with heinous consequences. The castle's true inheritor was nearby, though not within the castle's walls, and their identity was shrouded by a cloak of shame.

That was important information I would draw out later, when I had time to sift through for specifics.

Lionel was flattered that a long-ago guest, horrified by something he'd seen, had coined his favorite nickname, the Collector. For him, there was joy in the hunt and bliss in the moment of acquisition. Though maintaining his prizes took work, and he disliked that kind of work.

Lionel coveted the Du Blanc's château. No, more specific than that, he coveted the orchards surrounding Grisette's ancient hut. I would ask the Crone why a fae lusted for a bunch of gnarled apple trees.

Oh, Lionel Vigne, you are a liar.

As we suspected, he had no intention of allowing Tanner to move the Magicals across the border marking the separation of the Vigne lands from the Du Blanc's. Lionel had fae loyal to him stationed along the steep road we'd driven to get here and an air mage eager to create a diversion and collect his hefty payment.

« Beryl. Clementine. »

Cat's voice entered my ears with urgency.

"What?"

« We're done. Everyone's in the cars. Lionel's ready. »

« *And we're in.* » It took me a moment to register Sidan's voice.

"In the castle?" Clementine asked.

« In the section of the castle with the cells, where Alderose was kept. There are Magicals down here. They've been neglected. A couple are not in good shape. »

« We can free them and get them to the portal tree, » Alderose said. « We're going to need help getting them out. »

Cat cut in. « I'm sending Oscar to you with portal stones. Make sure your trackers are on. »

"Cat, wait. This is Beryl. There's an air mage and at least three fae waiting to ambush the cars. They're going to create a diversion and bring the Magicals right back to the castle."

« Shit, » she said. « On it. We'll pull the cars over and wait for Tanner and Kaz and the other two to get their asses to us. »

I was relieved I got that warning out. I had barely a moment to take a breath when the filaments told me Lionel's demeanor changed. He went icy. Demanding. Aggressive.

"You have everyone you came for," I heard him say, then add, "It is time for *you* to show *me* what you are offering in trade."

"We have papers for you to sign, then we make the trade."

That was my cue. I felt for Clementine's fingertips.

"Clemmie? May I draw more of your magic? I could use a boost."

"Take whatever you need," she said. "You're the one who's going inside. If something happens and I need more, I'll deal with it."

"Thanks, Sissy." I kissed her cheek and held onto her forearm with both my hands. I found her love for Laszlo and the richness of their sexual chemistry, wiped her signature from it while keeping the core energy intact, and wound that through the Beguilement. Featherweight threads I'd sent out earlier thickened and became more purposeful.

Inspired by my aunt, I added a spark to the end of each of those threads, something sharp that would pierce Lionel and provide the frisson of pain he sought, apparently, at the frequency with which I reached for the comfort of a new purse or pair of shoes.

Though he usually sought to inflict the pain, or watch others giving and receiving pain, he had a deep desire to take it on himself. I learned that decades had passed since he'd last found someone willing to give him what he craved. Even then they had declined to deliver the final, conclusive step.

If I could get him to reveal the shape of that elusive release, I might be able to give Lionel Vigne everything he wanted. Question was could I and would I?

I tightened the ties on the eye mask my aunt created when she was working on the dress. She had spelled both items so I wouldn't have to worry about them coming off or being taken off against my will. Though the skirt part of the dress had the freedom to float away from my legs and some of the butterflies could fly away.

Armored by the garments' construction and beauty, I scooped another cupful of my magic from its deep well. I poured it into the Beguilement and absorbed the repercussions of Lionel Vigne's presence as he moved closer to the limousine.

"I'm letting go now," I said. Clementine unlocked the doors and whispered *Good luck*. She climbed over the seat back and hid where Tanner and Cat had been sitting. River grabbed hold of the handle on my side of the car and opened the rear door. Lionel took a measured step back as the druid extended his arm to help me disembark.

I closed my eyes for a mere moment. It was my turn now to act a part. I swung my legs to the side, placed my feet on the cobblestones, and set my fingers on the hand on offer.

I almost recoiled. Lionel must have moved River aside. The gloved hand drawing me out and to standing was more often engaged in cruel activities than helping witches disembark from cars.

"Welcome to Clan Vigne." Another fae appeared beside Lionel and shielded us both with his black umbrella.

I kept my gaze to the glistening stones, even while offering the hint of a smile, and infused the Beguilement with the flavors of rare wine and red meat and the velvety softness of rose petals. Lionel sucked in a breath across his teeth and tongue and exhaled his pleasure at the sensation. He brought the tip of a finger under my chin and slowly drew my gaze up the front of his body to his eyes.

I didn't think I would remember his appearance—or those eyes. Prior to this moment my memories of what happened at the demons' ball ended when I arrived at the top of the grand staircase and called to Clementine. But I *did* have other memories. Of a merciless hand grabbing me by the neck and dragging me toward a man in an exquisitely tailored suit. Of Lionel's cold-eyed snap appraisal determining I was expendable. Of him ordering Guillaume to drain me and leave me for dead.

I resisted the urgent need to press my hands to my belly and shut my mind to the memories of everything that had come after Lionel made the decision to toss me away.

He was taller than I remembered from that brief moment, though not as tall as Tanner or Kostya. Everything about his physical appearance read as controlled, calculated, compact, and exact. Not a dark silver hair out of place. Not a blemish on his bluish skin. Full, thick lashes framed dark blue eyes. Lionel Vigne was brutally handsome—but brutal beauty wasn't my catnip.

I didn't allow any of that to cause a break in feeding the Beguilement out and drawing it in, absorbing what it brought me, and refreshing its purpose.

Lionel pressed his thumb to my lower lip, as if testing for fullness. His gloves were skintight, made of a pearlescent, lavender-gray material so fine I could see the tendons in his hand.

"She will do for now," he said, loud enough for everyone to hear. "If I find her lacking, you will find her outside the Du Blanc gate in the morning." He took my wrist and walked us between Tanner and Cat and the druids. Two fae opened the castle's ornate doors wide enough to let us pass and promptly shut them as I crossed the threshold.

« Beryl, we have eyes on you. Stick with the script. This will all be over soon. »

Lionel's grip was tight. Bars groaned as they were lowered across the doors from the inside, sealing us in. I gave the subtlest tug with both my magic and my arm, requesting he slow down. He followed the suggestion, even relaxing his grip and switching to a gentler hold on my elbow as he guided me down a long, wide hall. We passed numerous closed doors, all carved, painted, and gilded, and statuary, paintings, and tapestries.

"Is this the express tour of your castle?" I asked.

He stopped suddenly and released my arm. He took his time letting his gaze wander all over me, ending with a lengthy visual examination of my face. He reached out to trace the edge of the eye mask and its knotted trim. Using both hands, he slid his fingers behind my earlobes, detached the earrings and the cuffs, and dropped them on an area of bare stone.

"You won't be needing those," he said, crushing the metal and my connection to my sisters and my friends with his heel.

"Do you plan to replace my things?" I asked. "Those could have been family heirlooms." From one moment to the next, a major crutch was ripped away. I held my breath and focused on the single, tiny pearl button on each of his gloves.

"It should be obvious I have an eye for what is *truly* of value." He swept his arm to encompass the gallery-like hall, brought his hand to my lower back, and guided me toward a set of wide stairs. The second landing opened onto a spacious anteroom, furnished with antique love seats and side tables. Thick carpets deadened the sound of our steps. More sets of double doors were closed. Lionel steered me toward the set on the right and turned the polished handle. Another smaller, more lushly appointed room greeted us.

I entered first and waited. Lionel closed the door, tugged off his gloves finger by finger, and undid the button on his tailored suit jacket. Shrugging it down his arms, he folded the jacket in half and draped it over the back of a Louis XVI chair, all while keeping his gaze on me. He shoved the chair's matching footstool into the center of the room with the toe of his polished shoe, unclasped his cufflinks, and dropped them onto a jewelry tray.

"Stand on the stool. I want to look at you."

I lifted my knee. Lionel rolled up his sleeves as I slipped my finger into the heel of my ballet flat and pulled it off. I did the same to the other shoe, set them side by side, and followed Lionel's directive. Only, I chose to take the long way to the stool. Exploring his room would buy me time. I touched surfaces, ran fabrics through my fingers, removed glass stoppers from the bottles of liqueur on one tray and perfumes on another and sniffed in the unusual aromas. I even opened drawers and poked through stacks of silk socks, undergarments, and sleeping attire.

I approached Lionel's bed. The most remarkable thing about it was its normalcy. I wasn't sure what I was expecting. I finished my stroll, noting the rampant use of heavy drapery throughout the room, and the lack of windows, and made my way to the stool.

Lionel bent from the waist to examine one of the butterflies stitched to the bodice of my dress. He slid the blade extending out of his forefinger along the back of the appliqué, flicked the bug into his palm, and sliced its thorax. He went to the next one, and the next, until there were no more butterflies left on my dress. I looked down to see them littering the rug in a circle around the stool, wings twitching.

"I liked those butterflies," I said.

"Remove your dress."

"No."

Lionel stifled a smile. "I haven't heard that word in so long." He went to his knee beside the stool and took hold of my dress's lacy hem. Using the same nail blade, he poked at the black thread until he had teased out an end.

"If you won't remove your dress, I will," he said, rolling the unravelling thread into a ball as he pulled and pulled.

"Why do you want me to take off my dress?"

"To verify that you are hiding nothing."

"You could have simply asked me."

He continued his pulling and winding. My feet were beginning to get cold.

"It's quiet in here," I said, shifting my weight to one leg and rolling the other ankle and spreading my toes. At this rate it would take hours for the dress to disappear. I hoped my aunt's magic would prevent its destruction once my legs were exposed.

Lionel remained on one knee, intent on his task. I gave into temptation and brushed my fingertips across his hair. It was surprisingly silky. He froze. I loosened the Beguilement. Ribbons of magic flowed from my chest and along my arm, quickening their pace as they wended their way through locks of his hair and around his neck. They continued around his chest, crisscrossing like the ties of a traditional corset. I brought my other hand to his head and mimed drawing the invisible ribbons tighter and tighter.

He set the tiny ball of black thread on the floor, lifted his face to the ceiling, and closed his eyes.

"More," he whispered.

I directed another set of the magic-soaked ribbons down his

arms and pulled, tying his wrists together behind his back. This was a first for me, binding another being with my magic in this way. I wasn't sure if the binding would stay, and I wasn't clear about what to do next. The earlier version of Lionel, the one who revealed he'd stolen the castle from its rightful owner and had no intention of permanently letting go of the Magicals he'd collected, was inside the man kneeling in front of me. I couldn't lose sight of that, even as my curiosity about this aspect of my magic bubbled.

Someone knocked on the door. Lionel's eyelids fluttered open, his eyes unfocused. He rolled his shoulders.

"Undo the restraints, witch. My sister doesn't like to be kept waiting."

I ignored his urgency, keeping tension on the ribbons as they slid across his skin with each uncrossing.

"You're free," I said, slowly drawing the last bit of the Beguilement toward me.

"And that is where you are mistaken."

16

Lionel massaged his wrists and rolled onto his feet. The banging continued. He glanced over his shoulder at me before he opened the door. An impeccably dressed woman in one of the most iconic silhouettes in fashion history pushed past him and entered the room. My gaze was drawn to the plunging V neckline of her navy-blue dress and its nipped-in waist. She stopped when she noticed me, a witch in a hand-knitted dress standing on a footstool in the middle of the room.

"Really, Lionel?" she said, cocking her hip to the side and smirking her bright red lips. She circled the stool, allowing me a closer look at her glossy, dark brown hair and flawlessly made-up face. "What makes you think now is the time to indulge in one of your *scenes*? Guillaume is missing. Larch is missing. And I can't find Arnaud in any of his usual places. What have you done with my boys?"

"Guillaume is not and has never been your *boy*, sister. He has always been mine. I sent what was left of him to the druids as a warning. Same with that faun you find so entertaining. The pleasure of a big cock lasts only so long, and I've grown tired of his antics. You really need to move on."

This was Linette Vigne. Where so many fae were tall, lithe, and contained, she was curvy. And outwardly furious. Something about her piqued the interest of my magic. I almost didn't send out an exploratory thread—but then I did, just a light, dainty ribbon, bright with innocence. Nothing about it pointed a finger to me.

She brushed her hand down her arm, smoothing the wrinkles in her elbow-length gloves, and opened her mouth as if she was about to speak.

"I did nothing to Arnaud," Lionel said, sliding his hands into his front pockets. "Though knowing how strongly he feels about Guillaume, I wouldn't be surprised if he's jumped off the castle wall or thrown himself into the well."

Linette strode to her brother, smacked him across the face, and turned to leave. Lionel grabbed her forearm and jerked. A bone snapped, and as Linette screamed, Lionel clamped his hand over her mouth and marched her into the hall. The door was left open for the rest of their heated exchange, which seemed to center on the endless supply of lovers Linette dragged into the castle, and the impression that had made on her son when he was younger. Linette stormed off, sobbing. There was silence before Lionel re-entered the room and shoved the door closed behind him.

"My sister is spoiled. She has never wanted for anything. It would be prudent to forget she was here in the first place."

While they were in the hall, I had added a thickener to the Beguilement to strengthen me and add weight to the magic.

"So. You flayed Guillaume."

He barely blinked.

"And you tied Larch to his portal tree and magicked him and the tree to Château de Blanc. Or hired someone to do that for you." My vote was on the air mage waiting outside the castle—

and my hope was the mage had been grounded before their powers could be used against my friends.

More silence from Lionel. No blinking.

"What did you do with the third man?" I asked. "The one I assume is the Arnaud that your sister referred to."

Evil leaked from Lionel's smirk. "Arnaud is my nephew. Arnaud and Guillaume have at times had a relationship. Which has never bothered me. What bothers me is that Arnaud lacks certain familial traits, a certain...world outlook. I used a recent event to drive home the point that I will not be betrayed. And as my sister knows all too well, hurting strangers is too easy. Pleasure becomes much more nuanced when we hurt the ones we love."

"Are you planning to hurt me?" I asked, bending my knees and picking up the ball of rolled up thread still attached to my dress. I wished I had a pocket to tuck it into. I was aware of Lionel tracking every move I made.

"Have we met before?" he asked, extending his arm and opening his palm.

I weighed my options, including whether to return the ball of thread.

"You haven't answered *my* question, Lionel. Are you planning to hurt me?"

"I'm planning to *test* you. Whether my tests cause pain is up to you."

"Fair enough."

He used his nail blade to cut the thread attaching the ball to the hem of my dress. "I answered your question. Answer mine."

"Yes, we have met," I said.

"If you would remove your eye mask, perhaps I could recall when and where that propitious moment was."

"You could try to take this off me." I sent another wave of

Beguilement toward Lionel and had it focus on filling his palms with the sense that he was touching the skin of someone he loved. Confusion swept his face.

I slid my magic along his arms and interlaced slender ribbons behind his neck. Tugging, I brought him closer to me, close enough there was no space between the fronts of our bodies. He gripped my hips and lowered his face until his lips hovered above mine. The tip of his nose bumped my temple. I closed in on him only enough to brush my lips across his jaw.

"Who are you?" he whispered.

I moved the metal nail file I'd picked up from the grooming kit on his bureau from where I had secreted it in my dress to my hand. Beguilement kept Lionel where he was. I brought the dull tip to his neck and pressed until I felt the skin give and smelled blood.

"I am exactly the one you want, Lionel. Stop toying with me."

He curled his fingers around mine and pressed the nail file deeper into the side of his neck.

"I want you to hurt me," he said. "I want you to hear my confession. I want you to tell me I have been a very bad man, and I want you to tell me in such a way that I shall believe you. Others have tried."

"Then what are we doing in here?"

He slid one finger between mine and the file and made me drop it on the carpet atop the pile of lifeless butterflies. Red droplets soaked into his shirt collar as he straightened and offered me his hand. I took it, noticing the blades on his finger-tips had retracted.

Before I let him lead me out of the room, I slid my feet into the ballet flats. We passed one assistant, then another, on the stairs. I glanced over my shoulder, only to see them doing the same. Both wore looks of wide-eyed wonder and walked too fast for me to read more from their expressions.

On the ground floor, Lionel proceeded in a different direction from where we'd come. I lost my bearings, which created the perfect opportunity for me to reach for his hand and begin to siphon off his magic. This would be my first time working with fae magic. To have blades sprout from my fingertips would raise Lionel's suspicions. I found and latched onto the fae's intimate knowledge of glamour and the myriad ways they disappeared behind masks.

Lionel held my hand in a steely grip. He steered us into a circular stairwell, one that was much wider and more polished than the one at the druid's château. He placed each foot in the center of every step. I lost count after thirty or forty. I replaced counting stairs with my first go at creating something from the borrowed fae magic. I conjured an invisible cloak and hoped it would give me at least a bit of protection against the bite of the growing cold.

"May I ask where we're going?"

"To the chapel of la Dame aux Trois," he said, gripping my hand tighter and steadying me as we came to the landing. The opened exterior doors explained the drop in temperature.

Columns to either side marked the start of a covered walkway. At the other end was a tower that looked entirely disconnected from the main body of the castle. Snowflakes whipped through the opening, and the spaces between the columns, sending white eddies swirling through the landing area and chilling my skin. Lionel's body ran colder than mine; there was no heat for me to pull on and use for comfort. I again hooked into his ability to create illusion and made the wool of my cloak thicker and added a deep hood. By the time we crossed the walkway and were at the closed door to the chapel, I felt better.

Lionel turned and brushed his gaze up and down my figure. "You found something to keep you warm."

I didn't understand how he could see something that was an illusion, except that I'd created it using his magic.

"Can we please go in? I would like to get out of this cold."

The interior of the chapel was spare and unlit. Directly across from where we entered, light filtered in through wide French doors fitted with blue glass. I could see a balcony with a stone rail through the narrow windows beside each door.

Candles on tall holders, shelves, and antique tables lined the curved walls. I raised both arms, whispered *lucerna lumen*, and began to light the wicks within my reach. I started with the candles closest to the door and worked my way around the room, touching the wicks two at a time with the flame at the tip of each forefinger.

"When you have finished with your task, come here."

Out the corner of my eye, I could see Lionel in front of a free-standing wooden wardrobe, contemplating the contents. He used a cloth he pulled from a drawer to wipe down the chapel's altar. He moved one of the small side tables and set it nearby and asked me to bring him one of the taller candles. He placed other objects on the table.

I paused my circuit at the first window, hoping to get a sense of where we were in relation to the rest of the castle. Panels of more blue stained glass filled the window's upper half. I took my time finishing my tour of the room and ignored Lionel.

I ended my survey back where we had entered. With all the candles lit, mellow light infused the space, and I closed my eyes to absorb the strangeness of my situation. I had expected Lionel Vigne to do something to me, something hurtful, painful, along the lines of what I'd seen when the Beguilement brought me scenes from his mind and his past.

I hadn't expected to be standing in a chapel at the far end of the castle, with a fae who wanted to be on the *receiving* end of pain he wanted me to deliver.

"I am ready," he said.

Opening my eyes with a deliberate lack of urgency, I reminded myself that Lionel liked the elements of surprise and shock, and how they had the potential to instill immediate, visceral fear.

He stood between me and the altar. He had stripped and changed to a pair of skintight pants the same lavender gray as his gloves. I absorbed the expanse of his pale, blue-tinged skin. Scars of all shapes and sizes decorated his torso and arms. I could see more continuing down his legs, even across his sex, underneath the translucent material.

"Turn around." I dowsed the flames at my fingertips, indicated the direction I wanted him to move, and watched the graceful way he obeyed.

The scarring was evenly distributed on the side and back of his body, especially across his buttocks and the backs of his thighs. I drew the cloak I created tighter around my shoulders and began to feed the Beguilement as one would feed a hungry fire. I pulled out the biggest guns from my emotional repertoire, love and family, and shot that right into the core of my being.

Whatever Lionel wanted from me was going to take a lot out of me. And I wanted to walk away from this castle alive.

I moved closer to his back. Studied the scarring in the flickering light.

"Drop the glamour," I whispered.

"This glamour?" he asked, shedding his scarred skin and showing off the plumped and unblemished skin of a young man in his twenties.

"Or this one?" The skin he offered next was wrinkled and aged, making him look far closer to his physical age. He grasped the altar to steady himself, laughed, and returned to the scarred version.

"Which one of those is real?"

"They're all real. The Vignes come in threes, every generation, and those born in a full lunar moon stand the chance of becoming three within themselves. My sister Laurentine is such a rarity."

Not even the Beguilement could keep the tremor out of my hand. I threaded my fingers through the knitted holes in my dress and waited for Lionel to say more. A fae able to become three within themselves sounded like the same fae who had killed my father.

A fae able to become three within themselves confirmed what Alderose thought she remembered when One-Becomes-Three tried to kill Sidan in New York, captured my sister, and brought her back to the Vigne's castle.

One step at a time.

"Where is this gifted sister of yours?" I asked.

"Here. There. She is the only one of us able to move freely between this realm and our homeland. She could be anywhere." He turned his torso and glanced at the altar behind him. "Please find something suitable to place on the marble. I am ready to begin."

Vintage capes, shirts, and other articles of clothing hung from wooden hangers. Everything was pressed snugly together. Folded velvets in jewel tones of ruby, emerald, sapphire, and gold were stacked on a low shelf. The blues were the prettiest. Lionel Vigne didn't deserve pretty. I chose a red silk velvet so worn and faded it was almost brown, shook it out, and saw it was stained in spots.

"Of all the altar cloths you had to choose that one," Lionel murmured. "Don't put it away. Maybe this will be my lucky night."

I folded the cloth in half and centered it over the altar. Lionel sat on the side, brought his legs up one at a time, and lay on his back. He fidgeted with the positioning of his arms and legs and asked for a bit of padding for the back of his head. When I said no, irritation flashed across his face.

"Twice in one night."

"What do you want me to do?"

"I want you to tell me how it is I know you."

17

"Five, six nights ago you thought I was expendable," I said. "You were in the Reformed Realm, at Queen Violetta's ball. You instructed your vampire to kill me. He chose not to. He drained me to the point of unconsciousness instead and left me in the Barrenwood. I've been told he did what he could to make sure I didn't die of my wounds. One of my sisters used her magic to find me.

"You might remember her. Clementine. You tried to take her from the party at the palace. She conjured a bird and saved herself and the child you were deliberating over. You brought the child's mother *here*, to the Facility.

"Her name is Sheenah. She's safe now, did you know that? She's back in the Reformed Realm with her daughter."

"I remember Clementine. She was dressed in white. She was going to be my angel."

I switched my attention to the objects Lionel had placed on the tray. Many of them reminded me of the small charms I would see attached to shrines in México on my visits to my grandparents. Those metal milagros depicted things like body parts, or relatives and animals the person wanted help with:

legs, lungs, the heart, a daughter, an alcoholic spouse, donkeys and other creatures. I collected them on each trip and had a boxful stashed somewhere in my closet.

I lifted the charm of an angel with outspread wings and searched for its corresponding scar on Lionel's torso.

"I believe that one is near my throat," he said. "I'm afraid I made so many transgressions I was running out of room."

I found the spot, close to one of his collar bones, and set the charm on his skin. He hissed in a breath, and relaxed.

"That wasn't so bad," he said. "Next."

His recent crimes included flaying his purported friend, Guillaume; uprooting Larch's sacred portal tree, with the faun tied to it; and separating Sheenah and her daughter.

"Does breaking Linette's arm count?" I asked, searching for a charm of an arm.

He rolled his head away from me and stared out the windows. "That was nothing. Just the latest sortie in a war we have waged since..." He shrugged. "I suspect that even now she's plotting how she'll balance our scorecard."

I shook my head. The entire Vigne clan was infected with a similar sickness. If this was a side effect of living for hundreds of years or more, I was grateful for my own mortality. I chose a monogram with the letters LGM and found its scar underneath Lionel's arm. Pressing it there, he flinched. I pressed harder until it stayed.

"Guillaume," he whispered.

"That's what I thought," I said. "Weren't these supposed to come with stories as part of your confessional?"

"Continue with what you are doing. If I feel called to speak, I shall." He turned his head to look at me. "Are you going to tell me your name?"

"Later." I continued with choosing a charm or small object, searching for the corresponding mark on Lionel's body, and setting it there until his skin held it in place. He twitched every time, sometimes more violently than others, and spoke names, dates, locations. When I ran out of visible scars, he directed me to pull another tray out of the cupboard. He turned onto his frontside while I did, exposing his back.

I hesitated before resuming this odd ritual. The sky was growing darker. The wind was picking up.

"What comes after this?" I asked.

"We have a way to go, witch. Every scar has its token. They must all be matched with their scars."

"And then?"

"And then you may go."

"If it's that easy, why has no one else succeeded?"

He laughed. I took that as a challenge, especially as Lionel could be a more willing participant. I called on the Beguilement and added the element of pleasure. My pleasure, and my target's desire to bring me pleasure.

"Help me. You know where every one of these goes. You show me, I'll set them in the scars, and we'll be done in no time."

Lionel laughed again. Or tried to. His demeanor changed when the Beguilement embraced him, whispered in his ear that he should want to be a good boy and help the pretty witch. I set the tray in front of him and he placed charms into the scars on his forearms and biceps while I finished his back and sides.

"There are two more trays," he said. "Set the objects directly on my second skin. There are as many nerve endings in the material as on my real skin."

I cringed at the thought of touching clothes made to closely resemble skin—and leapt into imagining the pants were made of real skin, taken off a living creature. I gagged. Lionel made a sound of contentment.

The door banged open, allowing snow to swirl in. I set the

last tray on the table beside the altar. Something more substantial than cold air brushed my bare arm as I latched the glass doors together. A crouching form shimmered to my left, then disappeared. I darted a look to my right, thought I saw a similar movement, and had a moment of relief.

Sidan and Alderose were here.

I was safe. I just had to see this unusual confessional through and then we were all going to get out of this place intact.

"We're not finished, witch."

The scars across Lionel's buttocks and the backs of his thighs were deeper and more numerous than the smaller ones scattered over other parts of his body. I glanced at the tray. I didn't have enough tokens and charms to fill every mark.

"What do I do about these long scars?" I asked. I touched one—I couldn't hold myself back. Lionel grabbed my wrist, twisted up to sitting, and pulled me right up against the side of the cold, hard altar.

"I said you were to place the objects on the correct scar. I did not say you could touch the scars," he said. He maneuvered me in between his knees and crossed his ankles behind my legs.

"You're hurting me."

"Good. I should not be the only one in here in pain."

I ground my wrist against his hold, met his gaze, and immediately wished I hadn't. Sitting up and holding me in such a way that I couldn't escape flipped a switch in him. Emboldened, he ran his fingertips over my breasts

"You asked me to do this," I said.

He stuck his fingers through the holes made by the knitted patterning. Twisting a handful, he pulled me up and even closer. I could see the pulse in his neck, the point where I'd stabbed him, and the bruised bluish red of his lips.

"Kiss me, witch."

I lifted my heels. Tasted snow in the air as my lips met Lionel's. Sensed a presence behind me.

"I wouldn't do that if I was you."

Lionel looked up, over the top of my head toward the door we had come through. "Always one to spoil my fun, Linette. What do you want?"

"There's room enough for two up there. I think the witch should do us both."

"The witch is not *doing* me. She is hearing my confession."

Linette laughed. "Oh, how rich, Lionel. For you to give a full confession, you would need my permission."

"And mine," said another speaker, who was neither Alderose nor Sidan. "Are we giving our permission for our brother to tell all our stories, dear sister, or is little Lionel just going to have to wait until the three of us can agree? And doesn't at least one of us need to have produced at least three offspring first? How's your try for a third coming along, brother?"

I felt Lionel's heartbeat speed up. "Odilon and Ophelie have no part in this. Leave them be."

"You think sending them to Canada will keep them safe from us?"

Now my heart's beat matched his. I was sure the second speaker was Lionel's other sister, Laurentine, who my sisters and I knew as Jadzia. And One-Becomes-Three.

She had never seen me. Kostya and I weren't at the quarry while everyone fought Laurentine's three aspects while trying to rescue Gosia and her daughter. I pulled the Beguilement up my legs and circled it around my body, creating a buffer, and sent ribbons flowing around Lionel's chest.

Protect me.

His grip on my wrist softened. He wrapped his arms around my back and drew me to his chest as he slid off the altar and gained his footing. "I want the two of you out of here," he said.

"What, you no longer want us to watch, Lionel? Getting stodgy in your old age?"

He hesitated.

Keep me safe.

The door blew open again with enough force this time to loosen one of the panes of glass and send it skittering across the stone floor. Lionel whipped around, his arms still circling me, and walked us toward the outer door.

He had to release me while he struggled to close it. Something was in the way. That something punched him in the gut and launched itself over the altar and into Linette. She fell back and her head cracked against the floor. The other sister, Laurentine, barked out a laugh and disappeared.

"Rosey!"

"We're here," she said, still invisible. "Get out, get yourself back into the castle. They've located you and they're heading toward the stairs right now"

I did exactly what Alderose said. I ran. I didn't make it far enough. Lionel wrapped his arm around my waist from behind and hauled me out the far side of the chapel and onto the big, curved balcony. Little drifts of snow made the surface slippery and the cold stabbed through every hole in my dress and the bottoms of my thin wool shoes.

"No," Lionel said. "You are staying with me. We're almost done. I have stories I must tell. Let my sisters fight. They live to fight."

Through the windows, lit by dozens of candles, Alderose and Sidan flew after Laurentine. She'd released herself into three, and each was efficient with their blade work. Efficient and trim. Lionel spun me to face him and placed my hand on the back of his thigh. "I have scars here. Only my sisters know the story of how I got them and why. I need to tell you, witch. I need—"

I slipped my eye mask off and pressed it into Lionel's hand.

"My name is Beryl Brodeur. I told you about my sister, Clementine. My other sister's in there, fighting your sister, the one who can become three. My money is on Alderose."

"Beryl. I have heard this name before."

"Yes, you did. Clementine shouted my name when I appeared at the top of the stairs at the palace. I was coming after her, to protect her, and you took one look at me and decided it was my time to die. Guillaume, the vampire who decided to not quite kill me? He doesn't like you, Lionel."

"*My* Guillaume? I knew he betrayed me but I...I thought he loved me. I thought he knew." He stumbled back. His legs hit the carved balustrade and my eyes caught the repeated motif of an acorn worked into the stone.

"Yes, that Guillaume. He's with healers and he's safe. My aunt helped to stitch him back together after what you did to his skin." I tried to pull away from Lionel. I didn't like being that close to the edge of the balcony. I wanted to see what was happening inside the chapel. I wanted to help my sister.

I got my wish. Alderose and one of the fae flew out of the doors, blades flashing. My sister had one of Tanner's short swords, and another sword. *Her* sword, the one I'd seen only a handful of times and never in serious action. Rosey's beautiful long hair was mostly gone, sawed off, the fae was bleeding from a wound to her shoulder, and my sister showed no sign of losing energy.

I turned to Lionel. "You have to come with me. The only way for you to truly atone is to relinquish yourself to the Magical authorities. My uncle—"

Lionel threw his head back and roared into the snow-filled sky. I was numb. I hadn't kept up the illusion of the warm, thick cloak and I wasn't sure I could propel myself to the door, across the walkway, and back into the castle, let alone haul Lionel with me.

He poured his body into mine, gathered me in his arms like I was his long-lost lover, and found my mouth with his. His lips were warm, and there was the Beguilement, draped over his shoulders and now mine, twirling its ribbons around two cold bodies standing on the edge of a parapet.

"I have never known true love," Lionel whispered into my ear. A body thudded to the ground behind me, followed by a slate tile shattering against the stone. I tried to turn my head to see if was Rosey, or Sidan, or some aspect of Laurentine.

Lionel gripped me tighter.

"Give me this, ma petite brodeuse, *give me you*. Give me us. Give me *one more*. I promise I'll be good this time. I will honor you. I will cherish you. I will be...be kind to you, be good to you."

Underneath my flattened palms, his skin began to change. Scar tissue softened, absorbed the tokens, trinkets, and charms. Every time he muttered his remorse or made me a promise, another scar dissolved and that patch of skin grew smooth. His list of all the ways in which he would treat me like a lady, a princess, a queen, his beloved increased while my sister battled behind me.

I could not move. My feet were numb. The wool covering my feet was freezing to the stone, and I was shaking from cold, not from fear. Maybe the altitude or the temperature or even the snow had frozen the fear right out of me.

"Get...me...inside...," I said.

He obeyed, darting around Alderose and her blades, and his sister, or one of his sisters. Two more were inside the chapel going after Sidan. Lionel tore the velvet off the altar, wrapped me in it, and carried me in his arms. We were through the doors and stepping onto the covered walkway when he was shoved repeatedly from behind.

He dropped me on the snow-slicked stone as he faltered.

Bundled, I rolled over and over, the cloth coming unwound and tangling in my legs until I could scrabble to a stop and look up.

Lionel and Linette had death grips on each other's necks. As soon as one would throw the other against the side of the column-lined walkway, the other would push back, shoving their sibling to the opposite side. Another roof tile clattered down the domed roof behind me. I glanced back and went to duck. Phineas leapt off the edge of the roof, caught the loose tile before it could hit me, and landed with a thud.

"Are you okay?" he asked. I nodded and pointed toward the chapel.

"Help Alderose."

He didn't look back as he dodged the brother and sister still locked together and launched himself into the fray. I expected more would quickly follow the gargoyle's arrival. Laszlo. Kostya. Jake. Tanner.

I tried to stand. Lionel and Linette reeled closer to me in their vicious dance. Linette even tried to grab me, take me as hostage or use me as a shield, I didn't know. I scrabbled backward, my heart in my throat, as Lionel hauled her to her feet and pressed her against a low section of the stone wall.

"Oh no, Lionel, if I go you go," she said, and she took his momentum and drew it toward her and over the side.

I saw their legs disappear.

I heard a screech, and another, and the *whoosh, whoosh* of wings, and I was too frozen in place by the cold and by the fear I'd held at bay so my magic would have room to work.

I couldn't hold it back any longer.

I screamed.

I didn't want Lionel to die.

Shame heated my cheeks. I crawled inside the fortress, dragging the ruined velvet with me, and sat on the top step, contemplating my descent. I decided to stay where I was. I was too cold to help, and I'd lost my connection to the Beguilement. Or maybe, like a battery, I'd run out of power.

I backed into a nook between two of the columns and wrapped myself in the blood-stained cloth. This way, I could hear when it was all over. This way, anyone coming up the stairs would see me, and when Rosey and Sid came running out of the chapel, alive and victorious, they would see me too.

18

RUNNING FEET. DEMONS AND WITCHES CALLING MY NAME.

"She's got to be here somewhere. Check every room and hallway and balcony again."

Alderose found me. She tugged on a corner of the velvet and hauled me out of my hiding place. Lifting me to my feet, she propped me against her bloodied side. She was breathing hard.

"You're alive," she said.

"You're hurt." I felt for her wounds.

"Ouch. Fuck. Leave that alone. I'll be fine."

"Where's Sidan?"

"Sid's with the birds trying to figure out what happened to Lionel and Linette. And Jadzia or whatever the fuck her name is, is down to one last...self. C'mon, let's get you out of here. The cars are waiting, engines on."

"What happened?" Kostya's broad shoulders filled the doorway. He strode toward us and gathered me into his arms.

"She was amazing with Lionel, Kostya."

"Can we just get out of here?" I asked. "I'm about to crash again."

Kostya helped me down the hall. Jake came jogging toward us, eyes on Alderose.

"Hey, babe," he said. "How can I help?"

"You can start by never, ever calling me *babe*." Alderose kicked at his shin. "Go see if Sid could use your help."

TANNER AND CAT first tried to run the debrief from the infirmary, which was already packed with the Magicals they'd transported from Lionel's castle to the château.

They gave up, herded us into the classroom, and corralled those with medical skills to see to the wounded. The gash in Alderose's side was the worst, and Laszlo and Kostya both sported some large bruises.

"Thanks to Phineas's excellent instruction, Kostya and I were able to fly," Laszlo said.

Kostya wobbled his hand and carefully peeled the bandage away from his mouth and cheek. "I wouldn't call it flying, brother. More like, assisted lift off?" That got a laugh. Kostya continued. "Because of his observations, Phineas was able to point out other places where Magicals might have been imprisoned. Laz, Jake, Phin, and I swept those outlying areas and did not find any more Magicals."

"Guillaume would like to know if you found Arnaud." Alderose had walked in after the rest of us.

"We did not."

"Then another full sweep of the buildings and the grounds tomorrow is in order," she said, "especially with the three Vignes gone missing."

"I don't think Lionel and Linette are missing," I said, raising my hand. "I think they're dead." The vision of them toppling over the walkway's low wall kept replaying in my head. "I don't think there's any way they could have survived a fall from that part of the castle."

"Can you tell us what happened leading up to that, Beryl?" Cat asked. "Maybe start with you and Lionel entering the castle. We lost contact with you very soon after."

Clementine shook out another wool blanket and draped it over my shoulders. I stared at my feet, searched for my magic, and came up with only a whisper.

"Lionel Vigne made it clear he enjoyed inflicting pain. He started by asking me to take off my dress. I said no. And when *I* made it clear I was not going to play his game the way he preferred, he challenged me to hurt him.

"When Linette came to his bedroom and interrupted us, then made a remark about joining his game, he broke her arm. I learned later this behavior between the two of them was not unusual.

"I was in contact with and in control of the Beguilement the entire time. I used it to create a set of arm and wrist restraints. That's when I felt the dynamic begin to change." I stopped speaking and glanced around the room. "Anyone have any questions yet?"

No one did. I continued. "Lionel insisted we go to the fortress's chapel. He said he wanted to confess. I got the sense his attempts at confession did not end well for whomever he was confessing to.

"While passing through the castle to the chapel, I got very cold. I was able to initiate my ability to tap into others' magic and used Lionel's glamour to make myself a cloak. He made a comment about the cloak, and he didn't ask me how I did it. Once we were inside the chapel, I lit the candles while he changed into pants made from the same translucent material as those gloves he wears.

"He pulled a few wooden trays from a cupboard and asked

me to place something on the altar for him to lie on. I found a stack of cloths in the same cupboard and did what he asked. He then stated he was ready to begin." I had to close my eyes against a rising sensation of nausea. I didn't want to remember the details of everything that followed.

"Begin what?" Kostya asked.

"Atoning. Lionel's body was covered with scars. Every one of them marked something he did for which he felt he needed to atone. And for each mark, there was a token and the shape of the token represented what he'd done. Or who he'd done it to. Like, a piece of metal with the initials LGM represented Guillaume.

"I had been handing him those pieces and listening to him recite things about his victims, when Linette interrupted us a second time. Alderose and Sidan, and Lionel's other sister, Laurentine, entered the chapel soon after.

"We also know Laurentine as Jadzia and One-Becomes-Three."

I paused again. I had reached the place where I used the Beguilement to get Lionel to protect me, and where my magic had done something unexpected.

"Phineas said he saw you kissing Lionel." Kostya's voice had an edge to it.

"Lionel did kiss me."

"Was that because of the Beguilement, or because—"

"Yes, of course it was because of my magic," I said, tamping down my rising desire to defend each of the choices I'd made and actions I'd taken. "I had to use it to keep him focused on me, to keep me safe. Rosey and Sid were fighting the fae, and—"

"Phin also said you were fighting to get to Lionel when he and his sister were going at it on the walkway."

I shook my head. "I wouldn't say I was fighting to get to him, I would say I was hoping he would leave his sister and come to me. My job was to get Lionel to my uncle so he could be taken away and interrogated."

"I think your magic messed with your head, Beryl, and that if we hadn't come along when we did—" Kostya's tone went from edgy to accusatory. He stopped mid-sentence and left the room. The door clicked shut behind him.

"What the hell was that?" I asked. The blanket slid off my shoulders, leaving me chilled by Kostya's abrupt departure.

"He's jealous, Beryl. That's all. It's been an emotional day for everyone." Iván came over and rubbed my arms. "I know it doesn't make sense."

"He owes me an apology."

"Yes, he does."

THE DEBRIEF WAS TABLED for the next day. I refused to join Kostya in our room and was given a new one on a different hall. Alderose, Sidan, and Jake were staying in the room next to me. It seemed a minimalist bathroom and an armoire were standard in every room, and I was comforted to see the familiar utilitarian garments stacked in neat rows. I pulled on pants, a T-shirt, a sweater, and a pair of socks and I even luxuriated in the feel of slipping my feet into the clunky slippers.

I tapped on the door separating the two bedrooms and told anyone who was interested that I was going to the end of the hall in search of food.

"They're bringing you a tray, Beryl." Jake opened the door and smiled. "Holler if you want company, okay?"

"What I'd like is a glass of wine," I said.

"Red or white?"

"Red."

"Coming right up." He ducked back into their room, took drink orders, and exited out their door. I rested my forehead on the old wood and listened to the comforting murmur of my sister and Sidan talking.

Jake returned with the glass of wine and the rest of the bottle and made me promise I would seek their company if I wanted or needed anything.

"Any time, night or day."

A kitchen worker showed up with my tray and a lit candle before Jake left, which let him very helpfully move the little table to the window and drape a blanket over the rickety wood chair. I waved him and the druid out their respective exits, turned off the lamp light, and sat to eat. Pulling the woolly cover over my shoulders, I peered beyond my reflection in the glass and looked for signs of life beyond the weightless snowflakes.

Could my magics be trained? I made a cursory review of my use of the Beguilement as I swirled my wine in its glass before sipping. Yes, it had worked better than I hoped. And yes, it had acted in ways I hadn't expected, like entwining me with Lionel in a way that felt overly intimate. I could accept there was untapped power in me, and I knew I didn't have to make any decisions about the future of that power tonight.

Tonight was for recovering. And there was a small crock of onion soup in front of me, complete with the requisite cheese-topped crouton, sending up an irresistible aroma.

I tucked into the soup.

Tomorrow, I would speak more about what Lionel did, and said, and count on my aunt's and uncle's wisdom and insight. I knew there was no reason for me to feel any shame around what happened between me and the fae. I knew a line had been crossed that maybe I didn't want to cross again. And that maybe I should also consult a counselor or someone who advised Magicals who were unsure about the ethical use of their magic.

And tomorrow, or the next day, my sisters and I would meet the Magicals who had been captured by Lionel. I wanted to hear their stories, every single one, and write them down in my mother's notebooks.

While I chewed, swallowed, and sipped, the château settled into sleep around me. I heard a few creaky bedsprings in the other room. A soft cracking sounded near the window. I rested my fingertips on the sill and invited the château's magic to show itself.

I waited. Sipped at the broth and chewed the softened onions and bread. Enjoyed being warm and fed and safe. Reviewed what happened after Kostya had carried me to the limo. In the ride from the Vigne's castle to Château du Blanc, Alderose and Sidan had recounted the highlights of their adventure.

Once they were invisible, they had been able to go from the limo to the castle without detection. Alderose had made a few wrong turns once they were inside before locating the underground wing where the cells were located.

Tanner's goddess-blessed blade had helped her slice through the locks and bars on the doors. Not all the rooms held captives. Those that did were dirty and lacking in bedding, reinforcing the idea that Lionel intended to bring those Magicals back to the Facility once the farce of my 'exchange' was over.

The Magicals in the cells were predominantly females of child-bearing age. There were four minor children, and one adult showing intersex conditions. Most were shifters, and every one of them had been captured within the past two weeks.

I wasn't sure what had precipitated this acquisition frenzy, and I might never know.

The death toll from the rescue operation was exceedingly low, and those presumed dead shared a common denominator: their last name was Vigne. Lionel. Linette. And two aspects of One-Becomes-Three.

Sidan had spent part of the ride speculating about what it

meant for Laurentine to lose two of her three selves—whether it would mean a diminishment of her power or a tripling of it. Sid vowed to continue to her hunt for fae, who'd left the chapel once it was clear two of her selves were going to fall to Alderose's blades.

Sid and Rosey had only compliments for each other's fighting styles. Going off the looks they were trading, I concluded there had to be an eroticism to battle.

Alderose had spoken about Guillaume. How once his body was healed, he would work on his head and his heart. She wanted to help him through that process. Sid agreed, and said they'd work out the logistics.

And then there was Jake. He had somehow become a member of Alderose's coterie, and I had no arguments against his presence at my sister's side. I had my own relationship troubles.

I finished the soup, set the tray outside my door, and wedged the chair underneath the latch. I wasn't sure why I felt the need for the extra precaution—only that I did, and the last time I'd fallen asleep inside the stucco-coated walls, there had been a fire demon ready and eager to curl himself around me.

My things had been moved over from my other room. I washed my face and brushed my teeth, lined up the slippers by the bed, and crawled between the covers. Sleep was waiting.

So WERE DREAMS. One included knocking and when I pulled myself out of that dream and rolled over in bed, the knocking continued. It was coming from my window, and the bird perched on the outer sill. I scooted to the foot of the bed and swung the window open carefully. Color was just beginning to lighten the sky.

The bird might have been the same speckled harrier that

brought me the apple and the vole. It side-stepped closer and kept lifting its beak, showing me it had something. I held out my hand. The bird curled its talons around the base of my thumb, dropped something small into my palm, and flew off.

Lucerna lumen. I brought flames to my fingertips in order to see and almost face-planted against the window. The bird had delivered a small metal charm similar to the ones I had pressed into Lionel's flesh. This one came complete with a tiny, red ribbon looped through the hole in the upper portion. I could hang this charm on an altar. Light candles for it. Try to intercede with the Goddess on its behalf.

The charm was a perfect miniature likeness of Lionel's face. When I tilted it slightly in one direction, his visage became more youthful. Tilted the other way revealed the Lionel I had sensed when I was sitting in the limousine, waiting for him to pluck me from my seat.

"What am I supposed to do with this?" I asked. Turning it over, I had my answer. The back was dusted with crushed gemstone the same pale, icy blue as Lionel's skin and in its center, a drop of ruby red.

I was the keeper of Lionel Vigne's soulstone.

I wasn't much for swearing, but I couldn't help the extended *fuck* I released on my next exhale. Uncle Malvyn was going to have to guide me through what it meant to be in possession of a magical object like this. Did I need to have it on me at all times? What happened if I lost it?

Uff. Kostya was definitely *not* going to be a fan of this latest development.

I went to the knitted dress my aunt made for me, found the loose end, and unraveled enough to finger crochet a temporary necklace. When I finished with that, I strung the soulstone charm on it and looped it around my neck. Too wired to go back to sleep, I slipped a bulky sweater over my head, snugged my feet into my slippers, and brushed my teeth.

The halls and stairwell of this section of the château were silent. Ni'eve was gone. Grisette had returned. I wanted to hear what was going to happen to the students and followers, and to this place. I surprised myself by finding my way to the dining room. Another surprise startled me as I entered.

"Beryl! You did it!"

Grisette walked toward me with open arms. Elaborate sleeves draped almost to the floor, and fabric swirled around her legs. Unlike her daughter's robes, the Crone's were made of layers of embroidered and hand-painted silk. There was something alive about the way the fabric moved on her body, and she'd gone for a color rich palette over white and black.

Receiving her hug was easy. There was a little bit of my mother, and my abuelas, in the way her arms circled me and in the deep rumble of comfort and understanding sounding through her chest.

"Your mother would have been so, so proud." She let me go so she could see my face. "You know that, don't you?"

I nodded, afraid to speak. I was on the verge of blubbering and I wanted no puffy eyes or flushed cheeks when I saw Kostya. Grisette led me to a seat at the same table where Ni'eve had held court.

"Let me bring you some tea."

I looked around to see if there were any cushions or small blankets, something to make the hard wooden chair more comfortable. Seeing nothing, I settled in. The armrests and slatted chair back and even the seat began to shift subtly. I went along for the ride and in a minute was enjoying comfortable, balanced support. I patted the armrests and whispered my thanks.

"Here you are," the Crone said, placing a tray between us. She poured mugs of tea and urged me to fix mine how I liked it.

"Lots of cream and lots of sugar," I said.

"Just like your mother."

That broke me. I couldn't hold the spoon to measure out the sugar. I folded forward, burying my face in my hands, and cried. There was a chance my mom would never know that her daughters had picked up her banner and completed the one task she likely would have most wanted us to.

There was also a chance that she would. She and my dad had shown themselves to Clementine once. Maritza was confident they would show up again.

With that, my tears didn't last long. I wiped my face with the cloth napkin Grisette handed to me. A look crossed her face. She reached for the collar of my sweater, withdrew the cord, and held the soulstone charm.

"So. He chose you." She shook her head slowly, never taking her eyes off the charm. "May the damaged boy inside that terrible man find peace at least. And may those he touched find healing."

"Do you know what I'm supposed to do with this?" I asked. "A harrier brought it to my window this morning."

"None of us wants to be forgotten when we leave this earthly realm, dear Beryl. Many of us find a way to ensure that something of us is left behind in the hope that at least one person will carry our memory forward. Considering the connection between his actions, and your mother's mission, there's...well, there's a twisted logic to his wish that you care for his memory. I think in time you will know what to do. Until that time, keep this safe. A loose soulstone is not a happy soulstone."

"My uncle's a sorcerer. I plan to ask him for advice."

Grisette *hmm*d and urged me to finish my tea while she hurried the baker along. She had ordered an assortment of treats to feed the château's overflow of guests and wanted everything piping hot and ready to serve once everyone was awake. She disappeared into the kitchen just as Jake barreled in through the doorway and came straight to me.

"Have you seen or spoken with Kostya this morning?" he asked.

I shook my head, dread filling my belly. "Why?"

"He and Laszlo were planning to head out at first light to do fly-bys of the area below the chapel tower to see if they could locate Lionel and Linette. I can't reach them on their comms, and there's some nasty weather brewing."

"What about the birds? Cat was working with the vultures, and Grisette's got a connection to that raven. She's in the kitchen and—"

Jake was at that door in seconds and on his way out.

"Gonna get Cat on it. We're heading to the castle right now."

"I'm coming with you," I said.

"Whatever you say, Beryl." He looked at my slippered feet and shook his head. "You're going to need much better footwear."

"My boots are in my room. I can get them and be at the front gate in three minutes." I turned to run. "Don't you dare leave without me."

"Wouldn't think of it."

IVÁN, Cat, Jake, Clementine, Alderose, and Sidan were milling around outside the waiting vehicle. Everyone was trying to reach Laszlo and Kostya using electronic means, and no one was succeeding. I jumped in the backseat and made myself small as the car filled up with witches and demons and a dragon. I pulled Clementine close. She wasn't looking good.

"Did any of you hear from Laszlo or Kostya at all this morning?" she asked. "Laz left before I woke up."

"Just the once," Cat said, "when they said they'd made it to the walkway and were looking for a secure jumping off site."

"*Fuck*. Why didn't they take a third with them?"

Iván scratched at his head. "Arkadi brothers don't always act rationally or with the best interests of their loved ones at the forefront of the brains. I'm as guilty as they are. I should have gone with them and insisted those noobs wear a rope."

Someone banged on the back of the SUV. When it stopped, Phineas popped his head in and saw the lack of legroom.

"Sorry I'm late," he said.

Alderose tugged on the knit cap covering her much shorter hair and shooed Jake over. "Make room for Phin. Sid and I are staying here. We'll monitor the comm channel and join you if we're needed. Good luck."

They waved us off. Cat said the vultures were in the air and reporting visibility was bad, especially around the section of the Vigne castle with the chapel. "Can't be that air mage. We've got him locked up tight."

The hairpin turns made me glad for my almost empty belly. We drove right through the gate and up to the front of the castle. Nothing was locked, and as we let ourselves in and jogged down the first long hall, one of us after another would stop to open doors and check the rooms.

"Place looks deserted," Cat said as we made it to the turn that would take us to the long staircase and the walkway to the chapel.

"Were the fae who were waiting with the air mage taken to Malvyn too?" I asked. I slowed down after the first few stairs. Adrenaline helped propel me forward, as did my concern for Kostya and his brother.

"Yes. Still, there should be some staff left."

There were no signs of the two Arkadi brothers at the stair's landing or along the covered walkway. I was glad for the second sweater I'd grabbed, as well as for the boots. I held my hair back from my face and looked over the side. All I could see was dark gray rock, slick with rain and melting snow, and low clouds.

"I'm ready to go down," Phineas said. "Is my mic okay, Catherine?"

"It's Cat. And you're loud and clear." Cat, Iván, and Jake were working on securing a rope around one of the wider stone columns. The gargoyle was straddling the stone rail and peering down into the mist.

"Is this about where Lionel and his sister went over, Beryl?" Jake asked.

I took a few steps back, all the way to where I had been when I last saw and heard the Vignes.

"Go one more section closer to the chapel." I had to squeeze my eyes shut and breathe through the memory of seeing their bodies tumbling into the void.

"I'm ready when you are, guys." Phineas was now standing on the narrow, decorative ledge on the outside of the walkway. I made myself go closer and thank him for what he was about to do.

"It's nice to feel useful," he said. "And I'm very sorry I got you in trouble with Kostya."

"We'll work it out. Though I think I know how you can make it up to me." It had finally dawned on me that Phineas might be able to help me locate Micah.

"I owe you." He smiled shyly and shook out his arms. "Do you want to watch me shift?"

Curiosity got the better of my queasy belly. "Absolutely."

"Let me hold onto you."

I stuck my arms forward. Phineas grabbed my wrists and

directed me to lean back, as that would counterbalance the weight of his wings.

He took a deep breath. The change rippled through him, from his core to his extremities. Silky wings snapped out of his back. A long, forked tongue snaked out the side of his mouth. His body transformed into the kind of creature immortalized in stone and crouched on rooftops across France.

The gargoyle let go of me and pushed off, diving backwards and flipping before he disappeared in the cloud cover.

19

"BEAUTIFUL, HUH?" JAKE THREW HIS LEG OVER THE RAIL ONE section over and found footing on the same ledge. I agreed, and gasped as two massive vultures, then a third, circled the air right in front of us before dipping into the cloud.

"Be careful, Jake."

"Always," he said. He winked, buckled his bright orange helmet under his chin, and exchanged a rapid-fire checklist with Cat. At her *Go*, he started to rappel down the smooth stone surface of the curtain wall. The rising cloud swallowed him almost as fast as it had the gargoyle.

"Cat, tell us the second you hear anything.". I leaned into Clementine and wrapped my arm around her waist. She was as nervous as I was.

"You know it, Beryl." Cat looked up from the equipment she was fiddling with and shook her head. "Leaning over that railing isn't going to help them find Kostya and Laszlo any faster, you two. Go wait inside. Neither of you is dressed for this weather and I don't have time to triage two frostbitten witches."

Clementine protested. I looped my arm through hers and reminded her Cat and Iván really didn't need to be worrying about us too. We had been standing halfway across the open walkway. My sister headed toward the chapel, rather than the main body of the castle. I hesitated. I doubted anyone had thought to clean up from the bloody fight. But the chapel would give us a clear view of any developments.

"You okay going in here?" my sister asked, her hand on the door.

"I think I'm okay. And if it turns out I'm not, I'll tell you."

Once inside, we stayed close to the glass doors. Cat and Iván were standing side by side, their attention on the empty space beyond the walkway. I glanced at the floor. There was broken glass, some clear, some blue. Crushed candles. Sprays of candlewax and dried blood. If the reason for me being here were different, I would want to explore the cupboard where Lionel had stored the piles of velvet cloth, the clothes, and the charms and trinkets.

"Before we go home, I want to come back up here and go through Lionel's things."

Clementine slipped her fingers through mine.

"And I cannot wait to leave this place," she said. "I need to be home, even though I don't exactly *have* a home right now."

"I know what you mean."

We stood there, keeping a silent vigil. Some long time later, Jake's helmeted head appeared. Cat handed him a first aid kit, and he popped back down. Clementine opened one of the doors and asked for an update. Cat gave us two thumbs up and yelled that both Kostya and Laszlo had been found.

"But are they okay?" She waggled her hand and said they were alive. Iván had been in the process of securing another length of rope. He donned more rock-climbing equipment and a red helmet and lowered himself over the side, one column over from Jake.

"This sucks."

"Sure does." I fogged the window with my breath and drew a smiley face with horns.

"You and Kostya going to be okay?" Clementine asked.

"Yeah, I think so. We just have to talk about my magic, and I have to get over my disappointment that it was Jessamyne who got his wings to appear."

"Don't hold back a *thing* about your magic, Beryl. What you have is amazing. My magic is..." She sighed in a way that hurt my heart.

"*Your* magic is amazing, Sissy. Don't you *ever* think it isn't."

Clementine got very still. "I'll sit with Lionel's things, if you want. The mascara will help me see what happened way before last night. That's exactly the kind of task it's meant for."

I swallowed hard. What Clementine was offering could give her visions she might have a hard time processing.

"Your magic has already helped me see into Lionel's past," I said, "and if I was a good sister, I'd forbid you from doing it yourself."

"It's not a question of good or bad, Beryl. It's a question of doing what's right, and if there are story threads here that will help us figure out what happened to the missing Magicals, maybe give their families closure, then I'm willing to do it. Especially since we can't ask Lionel directly."

"Then it's a date."

We didn't speak again until Iván's red helmet bobbled on the other side of the stone rail. Laszlo's unbound silvery white hair came next. Clementine tore out the door and skidded to a stop. She helped Cat bring Laszlo over the edge. I got there in time to hear Iván say even ice demons didn't stand a chance when they landed on their heads.

"Mild concussion," he added. "At least, that's what I think. Sooner we get him home, the better."

"Did you find Kostya?"

He nodded. "Phineas and the vultures made a sling and they're flying him directly to the château. His leg's shattered. He'll have to tell us what happened because I didn't see any bodies down there."

"Leave the ropes here. We'll send someone over to get them later," Cat said. "It's going to take the four of us to carry Laszlo to the car."

BY THE TIME we got to the ground floor and out the front door, Laszlo was coming to. One side of his face was bruised, and his wings were a little torn. In the car, Clementine cradled his shoulders and head, and I draped his muscled legs over my lap. Tanner and Phineas met us outside the château with the same stretcher that had carried Guillaume in only a day or two ago.

The gargoyle took me aside once they had Laszlo secure.

"Kostya's knocked out," he said, "and we're waiting for a medical capsule to arrive from the Reformed Realm. Alabastair's meeting the demon med techs in Paris and portalling them here. Kostya's parents insisted that he get treated at home."

Phineas looked almost apologetic for delivering that news.

"Did either Kostya or Laszlo say anything about seeing Lionel or Linette, or even the other sister?" I asked.

"No, they didn't. Though you might ask those vultures."

"Thanks, Phineas. That's a good idea." I felt my demon's pull. "I need to go sit with Kostya."

"I'm not going to stop you."

I was ushered into the section of the infirmary that resembled the emergency room of a country hospital. Four beds, curtain dividers, and a chair beside each bed. Guillaume's bed was tucked into the far corner, then came Kostya's. Attendants were loading Laszlo into the bed next to his. Curiosity nudged me toward the vampire; loyalty and love sent me right to Kostya's side.

His breathing was slow and steady. I wondered if the druids had given him herbs to manage the pain. Two splints were fixed to his leg, one on the thigh area, and one from the knee to the ankle. There was nothing high-tech about them. Or so I thought. On closer look, I noticed they were held together by fresh stems sprouting from the sticks. Healing energy flowed up and down and around Kostya's leg.

I turned the chair so I could face him and rested my elbow on the doubled-up blanket covering his torso. He freed his arm and felt for my hand, never opening his eyes. We stayed like that until Alabastair arrived with a demon I recognized from my stay in the palace's medical ward. He crouched beside me and asked how I was doing.

"Not bad, all things considered," I said.

"You know we'll take good care of the prince."

I slipped my hand out of Kostya's as gently as I could. He was lifted and placed into the capsule, strapped in everywhere a strap could be buckled. I kissed his forehead and said my good-byes. Iván helped Alabastair and the demon walk the capsule outside.

An emptiness scooped out my chest. I stepped to the next bed. Guillaume was awake.

"You can come in," he said. "I won't bite."

"That's the worst joke ever." His warped sense of humor tipped the scale in his favor. I again took the closest chair and turned it to face the head of his bed. "How are you?"

"I am grateful to have been taken care of by such skilled healers, including Maritza. Being cared for means that I lived and living means I can offer my wholly inadequate apologies to you for putting you through what I did."

"I spent a few hours with Lionel last night. You spent... decades and decades with him. I don't know how you survived."

Guillaume gazed into my eyes a good, long time. "I'm not sure how I survived either, Beryl. I had been given to Lionel when I was about fourteen years old. I have no recollection of why I was separated from my parents, only that I was. After we received news my father died, Lionel stepped in and declared that he would be my father. He married my mother the next year. They had two children, Odilon and Othelie."

"Were your parents vampires?"

He paled. "No. Absolutely not. After my mother's death, when I was nineteen, Lionel insisted that I be changed. I had no say in the matter, and I loathed being a vampire for years. Decades. Until Lionel's nephew, Arnaud, and I began an affair."

"Were you in love?" I asked.

"There were times when I loved him," he said, worrying his fingers along the fraying edge of his blanket. "And there were times when he loved me. It seemed as though we rarely loved each other simultaneously."

Guillaume's eyes watered. "I'm getting tired. And I can tell you this. For long as I can remember, December thirty-first of this year has been my beacon of hope. Something to aspire to. Live for."

"Why, Guillaume?"

"It marked the end of my two-hundred-and-fifty-year indenture to Lionel Vigne. It marked the end of me having to live with someone who could be so cruel, and at times, so kind. The bricks of Lionel's cruelty always outweighed the feathers of his kindness and once I was free, I was going to kill him for everything he and his sister and others had visited on this world, and on me."

He pressed the back of his head into his pillow. Tears streamed out the corners of his eyes and down the sides of his face. "I don't know if we will ever become friends, Beryl Brodeur, but I hope we can fashion something out of the wreckage. Your sister is very, very dear to me, and I plan to make a pest of myself."

"Get in line," I said, letting one half of my mouth twist into a grin.

"She's worth waiting for."

Guillaume turned his head and opened his eyes. We shared a long look before I stood and told him I had to pack. Leaning over, I refolded the end of his sheet over the blanket and smoothed his covers over his chest. The charm I wore caught his eye. He reached for it just as I went to cover Lionel's likeness with my hand.

"Are you sure?" I asked, encasing his cool fingers in mine. "This...it's Lionel's soulstone."

He nodded vigorously. I let him hold the charm. "This means he's dead?"

"That's my understanding of how a soulstone works."

"This means I am free."

"You *are* free." In that moment I realized who Lionel had stolen the castle and the surrounding lands from. "And the castle is yours. I don't know the entire story, but last night I saw into Lionel's past enough to know he carried shame, and some of that shame was tied to how he came into possession of that castle. No Magical court will fight you on it."

Guillaume leaned back against his pillows and stared up at the ceiling. More tears trickled over his cheeks.

"I knew it," he whispered. "I knew it. Too many tiny memories that I could not discount. In a way, I have always been home."

I patted his leg, kissed his cheek, and accepted his kiss to the top of my hand.

"Please," he said, "come visit my home. I want to hear all of your stories, Beryl."

"I shall, Guillaume. Bonjour."

"Bonjour."

I drew the privacy curtain partially around his bed and went to check on Laszlo and Clementine.

"Alabastair's coming back with a second medical capsule and another med tech. I'm going with them to the demon realm," she said, "just to get Laszlo settled in. Then I'll meet you and Rosey in Northampton. Because we're going back there, right? Finish what we started?"

"I think that's the plan. Tomorrow? Late morning?"

"That doesn't give me enough time to be with Laszlo and deal with portal travel. Let's meet on Friday, and I'll plan to spend the weekend."

Clementine stood to hug me. "I won't be able to look for threads in Lionel's things on this trip, but I promise I'll come back and help you. Or you could pack them up and bring them to Northampton and I'll look at them there."

I wished Laszlo a speedy recovery and went from the infirmary to the dining room where Grisette was presiding over a big pot of tea and a plate of fresh-baked deliciousness.

"Come," she said. "Pour yourself a mug and have a pastry. Get something in your belly and then come for a walk with me."

"But it's snowing out."

"Dearest Beryl, this is the Alps. It snows here. We have warm coats and mittens for you to borrow, and I see you already have your boots."

I couldn't argue with her there. I made a big mug of sweet, milky tea, chose a fruit- and nut-filled muffin, and scarfed it down. Grisette brought the promised sheepskin coat and mittens and led me along the path toward her hut.

"Have you always lived there?" I asked, pointing at the squat little building.

"Hmm, perhaps? I know I've been in that spot for many years and I had been enjoying my time as a tree. Ignorance can be bliss, you know. But the appearance of you and your sister as well as the recent events that confirmed my suspicions about my daughter and granddaughter have forced me to shed my bark. I thought I was done with la Crone. Turns out my retirement was a bit premature."

We passed a section of ancient apple trees, gnarled and twisted, and veered to the right just before her hut. Through a rail fence and down a slope, we stopped in a section of newer apple trees. As a group they were taller, more robust, and well maintained.

Grisette wound in between the trees until she came to the one she was looking for. She held the trunk in her hands, pressed her forehead to the bark, and began to chant an invocation. Under her touch and in answer to her call, the tree shifted. More gracefully than I'd seen in Grisette's hut, a young woman with twigs in her long hair and near my age emerged.

"Grand-mère!" she said, throwing her arms around Grisette. "I was preparing for my wintersleep. Why did you call me back?"

"I wanted my new friend to meet you. Beryl, this is Marthe."

I came closer and extended my arm. Marthe batted my hand aside and kissed both cheeks. "When in France, do as the French."

"Marthe is one of the youngest Keepers, which as you know is a small sect dedicated to seeing that the seeds that grow the trees that bear the apples of immortality are never lost. It is not a path for everyone, and yet it is the mission our druidic order was founded upon. Someday, Marthe or one of her sister Keepers shall take my place.

"I want you to know this is an option for you, Beryl, should you find yourself unable to harness your extraordinary magic."

Marthe's gaze was filled with understanding. She nodded, and gently stroked my arms before taking my hands in hers. "My magic was one of a kind. I will let Grand-Mère tell you my story, if you wish to hear it, as I feel the call of my tree."

She released me, yawned, and received Grisette's goodbye. Folding into herself, she returned to her tree form.

"Thank you for sharing that with me." I had witnessed Jessamyne's harsh change and felt her twisted magic. Seeing another side of the Keepers balanced my initial impression. "I can't say I would be cut out for this kind of life, but I'm learning to never say never." I offered Grisette my elbow, and we returned to her hut.

"I shall say goodbye to you here," she said, "after I've given you a little something." She ducked into her home and came back out with a slender stick planted in dirt in an eight-ounce yogurt container. "This is a little piece of me for you to have wherever you are. We've only just met, yet our connection through your mother makes me feel rather attached to you and Clementine and Alderose."

She handed me the cup, gave me one more hug, and watched me until I disappeared down a hill. I knew that she watched, because every time I looked over my shoulder, she waved.

20

By the time Clementine, Alderose, and I met up in Northampton we were deeper into November and closer to the season's first snow. High winds and a cold snap had torn the last leaves off the maple and gingko trees lining the sidewalk outside Needles and Sins. The shop's big front windows and the beveled glass panel in the front door were as grimy as they had been when we arrived in town in the middle of October for the reading of Serena's will.

Alderose stood in front of us jangling her ring of keys. Clementine juggled a box of croissants and pastries along with her shoulder bag. And I leaned my rolling suitcase against my leg and lifted the cardboard tray of to-go cups to my nose. The aroma of chocolate and coffee wafting upward was proving irresistible.

"The door's not going to open itself," I said, stomping my feet. "And my toes are going numb."

"Shall we try this again?" Alderose grinned and separated a single brass key. We followed her to the door, stepped through together once she had it open, and sighed in unison as it clicked closed behind us. You'd think we were sisters or something.

"Are the wards up?" Clementine asked.

"Yep, they are. If anyone we know decides to visit, they can always text us to open up. Kostya and Laszlo have their own keys." I'd made the executive decision to give the Arkadi brothers keys.

"Oh, and I gave keys to Tía Mari and Uncle Mal," Clementine said.

"Sid and Jake have keys too. And Cat. And Guill." At our surprised looks, Alderose added those four were her inner circle and given that trouble and troublesome characters had been landing in our lives ever since the reading of Serena's will, the more trusted friends with keys, the better. "But only the three of us get the emerald rings when Uncle Mal finishes copying Mom's original."

Clementine and I agreed as she circled the room and flicked all the light switches. Overhead florescent bulbs stuttered awake, and the little lamp our mother had kept on a stand behind the cash register gave off a cozy, yellowish glow. I set the cup tray on the counter and asked for help moving the rectangular cutting tables back into the center of the room.

"Stools or chairs?" Alderose asked.

"Chairs." While I wiped down surfaces, Clementine went to wash the dessert plates we'd last used for pizza. She set one in front of each chair, along with a single paper towel folded in half. I distributed the cups of coffee and café mocha, slid the tray to the end of the table, and held up the potted plant that had occupied the fourth cup slot.

"Petite Grisette survived the portals, I'd say." The apple sapling stood tall in its plastic container.

"She'll need a bigger pot soon," Clementine said. "Where's her soil?"

Grisette had uprooted the sapling from near her base, calling it a 'pesky little sucker', and insisted we fill a couple of muslin bags with soil dug from the orchard surrounding her house. We had orders to use only Keeper-approved soil—which could have been Grisette's way of assuring that we would visit regularly. I already knew I would be portalling to France at least once a season, for the soil, for more of the Crone's stories, and for buying trips for fabric for my wardrobe.

My sisters popped the lids on their drinks and chose their pastries. I set the yogurt container in the middle of our brunch, uncapped my mocha, and licked the cocoa-dusted foam.

"Where do we begin?" I asked.

I already had a list of action items in mind, but I thought the fair and prudent thing to do would be to open up the floor for discussion. I pulled a three-pack of notepads I'd picked up in France and a fountain pen from my bag. Clementine asked if she could use one of the pads and offered to undo the cellophane wrapper. Alderose nodded when I asked if she wanted one too and popped out of the chair to get the mug of pencils and pens underneath the counter.

"You start, Beryl," Alderose said. "You have that look in your eye."

"Clementine, that okay with you?"

She lifted her cup and grinned. "Goddess forbid if any of us should ever get in the way of a middle witch with an agenda."

For all the years we'd spent apart, it surprised me how well my sisters knew me.

"I think we need to bury Dad." I ironed the notebook open to the last page, uncapped my pen, and tested the ink's flow. Dad's body had been properly cared for by witches specializing in the care of the dead, and according to their latest email it was time to lay him to rest.

Glancing up, I watched as Alderose propped her heel on the chair's seat and nestled into the cushion. Clementine stared at her cup. I plunged ahead. "I think we need to plan a memorial for him and bury his body. Before we do that, I'd like to have Mom's casket exhumed and buried in France. Near Grisette. I've already spoken with the Crone about this idea. She said she would love the company and she's agreed to accept Dad's body too. Doubles her audience."

I sipped at my mocha and thought about how to phrase what I wanted to say next. "I need closure, Rosey. I never had anywhere near the relationship with Dad that you had, and Sissy, I can't communicate with Mom's and Dad's ghosts the way you can."

I shrugged and continued to doodle in the notebook. "Our parents are dead. This building is our inheritance. The magic *inside* this building is our inheritance. I have no idea if Dad left any of his clients or contracts to you, Alderose, but Mom left" –I swept my arm around the room– "she left a shop, she left her couture clothing and matchmaking businesses, *and* she left her rescue operation.

"What she *didn't* leave was...*uff*, so much. We don't have clear instructions for how she wanted the two ongoing businesses to proceed upon her death. We don't have a guide to what other rooms might be hidden by magical means."

Both my sisters nodded along. Alderose pulled apart the sections of her bear claw and popped one into her mouth. "I vote for burying Mom and Dad in France and for each of us finding the closure we need. I have a shit ton of guilt to process still, and I owe it to Dad to find his killer—which is something I'd prefer to take on on my own."

"What about Sidan and Guillaume and Jake?" Clementine asked, snatching the question right off my tongue.

"I intend to spend as much time with each of them as I can. Sid's been able to dig up more information about One-Becomes-Three-slash-Laurentine without calling attention to what she's doing. Guillaume's got decades of work cut out for him, with reclaiming his family's lands and making renovations to the castle. He told me I can have my old cell back any time and decorate it just how I want it."

Alderose laughed and tore off another piece of her pastry.

"Jake intends to stay based out of New York City. He knows I want to sell my apartment, and he's got a guest suite in his family's mansion I'm welcome to use. I'm comfortable in both France and New York—so for now, I'm adding bi-continental to the pansexual and keeping everybody guessing."

The truth of that made us *all* laugh.

"To be absolutely serious for a moment, I'm tired of living my life as though Dad's way was the only way. He was a loner. He trained me to be obscenely self-sufficient. And I'm tired of that. Which is not to say I'm ready to settle down and start a family." Rosey snorted and put up her hands to stop us from even picturing such a thing. "But I *am* ready to be part of a pack. Guillaume's calling us a clutch, even though he's the only vamp. I'm not sure what Sid and Jake and Cat will have to say about that."

She took one of the pens and used it to draw on the side of the paper coffee cup. "I like the idea of Mom and Dad being buried together near Grisette. It'll make visiting them all that much easier. I vote for burial in France and a memorial as soon as we can make that happen."

"What about you, Sissy?" I asked, turning my attention to Clementine.

"I'd like to hear what you want first, Beryl. Though I'm casting a vote in favor of asking Mom's and Dad's ghosts if they're okay with our plan. Or at least *trying* to ask them. They don't exactly communicate in full sentences."

I grinned at her assessment as I halved a chocolate croissant using the folding knife Kostya bought as a gift for me in France. "I'm ninety-seven percent certain I want to stay here. I never felt like merchandising was my true calling, and I promised myself when I started that if, in ten years, I was *still* in the kind of job that felt like I was going nowhere, I would do a serious career reassessment. Well, it's been almost a decade and everything that's happened since we first walked in the door of Needles and Sins has convinced me this building needs a Brodeur witch living in it.

"I'm happy to be that Brodeur. And I've decided to take over Mom's matchmaking service. I think I'd be good at it." I popped a slice of croissant into my mouth and savored the chocolatey, buttery goodness. "I just have to figure out *how* she did it."

"And Kostya?"

"Kostya really likes his new position with the Board of Magical Governance. And you know he decided to buy a condo in Boston, close to the Reformed Realm's portal. He needs to be able to get to his physical therapy sessions and assist his parents with whatever his new role is going to be."

Kostya and his brothers had a series of conversations among themselves, followed by a bare-it-all series of conversations with their parents, discussing their roles in the Reformed Realm's government. No one wanted Queen Violetta left to her own devices, and both she and Borya were thrilled to see their sons united in their desire to contribute to their home realm.

"And he's going to spend days and nights here whenever he can while we figure out—" All I could do was press my elbows to my sides and wave my hands in the air. I wanted to both keep everything to myself *and* shout it from the building's rooftop.

Clementine squealed and hugged me. "I'm so happy for you two. And it's fine with me if you want to take over the second floor as your living space. Rosey, how do you feel about that?"

"Could we talk about me and Clementine having bedrooms somewhere in the building for when we want to visit?" Alderose asked. "Maybe even sharing the third floor and dividing it into two apartments? And what about the shop?"

Clementine shook her head. "I like your idea about the third floor, and I don't know about the shop. Because to answer *Beryl's* initial question, I think I'm going to be dividing my time between the Reformed Realm, Uncle Malvyn's estate, and wherever else Tía and Alabastair travel. Threads are my thing. I want to study their magical properties with Tía, and I want to study clothing design with Laszlo's tailor. Joconde has agreed to take me on as an apprentice. Which will give me something to do besides get bossed around by my future mother-in-law when Laz and I are in residence at the palace.

"His parents have asked him—us—to spend six months of the year there however we choose, and we've agreed. Plus, we have our wedding coming up next June and his father is *giddy*, he's so happy to have a big event to plan."

"What about your dog?"

Clementine dropped her gaze to her lap. Fat tears followed. She wiped them away with the back of her hand. "Sitka really doesn't travel well, and he's terrified of going through portals. Leilani offered to take care of him, and James and Malvyn are willing to have Sitka for a trial run."

"I would love to have the second floor as my home base," I admitted. "If you two are willing, we could table the idea of doing anything with Needles and Sins for now, and give ourselves three months, six months, however long it takes to honor Mom and Dad and get ourselves settled into our new roles and relationships."

"What about Mom's laboratory?" Alderose asked. "And any other hidden rooms?"

"We know Alabastair wants to research the calcified portal tree in the other section of the cellar." I rested my elbows on the table and propped my chin in my hands. There were so many logistics to consider, including what to do when other hidden rooms appeared.

Clementine reached across the table and patted my arm. "This is a lot to sort out all at once. Rosey and I can talk later about sharing the third floor. Today, let's start with something really practical, like cleaning the apartment. That'll give you a place to stay and all of us the opportunity to look through Mom's and Dad's personal things and talk about what a memorial service for them entails. By the end of the weekend, you'll at least have a place that feels more like home, and we'll be able to leave with a plan of action."

We finished our drinks and our pastries and created a shopping list that assumed there was nothing usable or edible in the entire building. Alderose offered to be in charge of purchasing cleaning supplies, and Clementine said she'd stock the pantry and the refrigerator.

"I think a home-cooked dinner would be a great way to inaugurate Beryl's new home."

MY SISTERS LEFT with their lists. I sat in the quiet, hands wrapped around the paper cup still holding traces of the café mocha's warmth. I was in no rush to go upstairs by myself; it was enough to sit cocooned in silence and imagine this room could serve any purpose we wanted.

I tried picturing myself stepping into Moira Brodeur's matchmaker shoes. To generate the level of income she was making at the time of her death, I'd have to know her methods and access her list of contacts, and right then, I knew nothing and *had* nothing. Which sent me spinning in the direction of thinking not only was there no way I could pick up the pieces, but maybe it had been my mother's intention all along to let her businesses close upon her death.

That was a sobering thought.

On another hand, Alderose had used her magic to locate our mother's grimoire, which was no doubt where I'd left it on the desk in her workroom. The book had already given up information to both me and Alderose—albeit rather cryptically and delivered piecemeal—but it was a start.

With Clementine's help, we could communicate with our mother's ghost. Probably. Maritza was willing to use her necromantic powers to again give it a try. She had made a point of insisting that my sisters and I not get our hopes up and reminded us that Moira hadn't communicated with her at all until the past summer. Seven years of silence between sisters was a long time.

There were so many reasons why I was placing a lot of hope on my aunt's skills and my parents' willingness to do the right thing, even from beyond the grave. Plus, Malvyn needed a way to channel the righteous indignation he felt over what he perceived as my parents' neglect of our magical educations. I liked having my aunt and uncle on our sides, ready to advocate for their three nieces and go up against two wily, somewhat selfish, ghosts.

I gathered our take-out containers, added a little water to the sapling's soil, and rolled my carry-on to the stairs. The interior door to the stairwell was still unlocked, and my bootsteps echoed off the wood-paneling as I ascended. Though it wasn't a very long climb, only twelve steps or so, I couldn't help but feel those twelve stairs marked a major transition in my life.

I parked the carry-on by the apartment's door, took a breath, and turned the handle. The foyer and hall smelled...empty. Stale. I shouldered my handbag and walked toward the big sitting room running the length of the front of the building. Petite Grisette could use the sun, and I was curious to see the room again. Rosey had mentioned she thought the furnishings were fairly new and that the room might have been used as a kind of a gathering place.

My phone dinged with Clementine's distinctive ring and a text asking if I had any special food requests. Tucking the yogurt container into the crook of my elbow, I typed out a quick list of my preferred basics and a few treats, including Valrhona chocolate and fancy marshmallows for my daily cocoa.

Trusting my sister to fill the cupboards, I pocketed my phone, nudged the door to the sitting room with my hip, and nearly dropped Petite Grisette.

"Well, hello! *You* must be Moira's replacement. *My* name is Shasta and I would like to hire you to find matches for my two sons."

EPILOGUE

Sitting on the sectional couch, garbed in a smart navy wool suit, was a demoness of indeterminate age. Her folded overcoat was placed beside her on the couch and her briefcase-style bag was tucked against her leg. Understated gold rings dangled from the ends of her horns. A large, cushion cut aquamarine adorned her ring finger.

Behind her stood two young demons, one clearly a few years older than his sibling. Both were dressed in near-matching suits, and both wore completely different expressions.

"And these are..."

"My sons," she said with a proud smile, "Rupert and Phineas Junior."

"Right. I'm sorry, may I ask how you were able to get in here?" I asked, setting Petite Grisette on the marble-topped table just inside the door and pulling magic into my hands. A defensive spell was on the tip of my tongue, something with bright lights and loud noises that would give me time to dash out of the room and seal the door behind me.

"Through *there*." She turned and pointed toward the windowless wall our building shared with its neighbor.

I squinted. There was no visible door. Only built-in book-shelves and a lovely old tapestry.

"The instructions on the website were quite clear," she said. "I made an appointment—which you are a half hour late for, by the way. My confirmation included directions on how to get here and the code to the lock. I brought a cash deposit, as the website states you extend a ten percent discount for siblings. Fifteen percent if both the deposit and final payment are made in cash."

"I see, um—"

"Might we get started?"

I tucked my hair behind my ears, walked to the couch, and extended my arm. "I'm Moira's daughter, Beryl Brodeur. I'm so sorry for being late. I just got back into the country this morning, and I'm running behind. May I get you and your sons anything to drink?"

"Not at the moment, thank you."

An elegant table anchored one corner of the room. I set down my bag, removed the notebook and pen I'd been using earlier, and shrugged out of my jacket. Dragging the nearby chair closer to the couch, I sat and took a moment to compose myself.

"How did you hear about my mother's matchmaking busi-ness?" I asked, admiring Shasta's flawless skin.

"Oh, she brought me and my husband together! In fact, I hear him coming up the stairs. I sent him out to get us coffees."

The door she referred to earlier opened. A sharp-dressed man in an overcoat and a bowler hat entered, carrying a paper-board tray with four cups from the same café my sisters and I had stopped at barely a half hour ago. He closed the door behind him and turned. His face registered deep shock when he saw me, and something dropped out of his elegant overcoat.

"Phineas! Come meet our new matchmaker. I was *just* telling Beryl you and I have always felt so well-suited and we swore that *if* we had children, and *if* Moira was still in business, we'd bring them to her when they were ready to settle down."

Phineas walked to his wife and handed her the tray. He removed his overcoat and hat, and placed both on the back of the couch. And then he stepped closer to me. I couldn't help staring at the triangle-tipped tail curling itself around his leg.

"Have we met?" I asked, extending my arm and knowing full well the correct answer was, *yes*.

"Yes, we have, Beryl. And it's fine. I told Shasta all about my adventures in Chamonix. I had no idea, however, that you were the matchmaker my wife had settled on."

Shasta beamed a smile at me as she handed one of the to-go cups to her nearest son. He uncapped it and blew across the top. "Mumsy, I *never* said I was ready to settle down,"

"And I've been ready for years." Where the first son was on the petulant side and took his coffee to a spot near the window, the second son seemed eager to participate. He stepped around the couch and walked toward me, lifting another armchair and setting it near mine. This close, he looked barely out of college. "I'm Phineas Junior and I am quite ready to begin the process. How long do you think it will take before you find someone suitable?"

I darted a glance at his parents. They appeared absorbed in each other. I masked my surprise, nervousness, and lack of answers by uncapping my pen and opening my notebook to a clean page. Crossing my legs, I leaned toward the young man.

"How long are you willing to wait for the right individual— or individuals—to show up?"

THE END

ALSO BY CORALIE MOSS

Join Coralie's mailing list

for news & ongoing short stories (www.coraliemoss.com).

Many of Coralie's stories are also available in "closed door" editions (meaning there is no adult content).

Visit her website for more information.

The Goddessverse Fantasy series includes:

- **The Goddess & the Woodsman** (book 1)
- **Persephone Lost & Found** (book 2)
- **Demon Healer**, a paranormal romance novelette (book 3)
- **Medusa's Proxy**, a paranormal romance novelette (book 4)

The Shifters in the Underlands series includes:

- **Paper Dragon** (book 1)
- **Blood Dragon** (book 2)
- **Moon Dragon** (book 3)

The Sister Witches Urban Fantasy includes:

- **Once Blessed, Thrice Cursed** (book 1) Set in Northampton, Massachusetts, and introducing Clementine, Beryl, and Alderose Brodeur.
- **Demon Lines** (book 2) is the continuation of Clementine's story.
- **The Scarab Eater's Daughter** (book 3) gives us the sisters' continuing adventures from Alderose's point of view.
- **Beguiled, Bewitched, & Broken** (book 4) features the middle sister, Beryl.

- **The Sister Witches Urban Fantasy Series: Box Set 1** (includes book 1-4)
- **Witches Everbound** (book 5) completes the Sister Witches Urban Fantasy series.

The Witches of Salt Spring Island series includes:

- **Magic Remembered** (book 1)
- **Magic Reclaimed** (book 2)
- **Magic Redeemed** (book 3)
- **Magic Restrained, a novelette** (book 3.5)
- **The Magic Series Box Set #1**
- **Magic Undermined** (releases 21 March, 2026)

ABOUT THE AUTHOR

Coralie Moss loves everyday heroines and complicated witches, layered magic and earthly moments, and will always believe in the power of love. She lives on Salt Spring Island, British Columbia with her family and two globe-trotting rescue cats.

Join Coralie's mailing list for book news, giveaways, and the occasional homage to sisterhood.